A Nebraska Apocalypse Novel

FELICIA JEDLICKA

Felicia Jedlicka
Find me on Facebook: www.facebook.com/feljedauthor
Visit my website feljedauthor.wordpress.com

ISBN 978-1-946092-29-8

For the man who gives me everything.

More titles by FELICIA JEDLICKA

DESTINY REJECTED
DESTINY RECLAIMED
DESTINY RAZED
DESTINY RESTORED

DÉJÀ VU

SAVE THE HUMANS

THE NECROMANCER'S CHILD

SISTER WITCHES
THE DEVIL'S SHADOW
THE DEVIL'S SOUL

THE NEBRASKA APOCALYPSE NOVELS
CORN COWS AND THE APOCALYPSE
COW TIPPING AFTER THE APOCALYPSE
CORN HUSKING AFTER THE APOCALYPSE

THE WARDEN SERIES
SUCCESSORS
RIVALS
LOVERS AND LIARS
BAD BLOOD
TENANTS AND TYRANTS
THE RING BEARER
GODS AND MONSTERS
BEASTS AND BURDENS
MAGIC AND MAYHEM
FORK IN THE ROAD
DETAILS AND DEADLINES

Corn Husking After the Apocalypse

Prologue

"T HIS IS JIMMY THE Card, bringing you up-to-date news straight out of the Metro. For those of you looking for a weather report, go the fuck outside.

"Today's news is a statewide want ad for dead bodies. No, that's not a joke. Our illustrious Mayor Thompson has decided to add more grim to our concentration camp. He is allowing the outlying towns to bring in their inactive dead, and has even hired a few suicidal men to collect the *live* ones.

"The mayor has gone on record to say, '*We need to take this burden off our neighbors. We here in the big O are better equipped to deal with this threat than farmers and housewives.*'

"I'm not sure Mayor Thompson is personally familiar with either one of those demographics, but I do know he shouldn't discount our small-town neighbors so quickly. He might be surprised to find out that shotguns and chef's knives can be wielded quite efficiently in the right hands.

"I don't know what the rest of you think about this little plan, but I for one am all for it. After all, the crime rate in the north O was getting uncomfortably low. Let's get that murder rate back up to an all-time high with the help of Mayor Thompson and his overpopulated-de-monic-zombie babysitting service."

Damn Dogs

I crouched down low behind the sundial at the south end of the park and waited for the ensemble of freelance jerks to get past me. There was a good number of people I avoided on a regular basis regardless of how well armed I was. First off, the grim. I was concerned destroying the walking portals to hell would make live humans more susceptible to possession, so lately I had avoided them altogether. That took a little explaining to my cohorts, but in the end they listened to whatever crap I spewed because they were finally convinced I knew what the hell I was doing. Not that I did, but lately I'd been putting up a front of stoic authority.

...and the Emmy goes to...

Next, I avoided the crazies. Aptly named, there were more than a few super survivalists, super religious, or super de-evolved citizens running around my small town. The survivalists generally stayed indoors or near their home, but I had fallen victim to that trap once already and I wasn't going to let it happen again. The super religious types were best avoided for personal reasons. The same reason everyone avoided Jehovah's Witnesses—they were just damn annoying. The super de-evolved were people who had given up every rational function of existence and basically went back to living like cave men.

They weren't really dangerous, but they smelled really bad, so avoidance was the best protocol.

The group of men I was currently hiding from, however, were none of the above. They were pirates. Some would call them a gang or a band, but I didn't like the implication that they were vandals or musicians. In reality, pirates were human traders. The only things of real value left in this world were drugs, ammunition, and slaves. The pirates were people who dealt in all three, but they usually specialized in slaves.

I was armed and I could fight pretty well, but they traveled in groups of three or more, and were heavily armed and could also fight pretty well. I didn't gamble much and the odds were definitely in their favor, so I hid.

At least, that was the plan.

The three pirates across the street were window shopping. By window-shopping, I mean they were looking for potential abductees who might have stopped into the stores for a few things. That was what I was there for, but luckily I knew to case the area before going in.

The human element in this rapturous hell was getting ridiculous. I almost wanted to shoot all three of them just to save someone else the hassle later, but gunshots would likely attract more attention than they were worth. I really needed to stop coming downtown.

I was nearly in the clear. The men were about to round the corner of the block and hopefully cross the tracks back to the hole they crawled out of, when a random stray dog started barking at me like I was a squeak toy under the couch.

I glowered at the yellow lab in the hope that I might have the ability to blow up his head with my mind. I had always liked dogs, but post-apocalypse they had all gone feral, or at least very not man's-best-friend-ish.

The men took notice of the animal, and crossed the street to check out the commotion. I really didn't want to get into a gunfight for the sake of a few toiletries, but it looked like the decision was no longer mine.

Screw it. What's another bad day? Bring it on.

I stood with my arrow nocked in my bow. The gun would have been safer in the short term, but dangerous in the long term. Gunfire drew grim like flies to meat.

The first arrow hit one of them in the chest and he stumbled back, shocked by his sudden imminent death. I loaded the second arrow I had perched in my teeth for quick access. I shot it and ducked down, already prepared for the gunfire from the third man. I afforded a glance back to see if my second arrow was a fatal shot. Unfortunately, the intended victim had caught it in midair and was looking at it with curious fascination.

"Oh, shit," I mumbled.

Shhhh!

I DOVE BACK DOWN in time to avoid becoming Swiss cheese. After a perfectly good clip was wasted on chipping the cement platform the sundial sat on, the men started the usual bad-guy dialogue.

"You shouldn't have brought a bow to a gun fight, little girl." The soon-to-be-dead one said.

I pulled my gun, jumped up, and shot the gunman while he was still loading a new clip. I, however, used one bullet, since I didn't have an endless supply of ammunition. "I didn't."

I only caught a glimpse of the surprise on the arrow-catching bad guy's face before I had to hide again. He ran off into the park to hide behind a cottonwood tree that was as old as the town. It might as well have been a house with the shielding it provided him. "I underestimated you," he called out to me. I heard the click of his magazine as he finished taking inventory of his bullets.

"No, you didn't," I yelled back as I scanned the park for grim. They would be coming soon. "I underestimated you, but only because catching arrows is a really rare skill."

"It's like catching a baseball. You just have to not be afraid to stick your hand out."

"Yeah, but baseballs can't go through your hand." I peeked out above my hiding spot. He was doing the same behind his tree. His gun was aimed, but he wasn't firing yet. He was decked out in a black leather jacket and black denim. There wasn't even a Harley in sight. The ragged dark hair reminded me of Priest's, but it didn't have the sheen. His beard was getting out of hand, but he hadn't reached mountain-man stage yet.

"I don't suppose we could call this a draw and walk away?" I asked, semi-serious.

"Sure, just bring me two of your friends to kill and we'll be even," he answered.

"Friends? Really?" I peeked over the dial again.

"Associates." I saw the edge of his shoulder shrug "I haven't really known them long."

"As far as I'm concerned slave traders deserve knives in the back, so don't expect me to feel guilty for giving them quick deaths."

He looked at the body of the man closest to him. My shot had hit him clean through the head. Haden would have been proud.

"They are a slimy bunch, aren't they?"

They?

"Unfortunately," he continued, ignoring my dipped brow peeking over the sundial, "they are the only ones with access to decent weapons. The military is hoarding the good stuff. The police have confiscated everything in the O. People like me have to come to po-dunk towns like this to get anything, and, of course, that means trading with these assholes."

"Wait, you're not—"

"Behind you!" he shouted.

I should have suspected it to be a trap, but who really uses that trick anymore? I spun around in time to see a grim silently sprinting across the grass at me. He launched himself at me like a long-jumping Olympian. With bullet conservation ever in the back of my mind—because I *won't* deal with assholes like the two I just killed—I gripped my brass knuckles and held out my reinforced fist, locking my elbow. The descending grim impaled his face on my fist, shattering the fragile tissues of his skull and brain matter.

In an ideal world, the little bits of him would *tink* and *ting* when they hit the concrete around me, but alas, they didn't. It sounded more like someone dropped a bag of M&Ms, minus the appeal of the chocolate.

"Impressive," the biker man said to my left next to the sundial. His weapon was still in hand, but only half raised.

"Hey!" I whipped back, pointing a finger at him as if it alone were a weapon. "Keep your distance."

"Do you want to take the next three, or should I?" he asked, motioning to the north end of the park where three track-star grim were barreling across the lawn.

"Goddammit!" I griped through clenched teeth. "I just wanted a fucking razor! Is it too much to ask to not have hairy armpits?" I was screaming, but I didn't care. The corner of Biker Man's mouth tipped up. He seemed genuinely amused, but a little uncomfortable as well. "You deal with them. I'm so sick of killing grim." I walked toward the pharmacy for my razors. "Waste of time anyway," I mumbled.

Three shots rang out in quick succession and I stopped midway across the street. I turned back around and watched the last grim fall from a fourth shot he used to finish it. "Will you stop shooting your gun! You'll only attract more of them. Not to mention it's a waste of bullets."

"Since when is killing grim a waste of bullets?" he asked, truly perplexed by my statement.

"It's like killing flies with a hammer. Yes, it will work, but why not just use a fly swatter?"

"Why would I need so many bullets if I wasn't going to shoot grim?"

I stared at him. He was the epitome of everything that was wrong with the human focus right now. "Because the bad guys—I mean the *real* bad guys—haven't even popped their heads out yet. If I were you, I would save every last bullet I could for them."

"Who...?" He trailed off when the yowl of a grim sounded down the street from me. He looked over and his eyes widened a little. I didn't even bother looking.

"How many?" I asked, more bored than frustrated.

"Eight, no nine. What are they doing?" he asked, like someone who had never really spent time with free-roaming grim before. He was used to the occasional escapee in the big O. He didn't understand that the grim were less feral out here. They had plots, plans, and human instinct, with a big helping of demon impulse.

"Are they lining up, waiting for someone to hike a football?" I asked.

He looked at me, baffled that I was able to guess their behavior without turning around. "How do you know that? Have you seen this before?"

"Yeah, right in front of me." I pointed down the opposite end of the street, where I was facing. He turned and saw the dozen or so grim that were lining up on the east side about to converge on us, sandwiching us in hand-delivered torture.

Quick Friends

I TALLIED MY ARROWS and I realized I was going to be about four short. If I could trust Biker Man he could help me dispatch the other four. Another shot sounded, and one of my east grim fell as a result of my potential partner's overkill tactics. "Stop shooting! It's like a damned dinner bell to them."

The grim charged forward.

"Speaking of dinner." The man shifted away from me, whipping his head back and forth to keep his targets in sight.

It was too late to conspire against our mutual enemy, and too soon to get a read on his trustworthiness. I would have to take this impromptu union on faith.

I started firing arrows in quick succession. "Bring me my other two arrows!" I yelled at him. He looked around for moment like he didn't remember where I had put them. He ran over to his fallen business partner and yanked the first one out. Then he picked up the one he had caught and brought them both back to me, placing them in my quiver.

"The west side is gaining. Can I please shoot them?" he asked, already holding up his gun.

I finished dropping the east line with only a few left stumbling forward. They were slow enough to displace by hand. I turned to the west and continued my quiet attack. "Let me put it this way," I said in answer to his question. "If you fire that gun one more time, I will shoot you in the leg and leave you here to distract the grim so I can escape."

"And the other option is, we both die?" he snarled lowering the gun and glaring at me.

"City folk," I mumbled. I fired my last arrow and dropped my bow. I ran into the remaining herd with two blades drawn—perceivably from out of nowhere. With my brass knuckles overlapping the knife hilt I got another good shatterpunch in before I had to start resorting to kicking and slashing.

Out of the corner of my eye, I saw my new friend/foe fighting the wounded grim on the east side. He was doing pretty well for a city boy. He caught on fast to their fragile nature. It took a pretty hard hit to stop one, but several battering hits could do the trick if your knuckles could hold out.

I dismantled the last grim on my side and panted while he finished up on his side. When he was done, he beamed with the exhilaration of a well fought battle. I wiped away a little blood from my cut lip. A jab I shouldn't have taken, but it was worth the pain to get the angle I wanted for the reciprocal hit.

"You're..." He looked me over. A funny little smirk played across his lips, like he was reading my life story and found it just as amusing as I did. "Who are you?"

He was asking me like I should be revealing my superhero identity to him, but I assumed my name would suffice. "Lenore Evans. You?"

"Ian Katz," he said carefully, in case I might be able to hurt him with the knowledge.

"If you're not a slave trader, what are you?"

He smiled proudly. "I'm a grim hunter."

"Oh, Christ," I mumbled. "Self-appointed? Or do you guys have a club now? Not that grim hunting is worthy of a club. I mean crap, I just incapacitated two dozen in the last ten minutes."

He lost his smile and glared at me. "I'm appointed by the mayor and I don't incapacitate them, I gather them. I hunt them, catch them, and take them back to the O for the tournaments."

I didn't know what to say about that. The mayor was now outsourcing for animate grim? He really was determined to destroy them all. It made me wonder if his motivations were his own, or if Adrian Dorn was influencing him.

The grim were a nuisance, but they weren't the greatest threat to humanity's tenuous hold on the Earth. As far as I had figured out, the grim were puppeteered by lost souls, the souls of former humans who had long since been trapped in hell by their own offenses. They were mad with the desire to share their pain and suffering with others, in any way they could. Usually that involved lots of pain and/or molestation.

Killing the grim, as it were, didn't actually kill the maddened soul. The crystalline dead were just marionettes to act out their aggression. If you did enough damage to the body, the soul was essentially kicked out, but that didn't mean you were truly rid of the evil. It was a fun pastime, but it wasn't going to save any of us. There were still bigger agendas for the Earth, and frankly, the remaining human population was as much an annoyance to those planning those agendas as the grim were to us.

"Don't tell me you've never heard of the tournaments," Ian asked.

"I've been to a few," I said, less than forthcoming that I knew several of the finalists.

"You should compete. They have an archery competition in a couple months. You would do very well." He looked me over again, this time a little slower, as if he were only realizing now that I was a woman and a reasonably attractive one at that.

I probably hadn't earned the title on his first inspection. I generally kept my reddish-brown hair cropped to my neck and layered around my face so it stayed out of my way. I hadn't worn make-up in... a long time. I usually wore jeans, but with so many weapons to carry, I had switched to cargo pants. They did nothing for my figure, but I was armed head to toe.

"That's what they keep telling me," I said mildly. It had always been in the plans for me to compete, but I wasn't sure it served any purpose, other than to show off. I wasn't sure I wanted to do that. Drawing attention to myself seemed like a bad idea.

"Who's they?" he asked, taking a few steps closer to me.

"My friends," I said. I made it a point to check the cartridge in my gun, just to remind him that I was armed. He may not have been a pirate, but that didn't preclude him from being an asshole.

"Your friends let you come out here by yourself?" His change in demeanor was unmistakable. He stood taller and his chest expanded. I wasn't sure if it was to impress me, or intimidate me. "I'm not sure I would approve of you being out on your own if I was your friend." His tone sounded almost scolding, but he had a subdued smirk on his face.

It occurred to me then that this was his idea of flirting. If I was any other woman, I might have found his impromptu protectiveness gallant. However, I already had a white knight in my life and this chump had no chance of out-flirting him.

"I'm not exactly defenseless." I nodded to the surrounding bodies.

"Oh, right." He cleared his throat, suddenly remembering who he was talking to. The tension in his shoulders relaxed and his efforts to peacock diminished. "Well, thanks for that... and not killing me."

"Likewise." I nodded curtly and headed back toward the park to get to my four-wheeler.

"Aren't you going to get your razors?" he asked.

I really did need some supplies, but I also needed to get out of there. Just in case the mismatch signals I was getting from this guy were more a miss than a match. I turned back and shook my head. "It's not worth the hassle. Besides, it's not like I have anyone to impress." I mentally kicked myself for sounding so pathetic.

"Do you... want... I mean..." he stammered. "I feel like I should offer to walk you home or something."

I smiled at that. He was still trying to be chivalrous. As unpracticed as he was, I did appreciate the effort.

"No, that's my ride over there." I pointed vaguely at the ATV tucked in beside the outdoor stage on the west side of the park. "Thanks though." I started to move on and stopped. "Oh, and I know it probably won't make a difference, but you really should watch your back around here. The smaller towns tend to be big on the crazies."

With my warning heeded he headed south and I headed north. I reached my vehicle by the stage and unloaded my empty quiver onto the back. I should have gone back to collect my arrows, but I was already late, and Haden and Devin would be worried.

Well, Devin would be worried.

I hadn't sensed the danger around me until a the twig snapped behind me. I whipped around to face my attacker. His eyes widened with surprise and I punched him. He stumbled back, clutching his bloody nose. Three more men came around the back of the stage. They were wearing black robes adorned with oversized rosaries.

The centermost robed man, the tallest and oldest, brandished his cross like a weapon. "The power of Christ compels YOU!"

"What the hell?" I grumbled before a sharp pain in my lower back forced me to the ground. The ancillary hit to my head knocked me out.

Step into the Light

"**I** don't suppose you're planning to baptize me?" I asked the man that was nearly quartering me with tight ropes when I woke up. I was sprawled on a church altar like a human sacrifice being offered to a vengeful god. I didn't recognize which church, but there were several in the area. This one was fairly archetypical: stained glass windows, statues of the Stations of the Cross between each one. The high vaulted ceilings asserted an authority that Priest's small church never could. It also made the religious experience seem cold and demanding.

"Hey, freak, what do you want with me?" I asked when my captor didn't respond to my first question.

He looked up at me warily and scampered off to the head priest to tattle on me. Three men stood in the chancel together whispering, while their disciples knelt in the pews at the front of the church. They each took their turn to glare at me and I started to wonder how worried I should be.

I checked to see if they had disarmed me all of my weapons, but they had. My boots were even off, so I couldn't hope to kick my way out. My only other chance would be to use my eloquent negotiation skills.

"Hey morons, I hate to tell you, but I won't work as a virgin sacrifice. My bloom has long since been plucked."

The head priest—designated by the size of his cross—ascended to the altar and leaned over me. "You are not being sacrificed, my dear. You are being cleansed. You have been taken by a demon, and I must release you from it."

"I am not a demon!" I screeched, offended that he could have come to such a conclusion.

"I know there is still a part of you that can be saved. I will separate you from the evil, and you will be free of its will."

"What the hell are you talking about? I'm fine. I'm all human. I can recite the Our Father. Well, most of it; I always get tangled in the middle on a perpetual daily bread loop."

"I'm sure you think you are, but I have seen this burden before. I can help you. Trust me."

"I can't do that, Father, but don't worry, it's not you; it's me. I've been burned by your type before. I have trust issues with men who wear crosses." He smiled as if he was trying to offer me a token of kudos for my humor, but there was too much pity behind his eyes to soften his face. "Okay, Father, so what are we talking: baptize me in holy water, group intervention, séance?"

He glanced back at his fellow priests and ushered them forward. They placed a Bible in his hands and he kissed it before returning to face me. "We are going to perform an exorcism, my child." He managed to say "my child" with as much empathy as condescension. This guy was definitely a priest.

"What happens if you're wrong?" I asked, testing my bindings.

"I'm not wrong," he assured me.

The two other leading priests joined him at the altar, effectively surrounding me. They threw holy water on me, and blessed me in Latin. The head priest began reading his Bible with determination, but the other two priests seemed nervous. I got the impression they were unfamiliar with the unwritten Catholic ritual. They held out their small crosses at me like they expected my flesh to burn in the presence of them.

I lay my head back down and watched the front row stare in awe of the ritual. I, however, yawned. I had already had my fill of blessings from Priest. This guy was not nearly as talented as he was, so I wasn't expecting any moving experiences.

I could feel my eyes close, but I still had a sense of the room around me. The priests hastened their chants, and the crowd gasped. I chuckled, thinking how ridiculous the entire situation was. I knew I wasn't a demon. Actually, I didn't know that, but I thought it might have come up before now if I were.

Despite the impermissible nature of this exorcism, it was actually quite relaxing—at least at first. I could smell the incense that had burned in the church a thousand times before. From behind my eyelids, I could see the candles flickering nearby. The priests' rhythmic chanting was almost a lullaby. I might have even fallen asleep if I hadn't been severely disturbed by the feeling of multiple minds reaching out to me.

I had a special knack for being able to see the truth in people, but usually I had to touch them physically. None of them were touching me, but yet I could feel their minds, all of their minds.

As I suspected, the two reluctant men were not priests, though father Edward had knighted them into the position after a few quick lessons on drinking wine and blessing bread. They were new to God, and by all rights had no business participating in this ritual, but it was mostly for show; an exhibition for the onlookers.

Father Ed was indeed a priest, but he was more of a televangelist. He sought power with his title and the apocalypse had not sated his taste for it. The thought of this hack performing a real exorcism was an insult to me, the priesthood, *and* several Hollywood movies.

I was about to say as much when I felt my body start to rip apart.

Pardon Me, But Your Standing on my Brain

I CAN'T OFFER ANY comparisons to childbirth, since that particular event never made it onto my résumé, but I can assume the pulses of pain that resonated through my body with increasing severity might have come in a close second to that.

I gritted my teeth before I realized I shouldn't be hiding my pain from Father Ed. He needed to hear what he was doing to me. I screamed, but the guttural sound that came from my mouth sounded far beyond my vocal range. I tried to open my eyes, but I couldn't. I tried to move, but I couldn't.

I could feel and hear my spine cracking and I had a horrible image of *The Exorcist*'s back bend in my mind. For a moment, I wondered if I really was possessed... but then I got over it.

"You fucking hack! You're ripping me in two!" At least my voice still worked.

"Fight the demon, my child!" Father Ed yelled over the other two men's chants, as well as the repetitive "Our Father" from the audience.

"I am! Get away from me!"

"Focus on the Lord and he will free you!" Father Ed stopped speaking to me, and was now showboating his grand boisterous voice that echoed nicely through the church.

"Son of a..." I mumbled before doing as he said and focusing on my imagined tether to God. It was a tiny little thread at the center of my mind. It didn't control me. It didn't even guide me. It was just a residual umbilical cord to God. It was metaphorical at best, but to me it was real enough.

I tugged on the line as if to check its strength, but really I was afraid, in the light of this event, that maybe it really was imaginary. Maybe I was kidding myself. As if responding to my question, I felt a warmth travel through my body. It didn't release the pain, but it did redirect me.

Instead of fighting the priest, I fought his words. The power he possessed was more potent than I expected, but it was hollow. I had once fought against Priest's mind, and I could do the same to this man's inflated words.

I drew in a deep breath, finding a place of strength within myself. I found someplace feral and instinctual. It wasn't warm and fuzzy, but cool and raw. I couldn't say it was evil—at least, I hoped it wasn't, but even if it was, it was a part of me. It was, at worst, my dark side, but it wasn't foreign. It felt vaguely familiar, and yet still barely recognizable.

I let that core of energy rise up within me and brim to the surface of my skin. The hum of power was alarming enough to worry me, but when I heard gasps from the brainwashed audience, I couldn't help but be pleased by this new superhero skill. Too bad I had no idea what I was doing, since I still couldn't open my eyes.

At some point, the pain stopped. The sound of the prayers and chants stopped as well. I released the energy and it snapped back into place like a rubber band. I opened my eyes. Everyone was staring at me as if I had grown a second head, and for all I knew, I had. I checked my shoulders for aberrant growths, but they appeared normal.

"I told you I wasn't possessed."

Father Ed furrowed his brow looking me over. "How did you...? I had it..." He paused, letting the events settle into his mind. When he looked back at me, there was no hiding his ire for me. He was more disappointed than I expected to have his sacrificial exhibition interrupted. He glanced at his two subordinate priests and then back at me.

"Kill her."

Buy One Exorcism, Get the Sacrifice Free

I T GOES WITHOUT SAYING anytime you are faced with bodily harm your instincts set in and self-defense becomes second nature. However, the demand Father Ed gave to his minions left me verbally blubbering, and mentally scavenging for the button to initiate the life preservation mode.

I was tightly restrained, and no amount of tugging the first hundred times had helped, but I continued to yank on my bindings as the minion priests came around either side of me. Though they were eyeing me warily, they didn't hesitate to raise two austere blades over their heads.

Where was my hero? Oh, right, *I* was the hero. Crap!

The two knives descended toward my gut and chest.

I took a breath to let out a hideous Faye Ray scream, but a gunshot reverberated through the church and interrupted the reason for my girlish display. I slumped back, sucking in air to console my panic, albeit feeding my hyperventilation. When I joined the others to look at the source of the disturbance, I saw Ian dolled up like GI Joe at the back of the church.

In addition to the handgun he had pointed at the ceiling, a rifle dangled from a sling around his neck, and if my eyes weren't playing tricks on me, he had a belt of grenades across his chest. He wasn't just any solider. He was Rambo.

"Cut her loose," he said forcefully. I hadn't known Ian for more than a few minutes, but I got the impression he was more an actor than any particular genre of man. He was wearing the tough-guy mask, but he was pulling it off. Or at least, the guns were pulling it off, and he was a necessary prop.

"She is not one of—"

"I won't ask again!" Ian didn't wait for the driveled objections of Father Ed. He positioned his gun lower, not necessarily aiming at anyone, but a firm reminder that he could if he wanted to.

Father Ed was furious, but guns still trumped the internalized power of God. At least, on Earth it did. He motioned for the men to cut me loose.

I leapt off the altar the minute I could. I took a quick glance around, wondering where my stuff was, but I wasn't about to ask. I found my shoes on the pew opposite the peanut gallery and quickly slipped them on.

There was certainly a lot to be said for my closest call with death post-apocalypse being at the hands of a priest, but it wasn't enitrely shocking to me. Human nature demands extremes. Neither side of the spectrum can be fully trusted.

I ran down the aisle to my savior, and new best friend. I slowed as I reached him. His face still bore stern resolve and I couldn't help but be intimidated. He turned half way, ushering me to the exit, all the while keeping his eyes leveled on Father Ed.

"Take heed my son, she is dangerous!" Father Ed hollered to him.

I continued to the door, not looking at either man, but I heard Ian mumble, "No shit," as he followed behind me.

So Long, Thanks for all the Rescues

I CHUCKLED ONCE I was outside of the church. I wasn't entirely sure why, but there was at least a little room for amusement. I turned back to Ian, but continued to walk backward across the street to the park. "Thank you. I guess we're even." I gave him a wave of goodbye and turned around.

"Wait." He jogged a little behind me to catch up "I can give you a lift," he said, creating some distance between us when I glanced over his weaponry.

"I don't need a lift. I have my four-wheeler," I said.

"I can see that." He nodded to my off-roading golf cart. "My van would be safer. I'd like to offer you some weapons. Free of charge," he added when I glowered at the sales pitch. "In exchange for a safe place to sleep, and maybe some food."

I slowed my stride when I realized he wasn't trying to sell me something, so much as begging me for help. "Clearly I don't know much about the small-town rhythm," he admitted. "Who better than a native to show me the ropes?"

I stopped and started shaking my head even before I started my speech. "Look Ian, I don't mean to be the cold, distant heroine that doesn't care about anyone but herself, except... if I bring home another stray, Haden is going to rip my ass." Ian's face contorted, unprepared for my reasoning. "She's not the type of woman I strive to anger. It just isn't worth the yelling... or bruising."

"Is she your...?" He tiptoed around the suggestion that Haden and I were family in a different way.

"No, no." I shook my head and he seemed relieved. "Haden and Devin are friends. We are kind of a team of sorts. At least, we're supposed to be." I looked down, finding sudden interest in the ground. To my surprise I locked eyes on my bow and quiver. I leaned down and picked them up. I was still missing several blades, my brass knuckles, and my gun, but I certainly wasn't going back for them.

"How many guns?" I asked as I rubbed my finger along the handgrip of my bow. When I looked at Ian he was smiling. The salesman in him couldn't resist the negotiation, and I knew Haden couldn't turn down new guns.

More Strays

"WHO THE HELL IS this?" Haden eyeballed Ian as we entered the living room through the kitchen. He did the same to her, but he managed to keep the sneer of derision off his face when he did it.

"Where the hell have you been?" Devin came from the laundry room with a folded t-shirt still in his grip. It wasn't what I considered clean, but pretreatment wasn't in his vocabulary. "I was about to go to town and find you." He gave Ian a cursory scan before looking me over for damage. Fortunately, I had none to show, or Ian might have been plastered to a wall before I had a chance to answer my first question.

"This is Ian. He checks out okay." I wiggled my fingers to appease their concerns. Ian hadn't known about my special gift when I offered my hand for a formal introduction before getting in his van, but that wasn't a story for short-term house guests. "He's looking for a place to crash."

"Crap, Lenore!" Haden sat back against the cushions on the couch to watch whatever movie she had chosen for a boring Sunday afternoon. Or was it Monday? At any rate, the weekend was gone and so was the drunk, loud-mouthed, fun Haden. Now it was just the hung-over, loud-mouthed, bitchy Haden. Which wasn't more than a stone's throw from not-hung-over Haden, but at heart she was still a fierce friend, so I put up with it. "How do you manage to get yourself wrapped up in so many men?"

I glanced at Ian, hoping he wasn't taking her question to mean I was a slut. When Haden glanced back at me I set my jaw and stared her down. For a split second she realized her statement was hurtful, but the remorse was there and gone, and I knew better than to wait for an apology. "As I was saying, he needs a place to stay and some helpful small-town camaraderie. In exchange, he is willing to gift us some weapons and ammunition."

Haden's eyes widened as she took another look at Ian. She had sized him up already—and a good deal faster than Devin, since he was looking for strength, and she was only ascertaining if he was armed. Even now, Haden's waistband strained from the gun tucked at her back. She wasn't afraid of strangers, so long as she had a gun within reach.

"What kind of guns?" she asked, almost childlike.

I saw Ian's mask of salesmanship slip into place and he smiled broadly at her. "I'd be happy to show you. I'll even let you pick the first one without any negotiation."

Haden was up and half way to the backdoor before Ian snapped to and opened it for her. They slipped outside and, within a minute, gunshots echoed over the fields.

I, meanwhile, settled into the couch and yawned, while Devin finished folding his laundry. He occasionally slipped back in to watch the action parts of the movie Haden had chosen. My recent state of sleep deprivation settled heavily on my eyelids and I started to doze off.

"How much longer are you going to let this continue?" I jolted awake when Devin spoke. I looked at him, but didn't answer. "He's punishing you for not going to the tournaments."

"I know," I said simply. I didn't want to discuss this subject again. "I don't know if it's wise for me to see him right now."

"Why?"

I took in a deep breath and looked at him. Devin had never been my lover, but friendship wasn't enough either, so our relationship had morphed into something like siblings. Talking to him about my feelings toward other men left me feeling guilty and ill all at the same time.

"I know I'm not supposed to be attracted to him, but I can't help it. Sometimes he's all I can think about."

"Absence obviously isn't helping."

"What if seeing doesn't make it better?"

"I don't know, Lenore, I just can't help but think you're running from this. You've come so far and yet you're still struggling to face your fears."

"That's just it. I want to go see him, more than anything in the world. I'm just not sure I'm strong enough. I'm afraid he'll hurt me, Devin."

Devin sat down on the couch and rested his hand on my knee. "Lenore, I would die to protect you, but I can't fight magic and nightmares. You have to face the man causing this. You have to compete in the tournament. You have to see Adrian Dorn."

Dream Boat

ADRIAN DORN STARED ME down from across a winding staircase that had no business being there. He was my own personal Freddy Krueger—apart from being a rich, handsome, suave, blond Ken doll. I was afraid of him, yet unnaturally attracted to him; and by afraid I don't mean he was a rebellious bad boy who could steal my heart. I mean I was afraid his seduction might lead me into the mouth of hell, where my soul would be taken.

We both took opposite approaches—in that he was circling the staircase to approach me, and I was backpedaling around it to distance myself from him. The frustration of the endless chase heightened my fear, leaving my hands and jaw trembling. The game of cat and mouse did nothing to change his cordial smile, nor did it change his pace of attack.

Consumed by the desire to leave altogether, regardless of the lack of exits, I jump-started my run before I had even turned my head. I crashed into a body. The strong arms embraced me warmly.

I abandoned my concerns of the Adrian stalking me and found another Adrian holding me tightly. His smile was the same. It was genuine, but with more innuendo.

I tried to pull away, or at least I tried to try to pull away. His face came to mine and he kissed me. It wasn't the deep, sexual kiss I had expected, and that surprise alone kept me from ripping my head away.

For a while, we kissed. I returned it, despite my understanding of him. When my desire bloomed, he pulled me closer, pressing our bodies together in a vain attempt to find our pleasure externally.

There was no removal of clothing, nor did we walk to another destination, but we were suddenly naked in bed together. He was inside of me, providing me with pleasure I had only seen faked in pornography. Unlike my first vision of him, there was no pain.

He towered over me, but after I had finished my lurid outbursts, he leaned into my ear and whispered the words that every woman pretends not to like. "You are mine." The words landed on my ear, hot and breathy. I forced myself not to say *yes*. I wanted to. I even nodded, but some part of me—obviously not my lower half—knew that saying it aloud was a bad idea.

He leaned back with no sign of disappointment on his face for my denial of his territory.

"Come to me, Lenore. I will bathe you in this pleasure." Though he was not perceivably plying his talents on me, I could still feel myself building to another climax. "I want to give you something. Something no other man can give you."

My orgasm shattered my mind, dispersing all logical thought into a puddle of goo. The ear-shattering bawls I offered in return were barely human and far from ladylike. When I recovered, panting and sweating, he was beside me, caressing my stomach.

The moment was perfect, until I looked down at my distended *pregnant* belly. I gasped, losing my place in my breathing altogether.

I hyperventilated as I stared at my foreign body. Instead of feeling the glow of motherhood, I felt the horror of an *Alien* victim.

I screamed, wanting to rip the creature out, but I was too afraid to touch my own body. The baby within shifted preternaturally and Adrian laughed. I screamed again and found the strength to rip at my body, but by then it was only me in my dark bedroom.

Until the light turned on.

Insomnia

"WHAT THE HELL?" IAN said with wide eyes scanning the room. He stumbled through the door in boxer shorts and a t-shirt with a rifle strapped to his shoulder. He was prepared to shoot anything that wasn't me or a doll. It was an honest reaction to a woman screaming in the middle of the night, and it only secured my opinion of his worthiness, but if I hadn't been trembling and whimpering I might have laughed at him.

"Put that gun away. It's just a nightmare." Devin shuffled in wearing pajama pants and nothing else. I knew for a fact he had only slipped them on to come into my room and check on me. He made no such efforts to do so for midnight bathroom trips. Despite our adoptive familial relationship, I had no objection to him doing so.

Devin crawled into bed with me, making no attempts to console me verbally. He just scooped me into his lap and pressed me to his chest. I murmured, "I'm okay," a few times, but it didn't mean it was true, and he only grumbled in response. He was still groggy and if the light hadn't been on, we might have curled up together and gone back to sleep in each other's arms.

"This would be easier if you would let me sleep in here," he mumbled in my ear, already shaking the sandman's hand despite the light and our position.

"Haden has dibs," I whispered back.

"Not above this," he said, finishing with a yawn. "Was it the same?"

I nodded. "You can go back to bed. I'm sure I'll be fine." He shook his head, but I could tell he wanted nothing more than to crawl back in bed and sleep. "Please Devin. One of us should get some sleep."

"I hate leaving you to deal with this alone. I could wake you when you start to rile."

"I can stay," Ian said from the foot of my bed. I hadn't realized he was still there until then. I assumed he had headed back to August's old room to sleep.

Devin chuckled at him. "Easy champ, you just met her. I'm not letting you sleep in her bed yet."

It was my turn to chuckle, but I didn't point out that it was solely my decision who slept in my bed. "I don't think that's what he means."

"No," Ian said slowly, as if he didn't want to rush the denial in case it would ever be an option. "I could stand watch for her. Wake her... like you said." He gestured to the chair by the window that he might sit in during his watch. It was far enough from the bed I wouldn't be unnerved by him watching me sleep.

Devin looked to me and I nodded my approval. He pulled me close and gave me a kiss on the lips I barely reciprocated. He was just marking his territory and making sure Ian understood I was important to him. Unfortunately, my past breakups had left me pretty sour to the pretense of affection. Especially when there wasn't a commitment backing it.

I was getting tired of being the girl that everyone sought out, but no one wanted to keep. That was a whole other issue though. First on the to do list: try to sleep so I don't go crazy.

Short Version

I SLEPT A LITTLE before Ian shook me awake. And by a little I mean maybe twenty minutes. The nightmares were becoming dangerous. If I didn't do as Adrian wished and go to see him, I was probably going to die of a heart attack overnight. I hated losing, but I was too tired mentally and physically to fight off a dream.

If Priest were around, I knew he would be able to stop the dreams, but of course he wasn't. The ironic thing was he left because he felt inadequate to protect me. Now that he was gone, I finally needed his particular brand of protection.

"What is all this about?" Ian asked from the shadows of his chair. The moon was full, and provided a silhouette of him and the rifle he had yet to set down. He either didn't trust me yet, or he just felt better with guns at arm's reach, like Haden.

"I'm not sure you want to know," I said, flipping and fluffing my pillow back to cool comfort. "This is a long story and you're coming in right in the middle of it."

"Who are you people?"

"We are the heroes. Or at least we're supposed to be. There's been a lot of confusion as to the specifics of our duties and the identity of our bad guys."

"You're the good guys though, right?" he asked again, nearly begging me to allay his fears. I nodded. "Back at the church... Why was the priest...? How did he...? What *was* that?"

"That's a whole lot of unfinished questions, Ian. Are you sure you want to proceed?" He didn't answer, but I didn't really take it as a *no*. "The rules have changed since the rapture. We aren't bound by physics and chemistry anymore. There's a few of us out there who have tapped into a power. You could call it magic, but in the end it doesn't matter what you call it. It just is."

"That priest had some pretty impressive magic?" He sounded like he was tiptoeing around the question he really wanted to ask.

"Yes, he was strong, but I know another who is far stronger."

"You," he said more than asked.

"No, actually I was thinking of someone else, but I do have some abilities. I can see into people. Not so much anything I *want* to see, but more their intentions or their character."

"But you're not possessed or anything?"

I furrowed my brow. I hadn't thought Father Ed was so charismatic as to convince Ian I was dangerous, but apparently something had stuck with him. "No, Ian, I am not possessed. I don't know what bur got up his butt. Some people think I'm special, but aside from my little psychic power, I'm just trying to do right by my friends. If that translates as evil to Father Ed, then I guess I'll have to endure the occasional attempted exorcism."

I smiled, but I couldn't see if he was amused or not.

"It's just... when I walked in... it looked like he was succeeding in exorcising something from you." He said 'exorcising' like he wasn't sure he was using it properly.

"What do you mean?"

He paused and I wasn't sure if he was choosing his words or debating what to tell me. "There was a lot of energy in the room. It seemed to be coming out of you."

I shrugged off the statement. "I've never been through one of those before, and unless you have a broad résumé, you haven't witnessed one either. Between Father Ed's power and mine, I don't think an impromptu fireworks display would surprise me. Maybe I have a built-in magical defense."

I was making it up as I was going along, but it made sense. I wasn't sure if I was convincing Ian, but I had at least convinced myself. Whatever Ian saw, or thought he saw, it was too far down my list of concerns to worry about.

"Ian, I know you're just a gun dealer and grim hunter. I didn't bring you here to join our little band of misfits. I appreciate you watching over me, but no one will think less of you if you slipped out before dawn."

"You should get some sleep," he said, almost cutting me off. "Do you mind if I move the chair closer?"

"Go ahead. I'd offer the bed, but Devin would have a fit."

He mumbled an agreement and scooted his chair over. "What's the deal with you two?"

I snorted. "He's my security blanket. It's innocent, but slightly obsessive."

"Oh," he said with no particular emotion behind it. He propped his feet up on my mattress and leaned his rifle against the chair so it was aimed away from both of us.

"What's your story, Ian?" I reached under my blankets and found a wadded-up afghan. I tossed it to him. "We're the good guys. You aren't bad, except the whole salesman thing. What's your backstory?"

He looked down at the proffered blanket, touching the worn yarn that Nicole's grandmother no doubt made for her when she was just a wee little one. After his pause to appreciate the textile, his eyes bore down on me from beneath his brow. "I'm a hitman."

What?!

THERE WEREN'T MANY THINGS that surprised me anymore, but this particular confession froze me. Since I was already lying in bed, I didn't think he would notice the change, but a smile crept onto his lips. For a moment, I panicked, thinking of every scenario that would inevitably end with my death building Ian's résumé.

In addition to being shocked into heart-racing panic, I was also really disappointed in myself. I had touched this man's hand and deemed him mostly harmless. Apparently the 'mostly' part left room for him to be a hired killer.

He laughed at me. "You've disappointed me. I thought you might be impervious to shock."

"No, not totally. Now if you said you were a reincarnation of King Arthur, that wouldn't have shocked me."

"I suppose it doesn't matter now if I tell you. I was a former Navy SEAL contracted by the government for *disposal operations*. I made certain low-priority persons disappear."

"You're kidding, right? You're a walking government conspiracy theory."

"Yeah, I guess I am," he said almost proudly.

"You don't really seem the type. I mean, you seem too nice to be a killer."

"It wasn't a hobby, it was my job. Besides, I'm whatever *type* I need to be. That's what makes me such a good salesman."

"Former hitman turned salesman. Kind of a sideways move in respectability, isn't it?"

"I didn't say *former* hitman," he said without a hint of flippancy.

He probably wanted to shock me again. He was indeed a man of many masks, but the ruthless killer mask must have been his favorite. He may not have been a vindictive psychopath, but there was still a part of him that liked to put people on edge. It could have been because the Navy had bolstered his ego to cumbersome proportions, but in his case, I thought it might have more to do with control issues.

To his dismay, my total of twenty hours of sleep over the last two weeks didn't leave me completely horrified at the idea of someone killing me. I let out an involuntary yawn that said as much as I felt about his skillset.

He smiled at me and spread the afghan over his lap and legs. "Tell me about your nightmares."

"Uber bad guy gets me pregnant via Earth-shattering sex," I said rather bluntly because I didn't want to do the long drawn-out conversation I had when I first had to explain the nightmare to Devin.

"That's a nightmare?" Ian asked after he rearranged the words a few times in his head to make sure he heard them right.

"The nightmare part is when the baby tries to rip me apart to get out, and I don't mean that metaphorically."

"Oh." Silence ensued for a little while. "Screw it." He grabbed his gun and crawled over the top of me, plopping not so gracefully into my bed with me.

"What are you doing?"

He laid his gun against the bedside table next to him. "Going to sleep, and so are you." I opened my mouth to object to a man taking liberties with the other half of my bed, but then I remembered I had offered it.

"Devin really is obsessively protective," I reminded him.

"Navy SEAL hitman, remember?"

"Suit yourself." I rolled to my side, putting my back to him.

Other Uncomfortable Conversation Topics

I PRESUMED THE ONLY reason Ian had slipped into my bed, was so he could nonchalantly make a move on me in the middle of the night. When he was subsequently sawing logs loudly next to me, I wasn't sure if I should be disappointed, relieved, or insulted. Either way, I was annoyed that the man designated to protect my sleep was preventing me from getting it. I was sitting up, determined to seek out earplugs, when I felt a familiar and devastating gush.

"Shit," I hissed quietly. I struggled to get off the bed while still confining the saturation to my pajama bottoms.

Ian snorted and reached out for me. When he found the bed empty his eyes fluttered open and he sat upright. When he saw me cupping myself like a four-year-old too eager for the potty, he crawled over to intercept me. "What's wrong?"

"Nothing." I turned myself from view, trying to hide my awkward and troubling situation. "Go to sleep, I'm fine." I tried to take a step, but found I was only allowing gravity to do more damage. "Damn it."

"Where are you going?" He reached for me again, but I shrugged him off.

"Just get away from me."

"Do you need the restroom?" he asked. "Did you wet the bed?" He managed to make the last question sound concerned, which did a small amount to dam my embarrassment.

"Please, Ian, I just need some privacy." I looked back and found him examining something on the bed. He reached over to turn on the lamp before I could stop him. "No!"

He looked from the bed to me. "What... Are you... hurt?" he asked, probing for the right word, the only word that would explain his findings.

I was still peering at him over my shoulder. I must have revealed everything to him by the look on my face. The shame was bad enough, but the fear of discovery was the real reason I hadn't let Devin sleep next to me.

Ian leaned forward and pulled me around to face him. There is no charming way to discuss the female cycle, even less so with a man, and even lesser still when I should have been prematurely dried up like every other woman post-apocalypse.

He already saw the truth, so I released my hands to show him the severity of the truth. He cursed at the amount of blood saturating my pajama crotch. Though I only bled once a night, it was all at once, and with little warning. It also hadn't stopped since the nightmares began.

"I don't understand," he whispered. "I thought... Aren't you...?"

"I was," I answered so he didn't have to pull out a health text book to continue the conversation. "Since the nightmares started, I've been bleeding at night."

"Do you need something?" He stood up, prepared to offer any assistance he could.

"Yeah, don't tell anyone," I said firmly.

"Including Devin?" he asked.

"Especially Devin. I..." I shook my head. "I don't know how I want to handle this yet. Avoiding Adrian Dorn isn't working, and in more ways than one, it's slowly killing me. However, taking this development into consideration with the prophetic nature of my dream..." I shrugged, trying not to cry in front of Ian so early in our association. I didn't really succeed, but I did manage to keep the blubbering to a minimum so I could continue speaking. "I just don't know if I'm going to get the happy ending, and I don't want Devin to do something stupid to try and save me."

"You mean like walk up to the asshole and shoot him in the face?"

I nodded. "I need to clean up." I started toward the door, but stopped and let out a sigh. "Shit."

"What?"

"I never did get my supplies this afternoon."

"Razors?" he asked, bewildered.

I smirked at him. "And tampons," I whispered.

"I have some."

"Razors?" It was my turn to be bewildered.

"No, tampons," he said, unabashed.

"Why do you have tampons?"

"I use them to clean my shotgun barrel." He was completely serious, but I could barely contain my smile. "Should I grab them, or wait for you to think of a joke?"

"I'll come up with something in the shower," I said as I waddled to the bathroom.

Jealousy

"TRY IT NOW!" DEVIN yelled from under the hood of his truck. I turned the ignition, but it wouldn't turn over. I went back to reading my book and waited for the next holler. I heard a high-pitched squeal that made me do a double take to see if someone had sneaked onto our property.

To my surprise it was only Haden. She was sunning herself on a blanket in the grass. Ian was sitting next to her, not quite sunbathing so much as enjoying the bikini-clad view. They had been flirting pretty heavily since their common interest in guns had been revealed, but squealing was something I rarely heard from Haden.

The part of me that wanted Haden to be comfortable with herself and fun-loving, smiled to hear her laugh with Ian, but the part of me that knew how much Devin loved her muted my gratification.

"Try it now," Devin said, leaning in the driver's side window. He made me jump, but I just pretended to be jumping to do his bidding. At last, the engine turned over.

"Yay!" I offered him a high five, but his attention was on Ian and Haden. The stone-cold stare he leveled at the back of their heads made me lower my hand and slump down so I wasn't in the path of it. The engine coughed and sputtered to a stop. I groaned in disappointment.

"It stopped," I pointed out the obvious, in case he was too absorbed to notice. "Should we give her another try?" I asked.

"No," he said simply. "It's time for a new model. I was getting tired of this one anyway." He pulled open the door. "Come on. Let's go find a new one." He practically dragged me to the four-wheeler. He jumped on the back, leaving me to drive.

I didn't question the offer, since I was more experienced with the four-wheeler. I slipped on in front of him and he scooted up to my back, resting his hands on my hips. I started the engine and pulled out slowly. I stopped in the drive across from Haden and yelled at her.

She turned around, still holding the smile Ian had earned. "Where you going?" she yelled over my engine.

"To look for a new truck." Devin's hands slipped down my thighs, but I ignored the attempt to make Haden jealous. Unfortunately for Devin, so did Haden.

"Okay. Be careful." She turned away.

Ian waved us off, and I saluted back. I hadn't mentioned the specifics of his occupation to anyone, but the Navy SEAL title did come up to impress Haden. He, in turn, had not mentioned my little biological anomaly to anyone.

Luckily, the bleeding had stopped completely, but since the tournament was in a few days, I was painfully aware of why it might have stopped. I had accepted that I needed to go to the tournament. I had even accepted that I might not have control over my attraction to Adrian Dorn. However, I had not accepted becoming a demon-birthing machine.

Devin's hands wrapped around me and stayed there even after we were out of Haden's view. I didn't question it, because he was my friend and I was used to him acting out against Haden via flirtation with me. When his hand dipped between my thighs, wrongly rubbing me the right way, I clamped the brakes. I almost flipped off the front, but Devin's wandering hand kept me down.

"Jeez, baby, slow down." He chuckled in my ear as he nuzzled my neck.

"What are you doing?"

"What I always do?" he whispered, dipping his other hand inside my collar, tracing my bra cup. "Keeping my girls happy."

"Devin, don't do this. Not now. Haden is just a little bewitched. She still loves you."

"This isn't about her. It's about me and you." He kissed my neck. "About what should have been a long time ago."

For a moment, I considered it. It was hard not to. Maybe this was right. Maybe that's why I didn't love Garrett. Maybe that's why Priest couldn't love me enough to be with me. Maybe it was meant to be Devin all along. He could be the one to once and for all rid me of my attachment to unavailable men.

At any rate, if I slept with Devin right now, I might be able to get Adrian off my back. First come, first serve is the rule in paternity, right?

I considered letting Devin and me wallow in our broken hearts through meaningful albeit uncommitted sex, but only because Devin was a beautiful man, and making babies with him would have been any girl's dream come true. However, I loved him too much to let him do something he could never take back.

"The hell it isn't about Haden. You do this every time." I shrugged both his hands away from me. "I love you, Devin, but I can't be your bait to lure Haden back anymore." I shifted the ATV into park and climbed off so I could look at him. "You want her back, go talk to her. Tell her you love her, and you don't want her to sleep with Ian."

"We aren't monogamous." He stated the mantra like a tired old catchphrase that everyone pretended not to be sick of.

"Ian's against the rules though," I said. His brow dipped. As I expected, Devin didn't even know his own rules. "You both go home with someone, or you go home with each other." He looked away like my prognosis was too simple. "Let's face it, Devin. If Ian was a one-night stand, this wouldn't even be coming up, but he's not. He's in our home. He's spending time with Haden outside of the bedroom. That's what hurts and that's what you have to fix. Talk to her."

"Talking doesn't work with Haden. She's emotionally closed off. That's why I just make her jealous. It's effective, usually."

"I don't know what to tell you. If you can't talk to her, and you can't make her jealous, you're going to have to find some way to convince her that you love her."

"How about I beat the crap out of Ian?"

I nodded. "Maybe, but be careful, he isn't as defenseless as he seems." Devin looked down at the ATV sheepishly. When he looked back up at me, he looked heartbroken. I stepped forward and touched his arm. "It'll be okay, Devin. I promise. As anti-feminist as it sounds, Haden just needs you to mark your territory so she knows where she stands."

His expression stayed fixed. "I'm sorry," he said, and rested his hand on my side, gently drawing me toward him. I didn't hesitate to go to him, since this was an acceptable expression of our love. I wrapped my arms around him and he scooped me onto the four-wheeler and his lap.

He pulled me back and kissed me. To a passing stranger the kiss would have been confused as sexual, but to Devin it was purely emotional. When a hug just wouldn't do...

When he released me from the kiss, he brushed my hair away from my face, and looked me over. I expected him to say, "I love you," but he didn't. "Sometimes I wish it could be you and me." I nodded, understanding how difficult it was to have such a strong connection, and yet still be in love with someone else. "Such is life, I guess."

"Yup." I stood and flipped myself around on the ATV to drive again. Devin took the opportunity to smack my ass to help me on my way. I yelped flirtatiously. Once again, things were back to normal, or as normal as things ever got in our perverse version of familial bonding.

Bows and Arrows and Grim, Oh my!

T HE ARENA WAS ALREADY thrumming with the vibrations of stomping feet and chanting. The rhythmic pounding matched my heart beat for beat. I was anxious, excited, and terrified. My tournament had finally arrived. The last few months I had avoided this place like the plague for fear of falling into bed with my sworn enemy, but too many things were driving me back to it.

I maneuvered through the crowd, wordlessly searching for the danger that had me on edge. I knew he was nearby, waiting for me. Thankfully, I had the competition to distract me or I might have been running through the stadium screaming his name like a victim of Cupid's arrow.

I announced my name at a small folding table outside the door to the arena. The robust woman with facial dermatitis wrote down my name and examined my arrows before marking my hand and directing me to the big doors. I ambled toward them trying to look confident, but my legs were shaking.

I knew my weapon well. I was skilled, there was no denying that. I wasn't afraid of grim. However, the chanting crowd, which was doing a rendition of "We Will Rock You" with structure-collapsing enthusiasm, was a whole other story.

I had never been on stage before, let alone competed against people. Even in school track meets, I just hung back and pretended not to know my own name. Now I was about to compete in the most infamous competition in the tri-state area.

Needless to say, I wanted to puke.

I pushed through the doors and was surprised by the brilliance of the lights. After a moment of blinking, I started to see shapes. A figure came toward me, and I shielded my eyes to get a better view.

"I was hoping I'd see you here," the deep male voice said, and for a moment I searched my brain, demanding the identity beyond the visual confirmation. "I missed you."

"Garrett?" The blond hair and burly shoulders started to come in focus through the graying spots in my eyes. "Oh, thank God." I hugged him unabashedly and he hugged me back.

"Is something wrong, or did you really miss me that much?"

"Oh, no, I mean yes, but no, I was afraid you were Adrian Dorn. I'm not ready to face him yet." I pulled away and looked over his bow. "You're competing."

"I always do," he said with a smile. Some people came up behind us, and Garrett pressed his hand on my back, ushering me to walk further in with him.

The arena was still covered in sand. There was no longer any point to it, but the lack of traction provided some amusement for the crowd. There were targets all around the arena, staggered at different distances.

"How are you?" Garrett asked once we had found an unobtrusive spot to stand. Several of the competitors were practicing, but I had no desire to reveal my ability, especially if I biffed the first shot.

"I'm..." I paused and wondered if this was the time to be completely honest, or just give the standard *fine*. "Next question please." He smiled, but only because I was attempting to add humor to an uncomfortable topic. "How's..." Speaking of uncomfortable topics. "...Chicago."

He nodded. "It's touch and go. We are struggling."

"Oh." I looked down sheepishly, knowing I was the cause of that struggle.

"It's good though. I mean, either way, I'm glad you pushed me to go back. Don't worry, I don't regret it, and I don't expect you to be waiting for me if it doesn't work out with her. In case you thought I had any motives beyond competing tonight."

"Oh." I smiled and nodded. It wasn't really a rejection as much as permission for me to reject him, but somehow I almost wished he had told me he wanted to come back to me. I could only assume that desire stemmed from my second X chromosome—the one that insisted I attach myself to the biggest strongest man that will have me. Fortunately for both of us, the first X chromosome—the universal one—knew that being with someone I didn't love wasn't right. "Thank you," I said.

"I'm sure you'll win this thing hands down, but remember, you need at least third place to get into the final competition," Garrett said, back to his usual teacher mode. "If you can't... What is he doing here?"

I didn't see Adrian since he was to my back, but I knew it was his presence that had diverted Garrett's attention. I could feel him. I wish I had something better to qualify that statement, like goosebumps or prickled hair on the back of my neck, but the truth was, I felt him via a wave of desire. This was not going to be an encounter I could win with violence or clever catchphrases. I was going to have to fight against myself.

Don't be a slut. Don't be a slut. Don't be a slut.

To Be or Not to Be…a Slut

T HERE WERE SO MANY things piling against my resolve. Adrian Dorn was already an attractive man in my eyes. I called him a Ken doll because he was handsome, with perfectly coiffed hair. Plus, his upscale clothing made it look like he had robbed a mannequin at Lacoste.

This evening, however, Adrian had bypassed his rich casual look in lieu of a bare chest. His body was far more athletic than I anticipated. He wasn't as muscular as Garrett, but he wasn't born with as much girth to begin with. His usual gel-frozen hair was sloppy and falling in his eyes. To top off the rugged appeal, he was glistening with a sheen of sweat, much like his appearance in my dreams. The dreams where we have hot, explosively orgasmic sex.

"Shit!" I averted my eyes from his approach, and Garrett tried to discern my emotion. He was clutching his bow. If I gave the word he would fire without any question. "I don't have time to explain, but don't let me do anything stupid. I seriously have so little control of myself right now."

"Lenore?" Adrian asked, as if he was verifying my identity. My eyes widened at the lurch in my stomach and I wondered if Garrett would mind if I suddenly French kissed the man who killed his sister.

"Adrian." I turned to face him, but I was no more ready than in my dreams. A frenzied mix of lust, anger, and fear tried to fit into my brain simultaneously. I wasn't sure anything could be stronger than my anger at this man, but somehow the emotion was building and feeding my desire. The more I wanted to rip his head off, the more I wanted to rip his pants off. "It's good to see you. Are you competing?" I asked, suddenly noticing the oversized crossbow against his leg.

"Yes, I've watched everyone else have so much fun I thought I should see if I can make the cut."

"I'm sure you will," I said warmly with a coy smile. "I hope you'll save room for me on the metal stand."

"I think I can make room for you just about anywhere you want." His voice was low and seductive.

I licked my lips and took a slight step forward that I didn't want to take, but damn it if I wasn't being reeled in like a fish. "I would like that," I said. I was about to take another step forward, but Garrett pressed something sharp into the palm of my hand. I glanced back, taking note of the arrow being stabbed into me, but I didn't object or cry out. I absorbed the pain and it shattered the hypnotic control Adrian had on me. "You remember Garrett. His sister was the one who died during the competition."

Adrian's libidinous expression blanked in shock, before annoyance puckered his lips. "I don't know that we were ever formally introduced." Neither Adrian nor Garrett offered a hand to make the introduction official. "I think I'll get stretched out. Lenore, there's an after party tonight at the mayor's house in honor of my win. I'll expect to see you there." He reached down and ripped my hand away from Garrett's arrow. He kissed it chivalrously. "I won't take no for an answer," he added sternly before walking away.

"What the hell?" Garrett mumbled.

"He's got me whammied."

"No, how arrogant to plan a celebration after party before he's even won."

"Oh, yeah, that's pretty rude." I rubbed my face. "Thanks for snapping me out of that."

"You looked a little lost. Is he getting into your mind again?"

I grimaced. I didn't want to get into the details. The details explaining that Adrian Dorn was in my mind, my dreams, my bed, and my body. That was a conversation best left for someone I didn't know intimately. "He's just making it difficult to resist his charms."

"What does he want from you?"

A demon-spawn baby of his very own.

"I don't know," I answered, feeling that it was only half a lie. I assumed the dreams were prophetic and not metaphorical, especially given my returned cycle. However, I wasn't the only woman available for reproduction. Why was he coming after me? And what was this baby going to be? Was I the lucky winner of the *incarnate of evil* prize drawing?

I never was the best Christian, but somehow I just never saw myself as the mother of the anti-Christ.

You Again

THE GRIM WERE LAUGHABLY slow. I managed to hit all my targets in the head during the first round. The second round called for moving targets, but I wasn't daunted by the lumbering puppets of the apocalypse. I even took my time to get the aim I wanted.

Garrett had done well, give or take a few off-target shots on the first round. He was good, but not as good as me. I found some pride in that.

Adrian, however, was very nearly beating me. He had been watching me carefully, observing my skill level with interest. I intentionally biffed one target just to see his reaction. As I suspected, his curiosity waned. I wasn't sure what that meant, but I decided second place would have to do in this competition. I didn't want to beat Adrian if it meant revealing my full skill level.

Round three was more of the same, but this time the grim were faster and more aggressive. Garrett went first, seizing his opportunity to shine under pressure. I clapped loudly when he downed all seven of his attacking prey with ten arrows. It wasn't a perfect score, but he did get points for speed, which was what he was going for.

The man Garrett had tied for third place in the second round didn't do as well on speed, but he got a perfect seven for seven. I deduced even before Adrian wowed the audience that I would have to get a perfect score and a decent time to make it into the finale. It would have been better if Garrett had thrown the match. That would guarantee me a placement, but that was like asking the wind not to blow. It just wasn't right.

Adrian flexed his muscles when he finished his seven for seven hits. I was focused enough, not to be turned on by his machismo attitude, but his bare-chested sinew was difficult to look away from.

I stepped up to the plate, as it were, and they released the hounds. I shot once, twice, thrice... by the time I made it to six I had lost count. The head shots were beautiful. I managed to shatter the last two, which made the crowd cheer.

I was eager to check my time and found my clock still ticking away. I glanced around the fallen bodies with another arrow already nocked, but nothing was moving. If not for the frantic waving from my friends in the stands, I wouldn't have even noticed the stoic grim that was waiting on the other side of the arena for me to shoot him.

I smiled at his audacity and raised my bow. I flexed for my upshot, but before I could release, the grim's head lifted slightly, revealing his face.

Once upon a time, the man would have been handsome and charismatic, and perhaps he still was, but whatever was inside of him made me seethe. The grim's demon that stared back at me was old and familiar. His villainous sneer promised of pain. I grinned wickedly at him, silently pledging to inflict just as pain on him. His mouth quirked even higher, blending amusement with his ire.

It wasn't as simple as *kill the bad guy* with this one. It went deeper. We had a history that stretched beyond my mind's memory. I wasn't sure I believed in reincarnation, but it was the only way I could ratio-nalize the amount of vengeance I wanted to take on him.

History

I T PROBABLY LOOKED STRANGE from anyone else's perspective. There was no way to alleviate the primal urge rising inside me. My jaw clenched just looking at him, and regardless of what was going on around me, I was only interested in killing him.

I dropped my bow entirely and was in a dead sprint before anyone could formulate the words to yell at me for my stupidity. I didn't have to wait long for my antihero to match my attack, stride for stride.

He roared his breathy hollow battle cry at me. He wanted blood, and so did I.

There was a united gasp from the audience, right before we careened into each other.

It occurred to me slightly too late that old grim have the speed legendary of vampire lore. He clotheslined me and I flipped through the air. Miraculously I landed on my feet. I was apparently tapping into my feline agility.

I threw my elbow back without looking. It met his face with a short-lived satisfaction. His fist hit my kidneys.

I swept my leg to trip him, but he was in front of me before I could knock him down. After two punches to my face, I remembered how to block.

The battle was not going as one-sided as I once thought it would have, and I was disappointed. I knew the sharpshooters could shoot him if I would just get out of the way, but I wasn't ready to give up. Even if my death was certain, I wouldn't and couldn't run away from this fight. Why my bravado had flared again for this creature, I didn't know. I also didn't care. I had gone from cowardly to feral with one look at this bastard.

I only needed to get one step ahead of him. I thought back to my almost-exorcism, when I tapped into my thread and touched the minds of the priests. If I could do that again I might have the upper hand I needed.

I mentally grabbed my thread—I expected it would take great concentration, but my instincts had boiled to the surface. I yanked on the thread, drawing a flood of energy that spurred through me. As a result, my retaliation increased in speed and force. It might have been the blazing lights of the stadium but my fists looked blurred to my own eyes.

I no longer felt the impact of my hand against the crystalline puppet before me. My fist, and its ghostly double extension, were going through it to the blackened shadow behind the human mask.

I felt and heard the demon within rumble at the offense of the assault. He increased his strength, and hit me, but he was no longer hitting my body either. I felt his impact, but in a different way. I bellowed back at him and latched onto his neck—or whatever was in place of his neck.

I felt tentacles wrapping around me as I struggled to keep a grip on him. The intangible vines poured pure hatred into me like a poison. I couldn't tell where his anger ended and mine began, but I tried to focus on my tether. There was no malice there, only a strange, unassuming love that shouldn't have housed the power I was receiving from it.

I felt a pain in my right side, like a burning knife stabbing into me. I couldn't see anything causing the pain. I heard the demon laugh and I saw in his mind the knife he had stabbed me with. Not now, but once upon another life.

I couldn't see the entire battle, or the reason for it, but I had fought him before, and I had won, but at a cost.

I echoed the pain I couldn't understand, and the grief I had spread across two lifetimes. The guttural thundering roar I offered was only concluded when I felt the presence at my fingertips explosively sever in two.

I felt the pain and the fear from him, but I didn't have any sympathy left to offer him. He was gone and he wasn't coming back, and I was glad.

When the crowd's cheers registered, I was leaning over the empty grim on the ground before me. I knew he was no longer a threat, but I pulled an arrow from my quiver and stabbed him in the head just to make it an official hit. The crowd laughed and hooted as they rose for a standing ovation.

I looked back at my fellow competitors. Among the shocked and confused faces was one particularly consternated one. Adrian Dorn did not like my performance.

So much for not showing my cards.

Poker Face

"WHAT DO YOU MEAN you don't know what that was?" Haden's voice pitched with disbelief. "Why didn't you just shoot him with a fucking arrow?" She ripped my quiver off my back and loaded it into the truck bed.

"He was too old to be bothered by an arrow. If he didn't block it, he would have simply stepped out of the way with his freakish speed," I defended.

"That's the point, Lenore," Devin chimed in, taking his turn. They had passed the lecture back and forth since I got out of the stadium. "You shouldn't have even considered taking him on." He opened the backdoor of the extended cab for me, but Ian thanked him and slipped in ahead of me. Devin gave him a sour look before taking my arm and pulling me away from the truck. Haden followed, standing behind me. "What did you do to him?" he whispered, assuming Ian was the reason for my reluctance.

I took a breath and thought back to the incident. I glanced back at Haden to be sure she was going to listen in to my answer. "I don't know!" I yelled.

Before I could throw my hands up and walk away, Haden gripped the back of my shirt and yanked me back with a stranglehold on the cloth. She tripped me and I landed just shy of goose egg.

"Haden!" I yelled at her as she straddled me.

The first slap was far from expected, but the second one was just insulting, and the third hurt me to my very soul. Devin tried to yank her off me but she racked him with a hard punch that turned his face red and made him cough.

"You are so useless!" Haden grabbed the front of my shirt and relentlessly shook me. "She died for you, and you are just as blind as she was! So, fucking capricious!" She slapped me again and I let her. She couldn't hurt me more than she already had. I kept my hands on her thighs, reminding her that my surrender was voluntary.

My cheeks were stinging like hell, and my eyes were crying from more than the physical pain of her assault. "I'm sorry, Haden. I want so much to have answers, but I don't. All I can tell you is whoever was inside of that grim was someone I hated. I don't know why or how that's possible, but I wanted him dead and... I think he is."

Her mouth was pursed so tight I could see the wrinkles in her lips. "He's dead?" She panted from her exertion.

I shrugged a little. "I think so."

"You didn't just kick it out? You killed it? How?"

"That's the part I don't know. The part I don't understand. The part that was just... instinct."

She shoved me down and dismounted in exchange for pacing the pavement. "Why didn't you just say that?"

"Because the ultimate answer is still, *I don't know*," I grumbled petulantly. "I wanted to piece together the puzzle a little further before

I said anything." I rubbed my face and got to my feet. I was thanking my lucky stars she hadn't decided to punch me. "Clearly you're frustrated, but the least you could do is not punish me for being an ignorant weapon."

"Your ignorance almost lost the competition! If Garrett hadn't stepped down from third, you wouldn't have even placed."

I shook my head. There was no negotiating with her on this topic. "I don't know what you want me to say, Haden. I can't keep apologizing for failing to live up to your expectations. You are the one setting them, not me."

She looked me over like she was mentally removing those expectations one by one. "You're right. I need to stop expecting you to be her. You are clearly an aberration of physics, but you will never be her."

I tossed back the hairs that were persistently being pushed into my face by the breeze, and tried to cover my fresh tears with a fake smile and nod. Haden had no idea how true her statement was. "I never wanted any of this, Haden."

"Oh, yes, please! Can we listen to yet another wailing attempt to dismantle your potential, so you don't have to be responsible for anything, ever! We all enjoy that so much!"

I bit my lip trying to keep myself from exploding into tears, but nothing I did stopped the streams that had already developed under my eyes.

Devin stood up, finally functional. "Haden, that's enough," he murmured and redirected me to the truck.

I slipped into the back seat next to Ian, while Haden and Devin had a heated low-toned discussion outside. Ian was sitting calmly in his seat, unfazed by the scene. I looked him over and he did the same to me. "So, you're on her side?" I asked bitterly.

"Not on anyone's side, really, but if it makes you feel any better, I think she was out of line."

"Not out of line enough for you to get off your ass and help me though, right?" I snapped and sniffled.

"No, not out of line enough for me to get off my ass." He narrowed his eyes and raised his right hand from behind his lap. It held a small pistol. "But I did have her in my sights the whole time, in case things got messy."

I stared at him a moment longer before relaxing back against the seat. He may not have been as overprotective as Devin, but Ian had my back, so long as my back was actually near death.

Haden and Devin got into the cab, simultaneously slamming their doors. Devin started the truck and put it into gear. "We're going to the after party," Haden announced before he could accelerate.

"Adrian Dorn will be there," Devin said.

"So what?" Haden double-dog dared him to give her a reason to be pissed at him too. "Let's corner the bastard and get some answers."

Devin glanced back at me for agreement, but I looked away. I couldn't object, not after what had just happened. However, Haden didn't really understand that going to the party was like setting me on a sacrificial altar.

Party Crashers

As we stepped into the foyer of the south O mansion, two things were abundantly clear: the city's public officials had been paid way too much, and we were shamefully underdressed.

I surveyed the people clustering around the winding staircase in front of us, as well as the subsequent rooms. They were all dressed to the nines, in clothing designed by names I couldn't pronounce. I immediately assumed our plan to get info from Adrian was off the table, since they were likely going to throw us out on our asses, right along with our blue light specials.

"Ladies." As I suspected, a tight-suited butler arrived with his hands wide, ready to usher us to the door. I turned to leave before he could give us the speech about being "a certain class of citizen." However, instead of pushing us on to the door, the man waved us to a bathroom just off the foyer. "You may select your outfits and change in here. Feel free to use the makeup and accessories if it pleases you. Shoes are optional."

Haden and I peeked into the bathroom that was bigger than our living room. It was filled with racks of clothes, most of them with the tags still on. Apart from a double sink near the entrance, there were four mirrored vanity stations filled with the kind of makeup displays you might see at a mall.

We looked at each other and back at the men. They were being ushered off to another room, outside of the foyer but away from the mingling areas. I couldn't tell if their wary sidelong glances were concern for us, or their impending itchy suits.

"Holy cow!" Haden hollered from inside the bathroom. "This is Gucci."

I smiled and joined her in the search for new clothes. I wasn't sure if this was all part of the prestige of a party at the mayor's house, or if it was a clever distraction. Either way, I wasn't going to let Haden one-up me with a better dress.

Party Dress

I MANAGED TO FIND a cream dress with a few simple black stripes running down from the left shoulder that worked with my skin tone and frame. It begged for a frumpy black Audrey Hepburn hat, but that wasn't an option in our accessory pile. I tried to find shoes, but there was nothing left in my size. Naturally, the most common shoe size is never available. Instead, I opted for barefoot as the butler suggested.

Haden, on the other hand, found black stilettos to go with a black tassel dress. It wasn't her usual skin-tight style, but she could hide the pistol strapped to her hip with a simple swish or turn. She eyed herself in the mirror for several minutes, trying out the movements so she didn't unknowingly reveal herself. While she practiced her catwalk, I took liberties with the makeup and made an effort to do something with my hair.

"You will let me talk to Adrian before you shoot his head off, right?"

Haden glared at me through the mirror. "What are you going to talk to him about?"

"It's not what he says that I'll be paying attention to."

"We should have done this months ago," Haden mumbled.

I couldn't tell Haden the reason I initially cowered from Adrian Dorn. I hadn't told her or Devin that August had become a silver saint. They didn't know our great and former leader—the one I could never live up to—might have been doing God's will.

To Haden, everything was cut and dried. Bad guy kill friend, we kill bad guy. As much as I felt compelled to avenge my leader, protect my friends, and take the Earth back from puppeteering demons, I knew it wasn't going to be as simple as shooting Dorn in the back. The secret I wasn't sharing with her was that I might unintentionally be working on behalf of a higher power. And if that was the case, who the hell was Adrian representing?

"Do you want to hear you're right?" I asked, teasing her ego in hopes so she would drop the subject.

"I don't want to be right, Lenore." She came up behind me and took over curling my hair with the curling iron that was available to us. "I want to be safe. As long as he is around, none of us are safe. I don't pretend to get your gift or what purpose it serves, but if you ask me, when it comes to him, it's defective."

"I think you're right." I tried to nod, but my head was otherwise occupied. "But I should try one last time to get a clear view of him. Something other than what he wants me to see."

"And if it doesn't work?" Haden asked, scrunching up the curls she had made for me. She wasn't exactly being gentle about it, but it still felt better than a slap in the face.

"Then we try it your way."

Die Hard Shoes

DEVIN AND IAN CLEANED up well in their new suits. They weren't a custom fit, but they looked pretty sharp. Devin winked at me as he put his arm around Haden and pulled her into what appeared to be the drawing room, a small lounge off the main dining room where the men had been grazing on hors d'oeuvres while they waited for us to preen.

I was about to follow them when Ian bulldozed me out to a veranda off the dining room. Before I could begin to wonder why he was pinching my arm, or figure out what the other two rooms feeding into the patio were, I stepped on a broken champagne flute.

I gasped and balanced precariously on the edge of my foot so the glass didn't go deeper, while I searched for a safe place to step. Ian cursed and lifted me into his arms. He set me down on a brick planter that sufficed as a bench, while he ran back inside for a towel. He returned a few minutes later with a waiter rushing right behind him. The waiter apologized profusely for the incident and started to clean up the fragments.

Ian knelt down to tend to my foot, but every time he reached to pull out a glass shard, I cringed and yanked my foot away. Despite the scolding glower he gave me each time, I couldn't seem to hold still for him.

"It has to come out. Do you want to do it?" he asked, but I grimaced and shook my head. "Okay then, quit being a baby and hold still." I closed my eyes and sang Jingle Bells in my mind until the task was done. After I felt a sting, I opened my eyes to look at the shard in his hand. It was not nearly as big as I thought it would be, considering the initial pain.

"That's it?" I asked as he tossed the broken piece into the flower bed for a gardener to cut himself on later.

"Yes, that's it," he scolded me and shook his head. "What happened to the fearless warrior from earlier tonight?"

"Excuse me, Mr. I Have Shoes On, these cute little tootsies are not warriors." I wiggled my toes in his face. "These are indoor feet."

He snatched my foot away from his face. "Is that so?" He smirked and started to massage the pads of my foot, being careful to avoid the wound."

"Hmm." I leaned my head back a moment to absorb the impromptu relaxation. "Almost worth the pain, for this." I raised my other envious foot. "This one kind of hurts too." I bit my lower lip, to keep my smile under control.

Ian's smile widened, but he shook his head. "I'm only doing this for our observer's benefit." He moved the massage up to my ankle and onto my calf. All the while he stared at me, but not locking at me. "He seems very interested in what we are doing."

I moaned in half-lidded ecstasy. "What *are* we doing? Because at this point I'm willing to marry you."

He chuckled. "Let's just see how the night goes, shall we?"

"Is it Adrian?" I frowned, suddenly realizing what he was saying. I was disappointed I hadn't felt his presence. I started to look around, but Ian pinched my leg.

"Don't look around, just look at me."

"Blond preppy Ken doll or blond with tree-sized biceps?" I asked.

"No, he's not blond."

I furrowed my brow and resisted the urge to rubberneck the crowd. I leaned down closer to Ian. "How do you know he's watching us? You haven't even taken your eyes off me."

"It's called peripheral, Lenore. It is of great advantage in my line of work." Ian perked his brow.

"What line of work is that?" Adrian asked from the patio doors leading from the dining room. Ian and I both jumped to attention and stood. It still hurt a little to stand, so I reflexively grabbed Ian's arm. We looked like quite the couple.

Adrian took note of the connection, but didn't lose his urbane demeanor. As an afterthought I looked around for the not-blond man that was watching us, but the only brunette men on the patio were paying attention to their dates, cigarettes, and/or drinks.

"I heard you hurt yourself," Adrian said, waving a small first aid kit in his hand. "But I see you've already been attended to." I opened my mouth to speak, but I only ended up giving a noncommittal shrug and head shake. My brain-body connection had apparently stopped functioning several hours ago, so it was no surprise my mouth was stalling out at a monumentally inappropriate time.

"I'm Ian." Ian threw his hand out, momentarily disrupting my grip on him. He might as well have thrown me into shark-infested waters without a life jacket.

"Adrian." The men shook firmly and only retracted when the sizing up was done.

"Congratulations on your win." I threw the statement out as if I had been working on it all day. Adrian nodded politely and stepped toward me.

"I was surprised at your directional change today. What exactly prompted you to attack that grim?"

"Um... in my experience the older grim are faster than arrows, so sometimes hand-to-hand combat is best." I made the excuse up as I went.

"I see. But what made you think you could defeat a grim by hand, when he was too fast for arrows?"

I shrugged yet another noncommittal gesture. "I really didn't expect to beat him. I just knew I was going to lose on time either way, so I might as well make a show of it." I laughed and glanced at Ian, who joined in.

Adrian smiled, but he looked uncomfortable. "Tell me, Lenore, why haven't you been to the other tournaments? I was... waiting for you." His eyes glittered with promise, and I felt my knees weaken.

"I was unwell," I answered a little too quickly.

"I see." Adrian looked me over head to bare toes. "You look..." He swallowed hard, like his mouth had suddenly gone dry. How the hell did he hide his true self so well? "...sublime."

"Thank you." I cleared my throat while my mind grappled for something else to say to keep me from launching myself into his arms.

"Ian, was it?" Adrian looked to Ian, who was either playing benign or had simply become bored of the entire conversation. If a platter of shrimp passed too closely to us, I might have lost his company entirely.

"Yeah." Ian snapped to attention.

"If you wouldn't mind, I'd like to steal Lenore away for a moment. I need to speak with her about something *privately*." Adrian reached to steer me along by my elbow, but Ian reached me first, pinching my arm a little too tightly.

"Actually, I do mind, Adrian. I was pulling Lenore aside for a private conversation myself, when we got sidetracked by broken glass. I wonder maybe if you could fetch her some slippers or something. We don't exactly have a health plan." Ian gave him a finger gun with a double tongue click that I couldn't keep from chortling at. "I'll be done with her by then." Ian's hand fell from my elbow and he dragged a finger along the side of my hip.

I wasn't sure how I was supposed to react to it, so I didn't. I'd lost track of what the game was and whether or not we were winning.

"I'm sorry, how do you two know each other again?" Adrian raised his chin resolutely.

Ian chuckled. "I don't know if that's really your business, but I guess you could call us... lovers." Adrian's eyes narrowed to thin slits. I half expected laser beams to shoot out of them and cut off Ian's head. "I'm not sure what the post-apocalyptic term is, but we're definitely sleeping together, aren't we baby?"

I couldn't help but smile as Ian's hand traced over my cheek. He was an amazing actor. If I wasn't afraid Adrian would slice him open right then and there, I might have enjoyed playing up my part a little more. "Ian, don't gush. It's rude."

"He asked." Ian shrugged.

"You two are recently lovers," Adrian persisted. I had more than one guess why he was so interested. My more recent female reproductive cycles were obviously in preparation for a conception, but once again, *first come, first serve,* was the rule.

"Yeah, we've been at it all week. I can't get enough of her, and apparently she can't get enough of me. Poor girl wakes up in the middle of the night begging for cock."

"Ian," I scolded in a whisper, but I wasn't faking it. The expression on Adrian's face reminded me of when he was facing off with Priest. I wondered what vision I would have if I touched him now, while his temper was high. "Adrian, we can talk now if it's important."

I reached to touch his arm, but Ian took my hand and looped our elbows. "Later toots." As he drew me away I looked back at Adrian. The anger on his face left his shoulders tensed and poised for attack. Instead of Ian protecting me, I might end up needing to protect him.

Colorful

"Y OU HAVE TO BE careful what you say to him," I scolded Ian once we were around the corner of the yard and heading toward the tennis courts—the landmark of the overly paid.

"Catch me up here, Lenore." Ian released my arm and took up a military stance before me, minus the salute. "Give me the short and dirty, and don't skimp on the dirty."

"What do you mean? You know more about the dreams than Haden."

"No, I mean you keep calling this guy evil, but as near as I can tell he's just a pushy guy. What's the history? What's the backstory?"

"Oh. The backstory is, after the apocalypse, AKA after God picked up all the good souls to take to heaven, the Earth became forfeit, which means everybody and their dog's uncle wants a piece of it. We got the inner circle of angels stabbing a piece out right now. The demons, as you well know, are peeping through the windows of our glimmer grim. I'm not even sure what kind of war is coming, but I guarantee humans aren't going to have a home court advantage."

Ian looked around the grounds. He was looking for the cameraman to jump out and tell him he'd been *Punk'd*. We'd all been waiting two years for that, and so far the joke wasn't over. "How does Adrian come into play?"

"Adrian is the one who organized August's death. We suspect he is an uber-demon that's strong enough to take over a human host. All I know for sure is that I am the only woman with a functioning reproductive cycle, and he apparently wants to use it."

"Are you sure he's evil, though, and not just an asshole?"

I took in a deep breath and let it out slowly. "He's two different people, Ian. I can read the bad in people, and when I read him, he is like you said: just a guy. But when he is distracted or angry, I see horrible things. I need to read deeper, but I've never gotten deep enough to see the whole image."

"So, what happens when— if he impregnates you? I mean, it wouldn't be human, right?"

"Even if it was, it would be like the kid out of the Omen. Plus, I kind of get the impression from my nightmares that I wouldn't be giving birth to a child, so much as incubating it until it hatches... ripping me apart in the process."

"Do you want me to keep you away from this guy or not? Is the information worth dying for?"

"I wish I had a better plan, but right now he's our only known link to... the bigger agenda. I need to try to reach him again. I need to know if this is all useless, before I risk my friends' lives to try and stop it." It was my turn to look around the grounds. "I'm sorry you're meeting me at this point in my life, Ian." His brow furrowed. "There was actually a brief moment, a while back, when I had backbone and I wasn't a complete waste of space."

"Wow, that's a little harsh. Are you sure Haden is the only one raising the bar for you?" Ian started to walk away, either out of disgust or simply because there was nothing left to say. Half way out of the court he turned back to me. "You know, if you interrogate someone long enough, they'll eventually tell you what you want to hear. Whether it's the truth or not, they'll say it just so you'll quit asking. But if you ask their friends and family the same questions, they'll prattle on for hours with unnecessary and excessive details. As they should—it's not a secret to them." He walked away to rejoin the party and left me to put the pieces of his anecdote together. I might not have been the brightest crayon in the box, but happily, my newfound friend was very colorful.

Networking

THERE WERE MORE THAN a few socially acceptable bad guys in the mingling elite at the mayor's house. As I passed through the gathering, elbow to elbow, I caught psychic glimpses of flagrant adulterers, a few high-end drug dealers, and more than one embezzler. None of them had the information I needed.

I searched yet another room that probably had an official name, but as far as I was concerned, it was just a living room with a piano in it. I could hear Jimmy the Card giving a throng of people a live performance of his comedic wit. I recognized a few other political players that usually flocked to the mayor like ass-kissing sucker fish. Finally, I spotted the bobbing bald head I wanted and headed over.

I made a quick scan of the room to check for Adrian, but my raging hormones told me he was farther away. Something told me he was still working out how to impregnate me if I had already been sleeping with another man. I hoped the answer was he couldn't, and he would just give up, but that probably wasn't quite what he had in mind.

"Mayor." I approached the red-faced version of the man I had seen at the tournament. He was either laughing too hard at his guests' jokes or drinking too hard with them. "Thank you so much for inviting us."

The mayor looked me over, still holding the smile he meant for the couple he was talking to. He didn't seem to recognize me at all. It occurred to me that he might not remember my name, so I offered it along with my hand.

"Lenore."

His smile shifted as he took my hand and kissed it instead of shaking it. I instantly sensed the many underhanded things he did for and during his term in office. The bribes, the money laundering, the prostitution was practically an addiction. Though pre-apocalypse his alcoholism was in check, it was no longer. The man was a typical red-blooded American businessman/asshole.

"I'm having a terrible time getting the couples to dance." He leaned in close enough for me to smell the brandy on his breath. "Would you mind dancing with me, just to start things off?"

"Certainly," I said, even though I knew it meant he would take the opportunity to rub himself all over me. At least I could keep delving into his criminal history.

He moved us to the center of the room where the floor stepped down into a pit. He waved to his piano player, who had been playing loathsome elevator music. The man jumped to and played a slow but playful rhythm that probably would have sounded better from a saxophone.

The mayor pulled me close and took liberties with his hand position on my back, or I should say my ass. I leaned in so I didn't have to look at him, which meant brandy was going to be my perfume for the rest of the night.

The glimpses I got from his present life were skewed, and vague. He had had a good number of dealings with Adrian Dorn, but in all of them he seemed to be just another employee. If the mayor was part of the evil plot, then he was a pawn and didn't have full disclosure.

"How are things going with the grim population?" I changed tactics to a good old-fashioned interrogation.

"Good, their numbers are decreasing exponentially. Soon we'll be rid of them and have the city back to ourselves."

"What made you decide to destroy them all? I thought the people were against it." I smiled to distract him from my reporter-style questioning.

He thought about the answer and I could sense the struggle in his mind to find the answer. "They are vermin. Vermin need to be exterminated. The people are beginning to understand that."

"How will you control the human crime when they're gone? Their fear of the grim is the only thing keeping everyone from running around like pack animals."

"The same way I control the grim. With armed guards... if need be," he added, since I wasn't smiling at his joke. If it was a joke.

"I see. May I ask what part Adrian Dorn will be playing in your leadership after the tournaments are over?"

He paused, looking me over. "You are a very beautiful woman."

"Thank you, but I—"

"I have several rooms upstairs available for private parties. Would you like to join me there?"

"No," I said coarsely, but quickly followed with, "thank you, I should be getting back to my date."

Instead of releasing me, he pulled me in a little tighter, and gave me a drunken smile he probably thought was sexy. If he cared one iota about my date, it wasn't deterring his hand from steadily creeping further down my ass.

I didn't want to make a scene, but I also didn't want to be in this situation any longer. I could read his many indiscretions of sexual harassment. Some of them were so aggressive they bordered on rape. More than one woman had given in to him, to keep her salary and benefits. Those that didn't were either silenced with bribes, or suppressed by the endless red tape of their lawsuits, leaving Thompson free to exploit more women.

His lips grazed my ear and I shoved against him. His bulky body didn't budge. He was just plain bigger than me, and that was frustrating as hell. Sure, I was supposed to be the hero, but I couldn't even pry a drunken louse off me. When his tongue dipped into my ear, I shrieked and pulled away. The mayor laughed and proceeded to kiss my neck. Short of screaming my head off for help, I wasn't going to get out of this, and judging by how many people were turning away from my predicament, possibly not even then.

Before I could activate my female alarm system, I felt a shift in the vibe I was getting from him. The human indiscretions faded and I felt something new. Power without restriction. Good, bad, and ugly all rolled into one. The energy rippled around me from everywhere. I expected to feel the creepy crawly fear I had with Dorn or the violent rage from my quick trip to hell, but this was different. This was alluring. This was addictive.

I dared a glimpse up at the mayor to see if he was doing this to me intentionally or if I was drawing it out, but his attention was no longer on me. His body and uninvited lips were indifferent to me. His eyes had ratcheted from lazy slits to perfect aghast orbs.

I looked behind me to what had disturbed him, and I found Adrian standing at the edge of the pit. He stared at the mayor with venomous intent. Anger filtered into my mind, disrupting my power high. The enthralling energy diminished, replaced by fury and lust.

I could see reflections of the crowd in the wall of mirrors lining either side of the pit. Images of Adrian and Thompson repeated ad infinitum between them, leaving each successive replication more distorted than the last.

Deep in the echo, I saw a halo of darkness over the men. The shadowy arch tugged at my primal instincts, demanding my observance in no small way. I couldn't tell if it was a vestigial part of Adrian's demon or if it was actually emanating from the mayor. I bobbed my head, trying to determine the origin, but my connection broke unexpectedly and I lost sight of the eerie uni-glow.

"Well, Lenore." The mayor abruptly broke contact with me. "I must be getting back to my other guests." He smiled genuinely, and he didn't seem unnerved or irritated. I couldn't tell if the power I had initially felt was from him or Adrian. A secondary read exposed nothing new from the mayor. I couldn't imagine someone so obtuse and self-involved could house anything that powerful. Then again, I was an ordinary person turned superhero—or something like that. "Dorn!" The mayor waved Adrian over, as if he were seeing him for the first time.

As Adrian approached, a wave of desire swept me around to face him. It was stronger than ever and despite what I had just seen in the mirror, I wanted to crawl up his body and saddle myself to him. It was the downfall to being human—we really were slaves to our hormones.

"Yes, sir." Adrian smiled at me warmly and I did the same, almost blushing since I knew he knew I was about ready to hump his leg.

"Would you mind keeping Lenore company? I have some business mingling to take care of."

"It would be my pleasure." Adrian offered his arm, and I latched onto it like a life raft. He walked us out of the piano room into what looked like the foyer we first emerged in, but in this room the winding staircase was varnished wood instead of painted white. We must have been in another wing of the house altogether. There were still a few people meandering through the area, so Adrian pulled me below the ascending stairs for a margin of privacy.

"I'm sorry about the mayor." He touched my fingers that were still clamped to his bicep. "He gets drunk. I'm sorry if he made you uncomfortable."

I nodded and shrugged. Apparently it was my universal response to everything I didn't know how to answer. "I should find Ian," I said, trying to compel my feet to move with the statement. It didn't work.

Adrian stepped closer to me. Unlike the mayor, his breath was minty fresh, as if he had brushed just for me. "Are you really lovers?" His face was filled with anticipation for my answer.

"No." I hadn't intended to disclose the truth. I hadn't even intended to speak, but the word came out. This was one time that honesty was *not* the best protocol.

"Good." He didn't smile or relax. His eyes stayed ardently locked on mine. "Are you ready for me, Lenore?" My eyes flickered between his and my mouth dropped open. "Are you ready to be with me?" he asked.

I screamed "no" inside of my mind, but when my vocal cords activated... "Yes." The damn word bypassed by brain and went straight to my lips. So much for my intellect helping me out of my debacle.

As much as I wanted to take it back, and run away, my feet had already surrendered to my captive desires. I trailed Adrian up the stairs to my inevitable fate. It was my fantasy nightmares come true, and all I could do was let it happen. Because as much as the little voice in the back of my mind told me it was wrong, my body told me it was right.

There was something poetic about being conquered by my own hormones. Damn you, estrogen! *Damn* you!

It took shuffling past several locked doors for me to realize we were not simply perusing the hall for a place to unfurl our lust. We were racing toward the nearest available space to get horizontal, like virgins on a honeymoon. Adrian's cool calm seduction routine had broken down into a frantic agenda. I wasn't sure what the rush was, but his hold on my libido was slipping with his effort to rush the process.

Seeing the chink in his armor, I focused on his frustration. I probed for an underlying motivation and found it. His actions were not born out of desire, but rather a mission. Impregnating me was definitely the goal, but doing so was not his idea. It was only a minor movement in a progressive strategy. Adrian was obeying orders, as any good soldier would. Unfortunately, he was a *very* good soldier, and short of raping me in the hallway, he was going to complete his mission. The only thing reassuring in my observations was that he hadn't chosen me for any grand reason—other than my physical tolerance to parasitic demon embryos. Catching his eye that first day in the arena might have been the worst thing I could have done. Then again, if it hadn't been me, his mission would be complete and devils-spawn daycares would be popping up all over the city.

I was still piecing together the information when Adrian came to a sudden stop. A torrent of anger seeped through our connection. Old anger, the kind that ferments through generations, and in this case, since the birth of the Earth.

I looked around him to see where his fury was directed, and my heart leapt and cracked at the same time. The joy of seeing Priest again was undeniable, but being abandoned was not something I got over easily. Especially when his absence had put me in this sleep-deprived state of vulnerability.

My mouth parted to speak, but the men were barely aware I was still in the room. Except for the vise grip Adrian had on my hand, I could have simply slipped away for a snack.

For a long moment, Priest stood rail-stiff in his designer tuxedo. The necklace I made for him rested unabashedly below his bow tie. He wasn't as clean-shaven as I had last seen him, but it looked intentional. His hair was sloppy, but it worked. It all worked.

"Let her go," Priest said quietly, offering as much authority in his tone as threat. Adrian kept a firm grip on me, refusing to do his bidding. Priest took a small step forward. I hadn't expected any reaction from the subdued threat, but Adrian backed into me, drawing away from the advance.

"Release her," Priest demanded.

Adrian yanked me forward. He gripped my head with both hands, one under my chin and one at the base of the skull. *"Is this what you want?"* A voice spoke, but it was not mine, nor Adrian's, nor Priest's.

It was the demon, and I suspected from the stereo surround sound it was in my head and not audible.

"Release her or I will end you." Priest spoke softly. The menace he exuded sent a shiver down my spine. I didn't know what skills Priest had gained over the last few months, but I was certain I wanted a little more distance between us before I found out.

"You don't have the power for that," Adrian's demon protested.

Priest looked at me for the first time. We were strangely close and I wanted to reach out to him. My fears melted away as I looked at him. He may not have had the skills to protect me from gun-toting crazies, but I was confident he would have just the thing to battle my demon-possessed Freddy Krueger stalker boyfriend.

Priest winked at me, and abruptly reached past my head to grab Adrian. While he was occupied in the stranglehold, I elbowed his ribcage and squirmed out of my containment. I stumbled over to the adjacent wall and watched the underlying power struggle that was somewhat transparent to me, despite my lack of contact with them.

The puppeteering demon was hard to make out, but there was a darkened blur looming over Adrian Dorn's human body. I could see seamless energy backing Priest, but his was a column that stretched from head to toe and beyond in both directions, raising him and grounding him.

For all the influence the demon had over Adrian, and the mayor, and my traitorous body, Priest had no trouble resisting its control. The shadowy arms that reached for him slipped away like oil from water.

Adrian's physical body collapsed under Priest's infused touch. Soon after, the demon showed signs of weakening. The darkness elongated into an arch that encompassed Adrian. As it stretched, the blur thinned until it snapped like a rubber band, breaking its connection to Adrian and this world. The demon was gone.

Adrian collapsed to the floor panting, struggling to get enough breath. Priest stepped back in time to miss the spray of vomit he emitted. I moved toward him to help him up, but Priest stepped in my way and shook his head.

Adrian stood and looked at me and Priest, but didn't seem to recognize either of us. He apologized, apparently for his vomit, and stumbled down the hall away from us. "It's only temporary," Priest said. "He's just a shell now. A host to demons. If I were less moral—or more, perhaps—I'd kill him to save him the misery, but that's not my place to decide."

I stared up at Priest, looking for the words to express anger, disappointment, relief, love, and so many twisted versions of the emotions that come right before you tell someone, *"fuck you."* Unfortunately, I was too tired to argue, too stubborn to talk civilly, and too damn hurt to want to look at his face another second.

I shook my head and walked away. I probably should have offered him some gratitude for saving my life, but frankly, a three-month-late rescue wasn't my idea of chivalry.

Hard to Get

I PADDED DOWN THE carpeted steps as fast as I could without losing complete control of my descent. When I reached the main floor, I knitted through the guests with the hope of getting lost in the crowd. Unlike most overdramatized female displays, I actually didn't want Priest to catch up to me.

There had to be a line drawn eventually. The rules of the world might have changed, but the rules for my heart hadn't. I had come to terms with being denied his love, but when he denied me his friendship, that was too much. I was not a toy doll that could be placed on a shelf between visits. I deserved better than that, and even if I didn't... I would rather be alone than endure it.

"Lenore," Priest half hollered, half growled my name from somewhere behind me, but I ignored him. He was too far away to stop me anyway.

I picked up my pace and darted down a hallway that provided doorways to several different rooms I hadn't even seen yet. My attempt to lose myself was thus far successful, since I had no freaking clue where I was. I was practically sprinting down the hallway in an effort to find a room with access to the outdoors. At least out there I could get my bearings again.

The end of the hall spilled into a three-way divide. I chose the straight path into the library since I could see several tall windows through the doorway. Unfortunately, they turned out to be only windows, and not patio doors. I cursed and turned back and found Priest fast approaching the room.

"Len—" Priest started to scold me, but his arrival was cut off entirely by Ian tackling him into an adjacent room.

I heard the hard landing and a scuffle of legs and arms before I could get out the door to see what had happened. As I suspected, Ian had Priest pinned to the floor of the... oh hell, let's call it the "plaid duck room." *Pretentious bastard.*

"What are we doing with him?" Ian asked. He didn't glance back at me, though I imagine he could see me in his peripheral vision.

"Let me go." Priest spoke as carefully as he had with Adrian.

"Not until the lady decides. Why were you chasing her?"

Priest looked to me. "Because she's a tenacious little pain in the ass," he grumbled and I rolled my eyes. "But she's worth the chase," he added in a softer tone.

I looked away, unable to hold his gaze. It was all useless. Useless sentiment for a relationship that was permanently on ice.

"Matthew?" Haden joined me at the doorway of the plaid duck room and furrowed her brow at the scene.

"Yes, it's me. Can you call off your new addition, before I'm forced to remove him?"

Ian leaned in close to Priest and whispered something about him being his bitch. Priest glared at him, but made no attempts to push him off.

"He's okay, Ian," Haden said. "He's one of ours. Or at least he was." Haden offered Priest a hateful expression before she brusquely cajoled me from the room.

I heard the men shift behind us, before offering first name introductions. The gasp I heard after brought my head whipping back to see what Ian had done to Priest, but it was the opposite. Priest was erect and shaking Ian's hand, while Ian was on his knees huffing for an indeterminate reason. "Good to meet you, Ian," Priest said civilly, before he broke contact and stepped away.

Priest caught me watching and I looked away. I tucked myself slightly closer to Haden as we walked. I wasn't sure what had happened to Ian, but I wasn't going to be shaking Priest's hand anytime soon.

The Billiard Room

"H E'S DEAD?" HADEN ASKED as she grabbed a bottle of vodka from the small bar in the billiard room. It was a continuation of her celebration of Adrian's demise. She poured me another half glass and shoved it over to me. She was doing her best to play the big sister part. It was probably partly to apologize for earlier, but also because she didn't want to leave me without backup against Priest. She knew how hard I had taken his departure.

The wood-paneled room was dimly lit, with focused lamps over three green-felted pool tables. Devin was playing on all three of them simultaneously, one against Haden, one against Ian, and one against me, but Haden and I had already forfeited so Ian took over, leaving the men to play three simultaneous games.

Ian and I sat on the stools next to the bar while Priest retold the story of our encounter with Adrian. He had made himself at home on a tufted leather loveseat with a club soda and lime over ice. He kept eye contact with whoever was speaking, but when he was between explanations he looked at me. I was doing my best to look entirely occupied with my drink at those times.

"He isn't dead. I just kicked him out like I do with the grim," Priest answered Haden.

"But he's a human, right?" Devin stepped away from his shot to tap the ash off his cigarette before returning it to the corner of his mouth.

"Yes, but it's the same thing. Adrian's demon must be very powerful. It's one thing to jump into a vacant mind, but it's an entirely different thing to get inside the mind of a conscious human being and make them walk, talk, and react against their will."

"Not to mention he's asserting influence on the people around him on top of that," I added with an unintentional yawn. The alcohol wasn't helping my sleep-deprived state. "He's been in my dreams since... you left." I cleared my throat and drank down my vodka in one big gulp.

"I still don't understand your dreams." Haden swung around the bar and sat on the arm of the loveseat facing Priest. "You describe it like an alien encounter, but if Adrian was a man, wouldn't that mean a human baby?"

"Yeah, but it would have a demon on the inside... right?" I looked at Priest for confirmation.

He nodded. "It could be a cambion: half human, half demon. Demons can't simply walk in and set down camp on the Earth. They have no corporeal bodies. Most are banished human souls, souls that were deemed unworthy of forgiveness and have thus spent thousands of years in the depths of hell becoming demons."

"So, it's like the prison system," Devin suggested. "You come out worse than you go in."

Priest nodded at Devin.

"I thought you said demons were here before man," I reasoned.

"Yes, but demon is a vague term. I am an animal and so is a fish, but I can't breathe under water, and I don't taste as good with tartar sauce."

He offered me a hint of a smile to help along his joke, and it drew a slight smirk from me, but as soon as I was able to, I put back on my business face. "Adrian's demon might be a high-ranking principality, which means he isn't simply a banished soul, he is one of the original bad guys. I suspect his primary purpose in impregnating you was not to create a cambion, but rather to create a body to possess. He was essentially planning to imbed his essence in the child at conception, thereby providing himself with a permanent body to walk the Earth in."

"Wait, wait." Haden waved her hands, not noticing that she was spilling her vodka as she did. "That's still not answering my question. My question is, how is a human man, demon-puppet or not, going to impregnate a human female?" She looked around the room for understanding, but the only one getting it was me, and I was pretending not to. "Guys, we are barren." Haden motioned between the two of us. "No cycles, remember? I don't know what the sperm counts are doing on your ends, but the only eggs in our bodies are poached."

I exchanged a look with Ian, but he was staying quiet per my request. Devin stopped mid-shot to ponder Haden's question. "How *does* that work?" he asked before sinking his next ball in the corner pocket. "I mean, I get that we're relying on a few dozen miracles a day by now, but don't you have to have the basic biological ingredients to make a baby?"

"Yes," Priest answered and looked to me. I wasn't sure he was looking for me to offer an answer or to admit the answer, but when Haden and Devin joined in on the nonverbal interrogation I decided my secret had held long enough.

"Since the dreams started... I've been... bleeding... again." Haden's eyes widened with offense, but as she realized what it meant, she sobered—emotionally—and moved back to the bar to pour more vodka in my glass. Devin barely reacted, but he hit his balls a little harder than before. He probably wasn't happy I had kept it from him, but given the personal nature of it, he probably also understood why I did. Priest didn't seem surprised in the least, making me wonder how much he knew about my predicament before tonight.

"He didn't get that far though, right?" Haden murmured while we were in close proximity. I shook my head. "Good." Haden turned abruptly back to Priest and raised her glass. "So, why aren't we killing Adrian before the demon comes back to him?"

"Because he's an innocent human, or at least as innocent as any of us."

"Well, that's a fuckin' stupid answer," Haden slurred slightly.

"Okay, how about this," Priest continued. "We need to be able to identify the demon, when he comes back, and he's likely to come back to Adrian because he's already got him broken in."

"Oh, yeah, that's a fuckin' *not* stupid answer." Haden laughed and joined Priest on the loveseat. He smiled at her as she leaned over to point her vodka-loaded finger at him. "You're a smart guy, Matthew." Vodka splashed out of her glass onto his tux, but he barely moved except to look down at his soaked shirt. "But you're not that smart. You know why?"

I could tell Haden was trying to have a private conversation with Priest, but her volume was stuck on high so she could hear herself, and consequently there was no hope of anyone missing it. Devin kept a sideways gaze on them. Ian got up to finally take his shots. Meanwhile, I took on my newly over-poured glass of vodka.

"Why is that, Haden?" Priest took the liberty of tucking a strand of Haden's hair behind her ear, since she was close enough to do so. The act seemed to throw off her increasingly drunken mind, but when she looked back at me, she remembered what her objective was.

"You lost her, Matthew. You walked away, and you broke her."

He looked over Haden carefully, not once looking to me. He must have seen the empathy in Haden's eyes that was meant for me. Haden's heart, turned inside out, was a rare show and definitely not to be missed.

"I don't mean you broke her heart," she amended, tapping the base of her glass on his chest. "I mean you broke her. The fight's gone, you know?" Priest nodded. "She had it. She really did, but now it's gone."

Priest rested his hand on her face and closed his eyes slowly. When he opened them I could see his emerald eyes had only the tiniest hint of pupils, like he had just stepped out into the sun.

"I know." Priest took her glass from her and rested it on the arm of the couch. Haden slumped down on his chest, apparently passed out. He brushed her hair back, perfectly content to let her add slobber to the wetness on his chest. It was a strange, unfamiliar interaction, one that left me with a twinge of jealousy. "Don't you worry, Haden," Priest whispered to her and then looked straight at me. "I'm going to bring back her fire."

He locked his eyes on mine and I couldn't look away. There wasn't any pleading or jest in the statement, just determination. Something had obviously changed for him over the last three months to make him so confident, but something had changed for me as well, and it was the opposite of confidence.

I found the strength to extract myself from his visual grip and made my excuses to get some air. I hoped, since Priest was pinned under Haden, that he wouldn't follow me.

Breathe

"YOU OKAY?" IAN STEPPED up beside me on the veranda. The air had turned a little cool since I had been out earlier, but the vodka was helping with some of that.

"Yeah." I nodded, looking out onto the lawn that was still perfectly maintained despite the world going to shit. Some things never changed for the rich. They were still oblivious to what was going on in the real world. "Thanks for not telling my secret."

He nodded. "For as much good as it did."

"Still, it's nice to have someone I can rely on for the little things."

He looked me over, and glanced back at the house. "Care to tell me who that guy is to you?"

"Former resident religious advisor," I answered tersely.

"Yeah, I got the memo on that, Chief. Now why don't you tell me how you really feel?"

I smiled thinly at him. "Because I don't want to cry on my dress."

"Oh, so its love." He smirked at me and my smile broadened.

"He's a former priest, thus my nickname for him. It's been difficult for him to come to terms with his relationship with God and how to serve him in this new world. Add a woman into the picture and you're liable to make his brain explode."

"He seems to be in control of things now."

I nodded and looked back to the yard. "Yeah, he does seem... put together."

"You mind explaining what the hell he did to me back there when he shook my hand?"

I smiled, though Ian didn't seem to find it funny. "I've experienced Priest's power first hand. It's not all his own, and it can be... humbling."

"Humbling? Hell, if my mother were still alive, I'd go crawl into her lap and cry."

I laughed even though I knew he was serious. "Yeah, I know what you mean. He seems to have gotten stronger. I've never seen him use it so nonchalantly."

"What happens now? Is he coming back with us?" I shrugged—back to my useless responses. "You know Devin will defer to you on that decision, and Haden's clearly done for the night."

"What do you think?" I asked.

Ian laughed. "Come on, Chief, I'm just the new guy."

"You've been helpful so far."

"Okay. I guess if I were about to go to war with a demon, I would want a priest on my side, former or otherwise." I nodded. I already knew that was what the ultimate answer would be, but it was nice to have someone else say it so I didn't have to. "You want me to have the valet bring the truck around, while you go gather the troops?"

"Yeah, thanks," I said and he started toward the house. "Ian," I called to him. He swung back around. "Earlier, when we were out here, was it Priest that was watching us?"

"Oh, yeah, it was. That's why I tackled him when I saw him running after you. I thought he was attacking you."

"Thanks for that too, by the way. Somewhat unnecessary, but it did save me from an awkward conversation."

"No problem." He started to move again, but stopped and turned back. "It must be love, because he looked like he was going to rip my head off just for touching your feet." He tipped his brow and headed inside.

Not Now

D EVIN WORKED ON GETTING Haden strapped into position on the passenger side of the truck with the addition of an ice bucket, in case she needed to ralph during the journey home. None of us had stopped to change clothes, but it seemed to be customary to take the outfits as a door prize. It wasn't like anyone had paid for them anyway.

The valet pulled up in Priest's Tahoe behind us. It had already been discussed that Priest would come back with us, but it was also mentioned that Devin's truck seats four comfortably. Priest didn't object to bringing his own vehicle.

Ian opened the backdoor for me to climb in. Priest cut me off and stood in my path. "Lenore, why don't you join me for the ride back? We can talk."

Part of me wanted to be alone with Priest, mostly to berate him for being an asshole, but that would only take about three minutes. The remaining forty or so were going to be awkward and heart-wrenching. I wasn't ready for that.

I shook my head and side-stepped him.

"Lenore," he said gently and reached out to touch me. I whipped away from him so fast that Ian jumped forward, prepared to break something on Priest. I wasn't interested in being manhandled, but more so I wanted to avoid being influenced by his power. If Priest wanted my forgiveness, he was going to have to earn it the hard way.

Priest's eyes widened as he realized how fervent I was in my avoidance of him. He looked more angry than hurt. I ignored him and headed to the truck cab. "Lenore." He started after me, but Ian went chest to chest with him. "We need to talk," he called after me. I climbed into the truck without another word.

"Lady doesn't appear to want your company right now," Ian said.

"Matthew, just talk to her at home!" Devin griped as he shut the passenger door and headed around to the driver's side.

"I think we both know I can get you to move," Priest said grimly to Ian.

"I think we both know that won't change whether she wants to be around you," Ian answered.

"Let's go!" Devin smacked his hand on the truck top before shutting his driver's side door. I knew I was part of the reason he was so mad, but I didn't want to deal with him either.

"Lenore!" Priest tried one last time, finally showing the desperation in his voice.

"Look, Matthew." Ian rested a hand on his shoulder. "I know you're new to the whole relationship thing, so I'll give you a hint: It's too soon to be demanding, and too late to be begging."

Priest looked away from me and examined our new recruit with new eyes. The anger and pain drained from his face before he looked back at me. "I'm sorry, Lenore, I just... missed you." I barely afforded him a glance, but I could see he wanted to say so much more. Instead, he patted Ian on the shoulder and headed to his vehicle.

Ian started to climb in next to me.

"Ian, you mind driving?" Devin asked as he got back out again. Ian was reasonably surprised by the request, but switched places with him.

Devin slipped into the backseat and wrapped an arm around me. When we were well on our way, I lost the battle with my emotions and started to cry. I hadn't afforded myself the luxury of tears after Priest left, but those saved up tears returned with interest.

Somewhere between wet cheeks and home, I also lost my battle with sleep. For the first time in months, I slept soundly against Devin's chest, and didn't wake from a nightmare.

The Morning After

I WOKE THE NEXT day well past noon, which was no shock to me since I was so desperate for sleep. I was more surprised that no one had woken me, especially since everyone was gathered at the table, deep in discussion, when I came downstairs.

Four faces looked up at me when I sauntered into the kitchen in my pajamas—thank you, Devin. Ian and Haden offered me a simultaneous sarcastic "good morning." Devin smiled warmly and put out his arm and leg for me to sit on his lap. I was still a little groggy, so I didn't take anything into account before sitting on his lap and looping my arm around his neck for balance.

Priest was cattycorner to us, and he locked eyes with me for a moment before I broke the connection to stare intently at my un-manicured nails.

"How did you sleep?" Devin asked, rubbing my back.

"No nightmares," I said.

"Good," he said, sounding relieved. "We were just catching up with Matthew. We told him about your incident with that grim at the competition."

"What did you feel when you were fighting him?" Priest asked.

I looked around the room at the faces anticipating further information. "Anger."

"Why?"

"I don't know, Priest." I stood up and left Devin's lap to dig in the refrigerator for some kind of breakfast—or lunch.

"I can find out, if you'll permit me," he said.

"No." I slammed the fridge door shut and set my jar of jelly on the counter and pulled down some crackers from the cupboard.

"Lenore," Devin said softly.

I turned around to face him. "You want to offer up your soul to bare, Devin, go ahead." I gestured to Priest. "I'm sick of being his test subject."

Priest stood up. Devin matched him and waved him off so he could reason with me. "Please, Lenore, let's just do this so we can have some answers." He sounded frustrated. He hated putting his duty between us, but he was sensing the impending doom like the rest of us. He wanted to know what he needed to do. "If you are destined to fight this evil then we should at least know what weaponry you're packing."

I probably would have fought harder to avoid Priest's voodoo, but I couldn't say no to Devin. Considering how deathly still Haden was being as she stared into empty space, I knew she was seconds from flipping out again. Ian didn't really care either way, but when I looked at him he tipped his brow and smiled at me. The tiny gesture amused me and called to my ego.

"Okay." I sat down in Devin's chair and crossed my arms. "Pick my brain, then." I leaned forward and whispered, "Just don't pull the thread."

Priest smirked slightly at that comment before coming around to face me. He stood in front of me, forcing me to look up at him. I tried to look brave, but I was already breathing harder. Devin rested his hand on my shoulder.

"A little space is best, if you recall, Devin." Priest looked to him sympathetically and his hand slid from my shoulder.

I glanced at Ian and he crossed his eyes at me. I shook my head at his method of dispelling the tension in the room. He was a strange cat, but his levity was oddly enough easing my fear. Priest glanced between us. He must not have enjoyed our little joke.

"This is just me, Lenore," Priest said before he started. "I won't use Him, okay?"

I nodded and took in a deep breath. I wasn't sure what was more nerve-wracking: my expectations of what was about to happen, or the proximity of our bodies. So close and yet...

Priest pressed his hand to the side of my face. He closed his eyes and murmured a nonsensical blessing. I wondered if the language was even Latin anymore or if he had jumped into the deep end of speaking tongues.

His thumb caressed my cheek. I resisted the romantic fantasy in my mind that urged me to turn my head and suck on his thumb. As the warmth descended over me, I closed my eyes and let my mind turn to goo.

"Lenore, I need you to think about that grim." I ignored him—he was threatening to harsh my groove, and I wanted nothing to do with it. "It's okay, I won't leave you alone. Just try to remember what you felt when you first saw him."

My head fell back against my will and a wave of rage flooded my mind just as it had when I saw the grim. As promised, Priest stayed with me during the tidal wave of emotion. I could feel his reassuring presence, looming and penetrating. "I hate him. I must kill him." My voice sounded hoarse to my own ears.

"Why?"

I shouldn't have had that answer, but I was speaking it before I could see the end of the sentence in my mind. "He did this to me," I hissed, feeling the pain in my side, where long ago a knife had wounded me too deep to heal completely.

"What did he do to you?"

"I lost my family, because of him." I spoke the words, but that was as far as my comprehension went. I could only assume it had something to do with my biological family. Perhaps I had blocked out a traumatic memory of my parents being killed.

"What did you do to him at the competition?" Priest continued. "You fought and won. How did you win?"

I opened my eyes and looked at Priest and the others. I could see their natural energies. Priest's ever-present connection to his God was thick, but inactive, like it was during his battle with Adrian. The others had a weak glow that only grounded them. They were leashed to the Earth like dogs. Fodder for demons.

"How did you win?" Priest asked again, more earnestly.

"I ripped his soul in two," I answered callously.

His mouth gaped, but he didn't open his eyes. "How did you do that? What power did you use to do that?"

"Mine," I whispered and yanked my thread. Priest gasped at the power it invoked. I felt him reaching for more of his power, compulsively trying to subdue me, but my instincts kicked in and I pushed him away.

Priest collided with the oven behind him. He stared at me, wide-eyed and panting, trying to discern what he had just witnessed. I wasn't sure why I had expelled him so abruptly, but I assumed that dark part of me was a little touchy after Father Ed's botched exorcism.

Devin moved to help him up. He glanced at me cautiously as he pulled Priest to his feet. I suddenly realized I was grinning like a crackpot. I relinquished the loony expression and shook my head. "I'm sorry. I don't know why I did that."

"Your directives kicked in. You're used to hiding it." Priest rubbed his elbow where it had hit a drawer knob.

"Hiding *it*?" I asked.

"The power inside of you," he answered.

"I don't have anything inside of me," I squealed. I glanced at Ian. He didn't meet my eyes long enough to assure me. "I'm not possessed!" I yelled, and moved out of my chair to get away from everyone.

"Not possessed, just endowed." Priest moved forward and I backed myself into the side door. "You've been given some very powerful defenses."

I glanced at Ian and he gave me a silent golf clap. I groaned and slammed my head against the door. "Fine! What the hell am I supposed to do with this power?"

"I would imagine killing the demon that's possessing Adrian Dorn would be a good place to start, but you may want to start a little smaller."

And I Shall Call Him Squishy

"**I** GOT YOU A stinky one." Ian smirked as he approached me in the backyard, chomping his gum. I knew his eyes were aglow with amusement somewhere behind his sunglasses.

"Why did you get me a stinky one?" I asked as he sidled up next to me.

"I think it adds a hint of drama." He moved in closer to me to whisper, "He really hates it when I get close to you."

"Devin?" I asked, not turning around to see my audience.

"No... Well, him too, but I think he's happier when I'm next to you than Haden. Your priest wants to castrate me."

"I can't see why. He's not exactly offering his bed."

"Give it time, he'll come around. In the meantime, I think I'll have some fun."

"Please don't, I already have an impending awkward conversation penciled in for later. I don't want to add to the topics," I complained.

"Oh, come on, can't we just see if we can make steam come out of his ears?"

"No, I'm too busy for games. I have to practice for a war. In case you haven't heard, I'm like *special* and stuff."

He chuckled and backed away slightly. "Would it make you feel any better if I told you you seem completely un-special to me?"

"Maybe."

"In that case, you are the most boring, ordinary person I have ever met, and just standing near you makes me yawn." He yawned for effect.

"Did you like killing people?" I asked completely out of the blue. I expected him to flounder for a response, but he only smiled at the sudden shift in conversation.

"I liked figuring people out. I liked observing their day-to-day habits and predicting their next move. I liked the hunt, but not the kill. That part was just my job."

"I liked killing that demon. I liked it a lot," I admitted. I watched his face for signs of judgment, but he had none. "What does that mean?"

"It means he must have been a really bad guy."

"What if I'm the one who's bad?" I mumbled.

"If you're gonna talk dirty to me then this friendship is going to get a little strained." He perked an eyebrow.

I scoffed. "I'm serious. What if that priest was actually exorcising some fragment of evil from me? What if I'm like Adrian and I don't even know it?"

Ian paused to think about his response. "What if what he was exorcising wasn't put there by a demon? What if it was put there by God?" I rolled my eyes but he was serious. "No matter how often religions glamorize peace, piety, and penance, when it comes right down to it, if God puts a hammer in your hand, you'd better use it." He shrugged and walked away, but not before slapping me on my ass.

I turned my attention to the chained grim some yards away on the barn. We shouldn't have brought him to our home, but if I was as skilled as Priest thought, I would be dispatching him very soon.

I walked over to him and he growled and bucked, trying to get to me. He was fairly young, but as Ian promised, he smelled like garbage. I offered Ian a scrunched-nose glare for his gifted *drama*, but he only offered me a big smile with thumbs up. Priest and the others were standing with him, watching me intently.

I wanted this over with, so I grabbed the grim by the neck and pushed into his mind, using my thread like an anchor to mine. A flood of angry, hateful, wanton thoughts ripped into me, demanding me to absorb them and foster new. His manifest destiny was to make every living person hurt as much and as deeply as he did.

I felt blindly for his soul, as I had with the other grim. At the back of his mind, beyond the hate, was a tiny shredded version of a soul. The light, long since extinguished, had no strength to rise beyond the pain. I gripped the tiny fragile fragment of humanity with my non-corporeal hand. I knew squeezing it would destroy it forever, but I couldn't do it.

The soul, crippled as it was, once belonged to a man. A man who had grown his own hell inside of himself, long before the demons got hold of him. I drew out the fragment, knowing it would never be enough to bring back the man he was, but that was for the best. At least the little pieces of him that weren't broken would be free.

I expected the soul fragment to float away like a dandelion seed in the wind, but the little bugger had more zest than that. A flash of light blinded me, followed by a tiny shockwave that knocked me to the ground.

I propped myself up and took an inventory of my body. My heart was racing, but I wasn't hurt. I felt energized and happy beyond words. I hoped that meant I did something good for the little guy.

Priest knelt down next to me, but he didn't ask the dozens of questions on his mind. He was only observing. He probably knew I had no freaking clue what I was doing.

"What happened to the grim?" I asked before Devin's arrival started an interrogation.

"He's empty," Priest answered without looking back at it. "Did you kill the demon?"

"No, this one wasn't a demon, just a lost soul. I think I freed it."

"Freed it?" Devin asked. "Like freed it from hell?"

"I think so." I shrugged.

"Freed it to go to heaven?" Priest asked suspiciously.

"I don't know," I said even though I was pretty sure that was what I had done.

Priest frowned, looking me over as if there might be instructions tattooed on me somewhere. He leaned forward and kissed my forehead. His mouth slid down my temple, dropping to my ear. "You are remarkable." He moved back and pinned me with his eyes as he helped me off the ground.

I withdrew my hand from his grip and walked away. There was no point getting excited about grateful kisses, even if they were hot.

The Talk

T HE NEXT MORNING, I slipped downstairs at a reasonable brunch hour. I had forgotten Priest was preternaturally awake at dawn. He was already pouring his second cup of coffee when I froze in place half way through the living room. No one else was awake, and this was the first time we had been alone together since he had returned.

He noticed me standing there and smiled warmly. "Coffee?" He raised the carafe. I nodded and moved forward while he poured me a cup. "Sugar?"

"Just cream. We like to save the sugar for important things."

"Like cream of wheat?" he suggested and handed me the mug.

"Yeah," I answered guardedly, as I tried to remember when I had revealed my favorite breakfast to him.

He handed me the powdered cream and leaned against the fridge. He seemed to be debating whether to return to his book at the table, or stay close to me.

When I was finished doctoring my coffee, he put the creamer back in the cupboard and pulled out a chair at the table for me. "Would you sit with me?"

I was already turning to leave, but I decided this was as good a time as any to break open my can of irritations. Not to mention his face was stricken with controlled panic, and refusing him might have given him a heart attack.

I sat, and he scooted the chair in behind me. "A little early for that much chivalry, isn't it?"

"Yes, but it's also far too late, so you can just call it sucking up." He smiled as he took the seat across from me. I smirked back, just to release some of the tension knitted in his shoulders. "Lenore, since we are alone, I have a thousand things I need and want to say, but before we start any of that, I need to ask you one question." He paused to see if I would object, which I didn't. "Are you and Ian *together*?"

I chuckled and took a slow sip of my coffee before answering. It was torture to him since he was again on the verge of a coronary. "Why so interested in my relationship status now?"

"I've always been interested in your relationship status. Your answer, please."

"No, we aren't together. I have actually been trying to peel him off Haden before Devin starts peeing on her. I'm not sure what difference it makes to you, though."

"Lenore." He reached across the table to touch or caress my hand, but I drew it back. His eyes scolded me, but pain quickly overtook them. "Why are you pulling away from me?"

"Because I'm not yours, Priest," I said boldly. "I'm not yours to touch, or toy with—I never was. I am especially not yours to hurt anymore." He stared blankly at me, unable to defend against such a statement. "I know you want to explain where you've been and I'm sure in the end there was some higher purpose in your leaving, but

I don't care about that. All I care about is that when I needed you the most, you were gone." I waited to see if he wanted to interject an excuse, but he didn't. He was going to let me rant as long as I wanted.

"I've got plenty of brawn around here to defend me. I don't expect you to be the one to save me all the time, but you left right when I needed you. That asshole was in my dreams, Priest. Mocking me with my own unconscious mind. You left me to fight him off by myself." I shook my head at his passive response to my anger and left the table. There was no point sitting in silence.

I heard his chair squawk and bang against the wall as he stood. "You misunderstood my reason for leaving." I stopped, but I didn't turn around. "I was stupid and careless when it came to that nut job hermit, but I wasn't surprised you outwitted him. I do blame myself for you getting shot, but that's not why I left." He took a step toward me and I turned to face him. He was careful not to get too close.

"When you were reading the grim—Avery—you started to cry and I assumed that meant it was hurting you. I tried to dispel it, but I couldn't. It was too entrenched." Priest's jaw twisted in disgust. "That's when I realized I wasn't prepared for the bigger threats lurking beyond our perception. All I've been doing, since I left, is strengthening the powers I've been given."

"You didn't have to leave to do that," I said.

He stepped closer. "Yes, I did."

"Why?"

"You know why." He loomed over me, sharing my air.

"Yeah, I know why." I took a long step back and crossed my arms. "Because I distract you from your *true* path."

"My path is with you, Lenore. I'm here for you."

"No!" I didn't mean to snap at him, but I couldn't help it. "You're here for Him." I shoved my finger up to the proverbial heavens. "I saw August's body, Priest." He took in a breath and raised his chin. "*You* are here to do God's work. *I* am here to save the people left on this Earth."

"Since when is saving fellow human beings not God's work?"

"Since He abandoned us here!" I couldn't have yelled any louder if I tried. I could hear the scuffle above me as one or more of my partners stumbled out of bed to help in the fight. "Since he left us to fertilize the next demon plague!"

"That's not what He did!"

"The fuck He didn't! We are good people, Priest!" I beat my fist to my chest, since there was nothing nearby to throw. "We may not have deserved a front row seat in heaven, but we deserved to at least stand in line for admission!"

Devin and Ian practically tripped over each other down the stairs, but when they saw me red-faced and yelling at the top of my lungs, they paused, not daring to move forward or back.

"Not everyone deserves that chance," Priest interjected.

"*Everyone* deserves that chance! Including that shriveled little soul I saved yesterday!" I paced, trying to find something to hit or break. "We deserve a chance to face our accuser and plead our ignorance."

"What do you think this is?" Priest motioned vaguely to everything. "This is the second chance!"

"Bullshit! This is extinction! We are the last starving animals after a cataclysmic event." Haden joined the party at the bottom of the stairs. "And what no one wants to think about, what no one wants to say out loud, is that no matter what we do—kill Adrian, destroy the grim, or overthrow a demonic invasion—there is nothing after this. The human race is dying! *These* are the end of days, right here, right now!" I shook my head, feeling the impact of the words leaving my mouth. "There is no point to any of this, except to negotiate for a belated general admission ticket. So don't tell me you are here for *me*, because you don't wipe your ass unless He approves." I avoided the crowd in the living room and decided to take my leave through the side door.

"You know, Lenore, I can't tell where your anger for me stops and your anger for God begins," Priest snarled before I could get through the door. "If this is about us, then let's keep Him out of it. If it's about something else, then I'm sure He'd be happy to respond to your accusations." He threatened with the authority of someone who could reduce me to a quivering blob with one touch.

I turned back to him and, with a small amount of amusement, turned his former favorite blaspheme back on him. "Fuck God." I slammed the door behind me on my exit.

Once Upon a Front Porch, a Backstory Did Live

I HADN'T BEEN TO the house in over two years. It was dilapidated, but then again it wasn't in great of shape when I had lived there. The white paint was peeled down to the gray wood underneath. The rusted screen door screeched just looking at it, but the porch swing still looked brand new.

I stepped up onto the porch and took a seat on the swing. I pushed off the railing and let the slow rocking motion remind me I was still somewhat sane. I spent most of the day mulling over my temper tantrum. I hated myself and everyone else for ever thinking I could lead them.

Haden had been right about me. I was finally grasping my role in all of this, but then Priest left and I fell apart. I could make as many excuses as I wanted about why, but the truth was, I was just sad. Maybe if I hadn't been so hurt, Adrian wouldn't have gotten so deep into my head or my bed.

It was clear my late-in-life adoption and my single-child upbring-ing—not to mention the death of over half the human race—had left me constantly craving companionship, but I had Haden and Devin for that. Priest was a different connection for me. I felt stronger when he was around. I could see more, feel more, and do more. Perhaps it was because I was in love with him, or perhaps it was because he was so special.

August had been special, and I latched onto her immediately. I had done more than I ever thought possible for her. The only time I had considered leaving her side was to go to Priest. That, of course, didn't turn out, since I thought he was dead. When she died, Priest came back again.

The last three months was the first time since my training I had been without both of them. It took me a good deal of time to get over that first little abandonment as well, but I did learn from it. Even now, I hated myself for taking so long to forgive her.

As much as Priest's desertion hurt me, I knew I needed to forgive him. He had obviously increased his power and if it took focused solitude to do it, then I couldn't hate him for it. Especially since he did it to protect me.

I heard a branch snap. I bolted upright and pulled my gun from the small of my back. Ian came around the corner of the house with his hands up. I offered him a chin thrust *hello* and holstered my gun back in my waistband. "They sent you to kill me, didn't they?"

He smirked as he stepped onto the porch. "Oh, Chief, if that were the case, you'd be dead already." He stayed standing rather than join me on the swing.

"I take it you're the search party then?"

"You've been gone awhile, and they were getting antsy."

"Sorry you had to witness that spectacle."

"After you left, Matthew explained to us about your fallen leader. Is she really crystalline?"

I nodded and sat back in my lounging position. "There's a hard conversation to have. Pass the potatoes, oh and by the way, August was sent by God to save the world, so you'll need to take over that job for her."

"She must have been pretty... special," he said, not finding a better word for it.

"She was my rock." I frowned. "When she died, I felt adrift." I chuckled. "I still feel adrift."

"I'm sorry," Ian offered. I shrugged. There wasn't anything to do but feel the pain and move on. "What is this place?" Ian asked, looking over my choice of thinking spots.

"My childhood home," I answered somewhat proudly.

"Are your parents...?" He reached for his gun and waited for me to answer the question he hadn't asked.

"No." I smiled. "They died a while before the apocalypse. They adopted me when they were in their fifties and I was already seven. I never had much hope of being with them long into my adulthood."

"That's an unusual union," he said, moving behind my swing to give it a gentle shove so I didn't have to keep pushing off the railing.

"They lost a child the first go around. She was 12. Car accident, I believe. My mother wasn't able to conceive after her. She was content with that, until life robbed her of the future she was planning on. They eventually looked into adoption to fill the void. I think they wanted a newborn, but by that time they were kind of in a gray area. My age and the fact that I had absolutely no living relatives was the reason they got me."

"They were good people, I assume?" he asked carefully.

"Yes, it was like being raised by grandparents. They didn't have the stamina to enforce strict punishments, so they played up their feebleness of age to get what they wanted. They were both very affectionate though. I had a nice childhood. Nothing to blame my current faults on." I looked back at him with a smile and he chuckled.

"What were your birth parents like?"

"I don't know. I don't remember them. I came into foster care around six. It's just a blur of new people every day between then and my adoptive parents. What about you? Anyone to blame your murderous tendencies on?"

"You mean besides the U.S. government?"

"Excluding them."

"No, not really. I had a pretty regular family life." He frowned and his eyes glazed over as he thought about something.

"Anyone still... here?"

"Nope," he said, snapping out of his memories. I nodded— there wasn't much more to say on that subject. The horse was dead, beaten, and long since buried. "Looks like rain." He nodded to the sky. As if on cue, a distant cloud grumbled about the storm about to roll in. "You should probably get back so you don't have to ride the ATV back in the rain."

I smiled and shook my head. "Are you kidding? That there is what separates the men from the boys, and the Midwestern cowboys from the west coast surfers." I stood up to peek at the sky beyond the roof of the porch.

"You do realize if I come back without you, Devin will raise hell."

"I'm sure you can handle him."

"Still doesn't mean it's my preference," he mumbled.

I looked back at him, trying to discern if this was his version of pouting. "What is your preference, Ian? Why are you still here?"

"I thought we were talking."

"No." I leaned against the railing and he backed against the wall of the house. "I mean why are you still hanging out with us? I get you have a thing for Haden, but come on. You gotta see the bigger picture here. We are the blind leading the blind, into a battle we can't see coming, and can't win. Don't you want to jump ship now, while you still can?"

Ian looked out past me. "You like the storms, right?" I nodded. "Well, you're like that storm. I can see it coming, and I'm definitely scared, but I kind of can't wait to see it up close."

I snorted. "You realize it's not just pretty lightening and petrichor. It's downed power lines, flooding, and tornadoes."

He shrugged. "Come on, Lenore. You said it yourself. This is the end of days. Might as well make it one hell of a last stand." He grinned wickedly. "You mind if I stay for the storm?"

"Front row seats two." I gestured to the swing. We sat down and waited for the rain to roll in.

Reign Down on Me

I T WAS WELL INTO the dusking evening before Ian and I came
through the side door in our sneakers, splotching wet footprints
across the kitchen floor. I could see Priest asleep on the couch with his
book on his chest. I motioned for Ian to follow me.

I took him into the laundry room and started removing my wet
clothes. He took my cue and started undressing as well. He managed
to get his clothes off with no trouble, but my jeans were a little tight
to begin with, and the rain had made my legs rubber.

Since I practically ripped off a nail to get them over my hips, he
decided to help me. He cussed and laughed when he had trouble too.
"I think your legs have swollen," he whispered.

"Nebraska rain will make anything grow," I retorted.

He yanked again and they gave way, but I slipped on the wet floor.
Luckily, Ian mostly caught me, so I didn't bruise my ass. He snorted
trying to cover his laughter, and I hissed with escaping giggles.

"Shhh," he hushed me.

His laughter slowed and stopped as he looked me over. I was in my
bra and underwear, and in most normal situations I would have assumed he was looking at my body, but I knew he wasn't. The purplish
puckered scars that peppered my flesh were in full view.

"Jesus, what is all this?"

"My stubbornness, I'm told." I smirked at his reaction. It wasn't nearly as sympathetic to the pain as empathetic, like he understood the pain a little more personally. Given that he must have inflicted wounds such as mine intentionally on other people, that didn't really surprise me. He touched one of the scars gingerly. A smile spread across his face, but I didn't get a chance to ask him about it.

"Priest," I gasped, suddenly realizing the shadow outside the door was a man. It took me a moment to realize why he looked horrified. I was lying on the floor in Ian's arms, down to my knickers—save the last quarter of my pants—and Ian was down to his boxers.

Ian seemed to find the situation more amusing than embarrassing. He didn't even look at Priest before he stood and yanked the remainder of my pants off. "Well, Lenore, I can honestly say, that's the hardest I've ever had to work to get a woman's pants off." He winked at me and I smiled despite my annoyance that he was trying to incite Priest.

"Gimme that." I stood up and yanked my pants from him. "Get upstairs." I started loading the washing machine and he gave me a mocking wide-eyed expression that Priest couldn't see before he brushed passed him to go upstairs.

"We should talk." Priest stepped out of the doorway and disappeared into the living room.

I slammed the lid to the washing machine and followed him out. "Don't do that."

"What?" He turned around, doing a full circle since I was already passing him up.

"Don't be... so damn reserved," I said, stopping at the base of the stairs to see his response.

"I don't know how to be with you right now. You're so angry."

"I'm not angry. I'm frustrated." I sighed and bit back my lips when I could hear that I did indeed sound angry. "I know there are bigger things at stake right now than you and me, and come tomorrow, I'm going to put on my big-girl panties and deal with them, but I can't face any of that without you. That doesn't mean you have to save me, or bless me, or hold my hand. It just means you have to be there. Can you do that for me, Priest? Can you be there for me?"

"Yes," he answered and stepped forward. He stopped and looked me over. I suddenly remembered I was mostly naked and cold.

"That was nothing in the laundry room, by the way. I just didn't want our clothes to mildew and make the house smell."

"I believe you, but it seemed a little more intimate than friends from where I was standing."

"Ian and I kind of broke into our friendship pretty hard, so what might seem like intimacy to you is just comfortable familiarity to us." He didn't seem to be satisfied with that answer, but he didn't say anything. "The only man I want to be intimate with is standing right in front of me and yet I couldn't feel any more distant from him. I don't know what this is anymore," I motioned between us, "but it's not intimacy... and I don't think you'll ever let it be. So don't go getting territorial over a toy you don't even want to play with."

He raised his chin, defiantly hurt by the statement, but again he was silent. I was sick of the silence.

"Good night, Priest." I turned to go upstairs, but he caught my arm.

Before he could answer for the delay or the intensity in his look, I heard Devin cussing upstairs, followed soon after by the sound of a struggle. "Oh shit," I whined before clearing the path for Ian's body to finish rolling down the stairs.

Broken Hearts and Noses

"ALRIGHT, LET'S DO THIS, you cocky son of a bitch!" Ian yelled upstairs as he wiped blood from his lip. Still in his boxers, he jumped up and shoved past me to go out the backdoor.

"Ian, what—?" I started to ask when Devin rumbled down the stairs in his boxers.

"Devin, what the fuck is wrong with you?" Haden yelled, coming down right after him in her fanciest nightgown.

They were both out the door behind Ian before I could get an answer. I started to follow, but Priest still had hold of my arm. When he tugged me from my destination, I ripped it away, not wishing to miss any of the unfolding drama.

As I stepped out onto the back porch, I realized how cold it was, and instantly regretted not going upstairs for more clothes. Ian and Devin were standing in the rain, facing off like kickboxers. Haden was latched to the porch post, transfixed by the fight about to unfold. Stunned silence was a strange color on her.

"What the hell happened?" I asked her.

"I was..." She looked over my state of near undress before crumpling her brow. "Why are you naked?"

"Here, put this on." Priest shoved a thin sweater at me from behind.

It took me a moment to realize it was the one he had been wearing. The intoxicating scent of him enveloped me as I gladly covered myself with it. It was the second time I had found myself wearing his clothes and it was no less enjoyable.

I turned to thank him, but he was already heading off the porch to stop the fight. The rain immediately drenched his V-neck white undershirt, making it basically see-through. Three nearly bare-chested men, wet from the rain. There were no words for it, only sounds of pleased satisfaction.

"I don't know what the hell set him off." Haden shook her head, perfectly bewildered. "It's not like we were together tonight. Ian and I just met on the way to the bathroom."

"And?" I was already picturing the scene Devin's already jealous heart had walked in on.

"We were just kissing." I heard the smack of Devin's fist hitting Ian's face, and the brawl began. Priest was skirting the fight, but he couldn't find an angle to touch them without getting black eyes himself. "What's the big deal? I've been with other men."

"Yes, but Ian is living here right now."

"So was August," she whined.

I didn't bother to remind her that August's death had changed our dynamic a great deal. "He wasn't in love with August." Haden glanced at me, but didn't acknowledge the statement as anything of importance.

Ian kicked Devin in the face and he landed in the mud. I cringed at the bruises already forming on his face and ran out into the rain. Priest had stopped seeking an opening to break them up. When I arrived at Devin's fallen side, he barely looked at me. "Get away, Lenore, I don't want you to get hurt." Ian waited patiently for him to get up.

"This is ridiculous," I said.

"Get away!" Devin yelled in my face, nearly splitting my heart in two. The only sliver that kept it together was the shame blooming in his eyes as Priest dragged me away.

"They need this," Priest whispered to me, pulling me close to him. I forgot about the last three months and huddled into his chest for warmth and consolation while I watched my friends beat the crap out of each other.

Devin and Ian were nearly a perfect match physically, but Devin had a slight upper hand with hand-to-hand combat. He was, after all, the champion in the tournaments. Unfortunately, Ian was well trained and too damn clever. He quickly learned Devin's weak points and took advantage whenever possible.

I could hear Haden gasp from the porch every time Devin's body received a particularly hard blow. I peeked over Priest's shoulder and saw the fear etched on her face and the distress expressed in her tangled, fidgeting fingers. The reaction when Ian was on the receiving end was different. She froze in anticipation, and when the hit was really good, she would smile proudly.

I sank back down and Priest looked down at me. "What is it? Why are you smiling?" he asked.

I touched my face, not realizing I was smiling. "She loves him," I announced with the same inflection one might use if you were on the receiving end of that love.

Priest smiled warmly and rubbed my back. "Of course she does. That's why I'm not breaking this up."

I looked back at the bloody mess Ian was becoming and realized Devin might win simply because the rain was draining blood into his eyes. Just as I came to that conclusion, however, Devin got a foot to the side of the head. I took my opportunity and started to pull away from Priest. He tightened his grasp. I looked at him. He wasn't half as much holding me back as trying to hang on to our contact.

"I'll be right back," I whispered, and he let me go.

I dove beside Devin like I wanted to tend to his injuries. It kept Ian at bay, but I think he was enjoying the break. I leaned in close to Devin and whispered, "Let him win, and she'll be yours. Now throw me off." He caught my wide eyes as I pulled back and he did as I asked.

"Get out of here, Lenore!" he added as he catapulted me away.

Priest jumped to my aid looking angrily at Devin, but I shook my head at him. "It's okay." He looked me over circumspectly and helped me up.

For a moment, we stood there watching the fight. I wanted to find a way back into his arms, but it seemed too familiar to simply wrap myself against him without cause, even though, I suspected he wouldn't push me away.

When a spray of blood shot from Devin's mouth, my honest reaction was to turn away. Before I knew it I was back in Priest's embrace where he could shelter me from the assault of blood, sweat, and rain.

Devin took two more blows to the face. I pinched my face and gripped Priest's shirt. I couldn't have felt guiltier, but when I peeked over Priest's shoulder, Haden's face was in her hands, and she looked near tears. It was working, but at what cost?

"You told him to lose, didn't you?" Priest eyed me suspiciously. I grimaced. "Aren't you little Miss Matchmaker?"

"Oh, poor Devin," I moaned seeing him flop against the ground, struggling to get up.

Ian moved toward him and kicked him hard in the side. Devin barely responded except to grunt. Ian brought his foot back to do it again.

"That's enough, Ian," Priest called to him. He hadn't yelled it, but the ripple of power I felt standing against his body gave my body goosebumps. I withdrew a little and he mouthed, "I'm sorry." Ian continued to pace beside Devin, scowling at his downed position. Priest stepped closer to him. "You've proved your point. Stand on your pride; don't wallow in it." Ian looked up at him, but the ire on his face dimmed and he stepped back.

I moved to help Devin, but Haden flew past me and took her place by his side. She cussed and yelled at him, all the while crying and caressing his face. I smiled at the revelation in play. Ian seemed to understand where he stood in the whole fiasco, so he stomped inside.

Sweet and Sour Grapes

I FOLLOWED IAN IN, and caught up with him on the stairs. "Ian, are you okay?"

"Of course, I won."

"Do you want some ice?" I frowned at the blooming purples on his face.

"No," he mumbled and continued up the stairs.

Priest came back inside and glanced up the staircase. "He'll be bitter for a while, but he'll get over it. You made the right call."

"I still feel bad."

"It was his choice to fight. He's just mad because he didn't get a prize for winning."

Haden came stumbling in the door with Devin draped over her. Priest jumped to her side and helped lift him from the other side. I ran to the kitchen and grabbed an ice pack, wet cloth, and our first aid kit, while they guided him upstairs.

When I arrived in Devin's room he was already in his bed. Priest was leaning him forward so Haden could prop another pillow behind his head.

I handed her the washcloth and she immediately started swabbing his face. I set down the ice pack on the night stand and started to open the first aid kit. Priest pressed his hand over the lid and took it from me. He set it on the nightstand, before resting a hand on Haden's shoulder. She looked up at him with mournful eyes. "Let us know if you need anything," he whispered and she nodded.

He didn't guide me out the door so much as herded me. I trotted out reluctantly and he closed the door behind us. "She can handle it."

"I was just going to—"

"You set this in motion, Lenore, but it's not finished. She needs to be the one to put him back together again."

I must have looked like a child with my face scrunched up, because he laughed at me. "Come on, Florence, I'll go slam my hand in a drawer so you can kiss it all better." He started toward the stairs.

"Does it have to be your hand?" I asked without thinking. When he turned around wearing a shocked smile, I immediately started shaking my head.

"What did you say?" He laughed. I shook my head faster. "I'm not sure how to take that. I'm appalled you might have another appendage in mind for the drawer, but intrigued which one you had in mind to kiss." He smiled relentlessly, enjoying my discomfort.

I forced my amusement away. "Don't. Don't flirt with me when you aren't going to let it go anywhere. I can't let you toy with my emotions anymore. It's too hard." I started to walk away, but he grabbed my hand.

"No, no, no, Lenore. No more running. No more hiding. You toy with my emotions just as much every time you walk away, so no." He waggled his finger in my face. "You are coming downstairs with me now, so we can once and for all hammer out some guidelines for you and me." I started to roll my eyes, but he yanked me closer. "Or I'll present my demands while I have you in the throes of passion right here on the stairs."

My mouth dropped and my legs nearly collapsed from my wobbling knees. I swallowed hard and took in a breath before I could answer in anything resembling my own voice. "That's an option?"

He smiled and winked. "It's not my preferred option, though. I'd like to have a legitimate discussion with you, so we don't end up like those two." He nodded to Devin's door. "I'll be downstairs, waiting." He stepped away, drawing his hand and body from mine.

Wait, What?

I T WAS ONLY EIGHT minutes, but it was the longest eight minutes of my life. I ran back to my room and shuffled through my closet for sexy clothing. I didn't have any, of course, because I didn't do sexy well. I decided my clothes shouldn't matter and switched to checking my hair.

I checked the mirror on my dresser and found I looked like a wet dog. Without pulling out a hair dryer there was no hope there. I checked my legs and discovered I was well beyond the bristly stage and into the furry one.

I ran to the bathroom and wet down my legs for a quick shave. My hands were shaking so bad I nicked myself three times. The bandages were in the first aid kit, so I had to let them clot on their own.

I decided to leave his sweater on, since it felt good, and I forwent pants, since I had gone to all the trouble of shaving my legs.

I arrived downstairs to find him stocking the fire. His white t-shirt was off, leaving only his silken skin. I could hear the dryer running in the other room. My and Ian's tennis shoes flopped around noisily in the metal drum.

He looked up at me with a relieved smile. "You had me worried."

"I was freshening up."

He scanned my body, probably trying to figure out what had been freshened in eight minutes. He stopped on my legs. "You're bleeding."

"I shaved," I murmured indefensibly.

He smiled broadly. "I appreciate that, but please don't hurt yourself to impress me. I'm quite fond of your legs, but I'm more interested in what's between them."

My knees finally failed me, and I swayed. Priest jumped to my aid, drawing me down to kneel on the floor with him. "Lenore." He laughed at my clumsiness, but his amusement faded as he looked me over. "Look at you, you look terrified. You're trembling."

"I'm just not used to hearing you speak so... salaciously... to me."

"Do you want me to stop?"

"No!" I whipped my head up, nearly clipping his chin. "I'm not uncomfortable just... nervous."

"Good, that means I have a chance of winning you back." I didn't point out that he had won me back the minute he suggested taking me on the stairs. "I do need to talk to you before I can... claim you."

"I'm tired of talking." I leaned in to kiss him. He lifted his chin to keep me away, but I decided not to let him talk himself out of anything. I nibbled gently on his neck, licking and biting at his throat and chin. I could hear his breath hitch and I moved forward to push myself against him.

He wrapped his arms around me and dropped me to the floor. Unfortunately, his purpose in subduing me was to actually subdue me. He drew back and pointed his finger at me. "I have spent a good number of years of my life fighting temptation; don't think for one second you can take me by the reins."

"I beg to differ," I said before wrapping my wetted lips around his brandished finger. I sucked it gently, tickling my tongue along the pad before drawing the remainder of it into my mouth. He gasped at my audacious teasing, but he didn't stop me.

"Are you prepared to give yourself to me?" he asked, not taking his eyes off my mouth.

I pulled his finger from my mouth and said breathlessly, "Yes!" I pulled at his arm to draw him down to me, but he wouldn't budge. "Yes!" I said again.

"No one else?" he verified sternly.

"Of course not! You know I'm practically the last person on Earth that prefers monogamy." I leaned up to him since he wouldn't come down to me. I suddenly realized that though I had imagined it many times, I had never actually kissed him before. The thought only paused me a moment, but it was a moment too long.

"Are you prepared to give your mind to me?" he asked sternly, but his eyes were full of apprehension.

"I... yes... what?" I stammered, trying to continue the moment, but I realized these were the demands he had referred to on the stairs. "I love you."

"And I love you," he said reassuringly, "but before we go on, I need you to surrender to me fully. There is a part of you that fought my presence before, and I want to know what it was that was fighting me. I need to see what secret your mind is hiding."

"What? No. You're just hijacking my hormones to get into my mind, which is so much worse than doing it to get into my bed." When he didn't offer a hint of apology or relinquishment, I realized the evening was lost, and he had once again dangled his love in front of me only to rip it away. "You son of a bitch." I cried this time instead of my usual tirade of volume. "Why are you doing this? This is what I was so afraid of. You keep toying with my emotions."

He tried to wipe away my tears, but I pushed his hand away.

"I can't believe I thought you were finally going to let us be together." I fell back and rolled over to cry into the floor. I was more than hurt; I was embarrassed. I had virtually thrown myself at him—again, and he had batted me away—again.

"Lenore, please understand, I could do this at any time, but I want your permission."

"You want my permission to mind-rape me. Well fuck you! Go reconstitute your harem if you want volunteers."

I felt him shift and he scooted his body in behind mine, spooning me in front of the fire. As much as I wanted to shove him away, I didn't have the will to deny myself the simple pleasure of his proximity.

"Do you even understand what I'm asking for?" he whispered in my ear while he rubbed my freshly shaved thigh.

"Yes," I sniffled. "You want to make sure you're stronger than me."

"No, that's not what I'm asking for. I already know you're stronger than me. I'm honestly not even sure I could get past your defenses to see what I want to, but that's why I'm asking you to give yourself to me." His hand roamed up under my sweater—his sweater—and stroked my stomach.

"You want to poke around my brain, and you want me to *let* you?"

"That's putting it rather indelicately, but yes. I want to see the power you're hiding. I caught a glimpse of it the other day, but I want to see more. All I'm asking is that you show it to me again, but in a non-combative way. Imagine trying to examine a wild animal, while it's still awake. It doesn't really give you a clear view."

I rolled over to face him. My tears had mostly dried, and I was starting to understand what he wanted. Part of me was just as curious about what he would find.

"You don't think it's evil power, do you?" I asked.

"Power is power, but you aren't evil, so no, I don't think it's evil." He moved his hand up and brushed my hair away from my temple. "I think it might be why August was drawn to you. I think it's why I'm drawn to you."

"Is that the only reason you want to be with me?"

"I want to be with you because when we aren't fighting, you and I are good together. Technically we're good together even when we are fighting, but it's just not as much fun."

I gave him a small smile. "Then why are you offering yourself conditionally?"

He thought a moment before answering. "Because I'm afraid what I'll find inside of you will make me feel unworthy of you."

I shook my head. "I always thought I was the one unworthy of you."

"You were never unworthy," he said strictly without qualification.

I took in a deep breath and let it out longingly. "Okay, what do I have to do?"

Surrender

"I FEEL STUPID," I said, still lying in front of the fire. To add to the increasingly sacrificial feel of the exercise, another front was passing through with lightning and thunder. Between that and the thumping from the dryer that might as well have been a steady drumbeat marshaling me to the hangman's noose, I couldn't help but lose my concentration.

"Stop talking," Priest said, kneeling over me with his hand on my forehead. I could feel the warmth that usually accompanied his presence in my mind, but it didn't seem as invasive as it had at other times. He was either holding back, or his power had become finer tuned.

"Just do it. You're driving me crazy."

"I've been trying to for the last three minutes. You are not making this easy."

"Can't you just... push?"

"Yes, but I'm trying not to *mind-rape* you. I want you to open up, and I don't think you are capable of doing it while your lips are flapping."

I pinched my lips, suppressing my laughter. I could hear him growl under his breath and shift, but I didn't dare open my eyes lest he skewer me with the ire on his face. "Okay, okay, I'll try harder." I cleared my throat and repositioned. After another half minute, I busted out laughing and could barely stop.

Priest shifted away from me, taking his hand from my forehead, but again I didn't open my eyes. I knew the minute I did he would make me feel like a jerk. "I'm sorry, Priest, don't leave."

"I'm not leaving," he said closer to my ear. He was lying down next to me. He was probably as tired of this as I was. "Let's try a different approach." Or not. "Something a little more personal to distract that busy little brain of yours."

"What, a mallet?" I giggled, very amused with my joke.

"Maybe if this doesn't work." I could hear the smile in his voice and I was pleased I had put it there. He placed his hand under my sweater and rested it on my stomach. The weight of it felt comforting, and I instantly focused on the small, intimate touch of the man whom I hoped to call my lover before the night was through.

"Do you trust me?" he whispered seductively, or at least that's the way it sounded to my love-starved ears. I nodded. "Say it out loud for your mind to hear, please."

"I trust you." I thought it was silly to say what I already knew I felt, but giving it voice did seem to help me feel it more.

"Again please," Priest said, shifting his hand lower on my stomach.

"I trust you." His hand slipped beneath my panties and I inhaled sharply at his touch. The touch I had waited a very long time for.

"Again please." He was so close to my face I wanted to kiss him, but I wasn't sure I could do it without breaking his concentration.

"I trust you," I said more as a moan of pleasure than a sentence.

"Will you submit your body to me?"

"Yes," I gladly moaned. "I submit my body to you," I added before he asked. I was writhing and grappling at the carpet, but he definitely had my complete attention.

"Will you let your mind succumb to me?"

He increased his ministrations as if he knew I might still struggle against that particular aspect of our arrangement. Although it still sounded somehow violating, I just thought of it like losing my virginity. If there were any man I would allow in the deepest recesses of my mind, it was him. Not because he was a proficient lover, or a man of God, but because he was flawed, and he could pass no judgment on what he saw there without passing it back on himself.

"I submit to you, mind and body." I wasn't sure any of it was intelligible, since my body was already climaxing, but I felt Priest's warmth move deeper inside of me. I could feel my mind open as I lost myself in the erotic pleasure of his tangible and intangible attentions. As perfect as the moment was, the descent from my euphoria brought me back to my physical reality as well as my mental one.

The rubber band effect it had on Priest sent him flying back as if someone had hit him. Apparently me. I opened my eyes and found him lying a short distance away. I crawled to him, searching for the damage I had inadvertently caused. He was panting and staring at me, wide-eyed.

"I'm sorry, I'm sorry, I couldn't control it." I didn't even know what *it* was, but it definitely wasn't answering to me.

"It's okay. You didn't hurt me, you just pushed me out."

"Did you see anything?" I asked. He nodded, but didn't answer. "What was it?"

I must have looked as terrified to hear the answer as I felt, because his face softened and he cupped my cheek. "Beautiful, just like you."

I was about to ask more, but he pulled my face down to him and kissed me. It was a sweet kiss, but full of intention. Before I could wonder if he intended to continue his mental prospecting, he unhooked my bra under the sweater.

I pulled back to disentangle myself from the clothing. As soon as I had, he pulled me down to him again, this time to suckle my nipples. Already primed for the occasion, a riptide of pleasure and astonishment forced a cry from my mouth that I was pleased coincided with a rumble of thunder.

He pushed me back and plied himself against me, pants to panties. I could feel his urgency and I was lost in the anticipation of finally having him. I didn't care that the world had ended. I didn't care that Adrian Dorn now knew how much of a threat we were to him. I didn't even care that someone might walk in on us if they wanted a midnight snack.

"Oh, Priest, please!" I begged for him to release himself.

He leaned down to my ear and practically snarled, "Matthew." I opened my eyes and nodded. "Say it," he whispered as he fumbled below with his pants.

"Matthew." It felt foreign to my tongue. He smirked and slipped off my panties. "Matthew." I said it again, since he seemed to enjoy hearing it.

I remembered a time when it felt too personal to call him by his real name, but that was when he was forbidden fruit. But in this moment, it felt perfectly right. We were finally on a first name basis, just in time for our most intimate of moments.

"Matthew." I whispered his name once more and he pushed inside of me. My head arched back and I groaned in instant relief. There was no more wonder, or hope, or anticipation; he was mine at last. I looked up at him and watched the same relief seep into his face. He smiled, sensing that we were both thinking the same thing.

He rocked against me, feeding my need and his until the immediate desire was quelled. When the thunderstorm ended and the dryer stopped, we moved upstairs, to my bedroom. I was more than ready for sleep, but he refused to let the night end. He exhausted himself more than once trying to make up for lost time.

In the end, we were back to talking. Apologizing, doting on each other, and even sharing memories. I told him about the house I used to live in and he told me about the many un-priestly things he did in his youth. It was probably the best night of my life pre- or post-apocalypse.

The Walk of Shame

T HE NEXT MORNING, I woke alone.

There was no measure for my panic. It was practically noon and Priest was a notoriously early riser, but I was far too stuck in old memories to think about that. I slipped on my jeans and a t-shirt sans bra and underwear. I ran downstairs to see if he was still there, but I only found Devin and Ian, the bruise-faced twins, at the table.

They seemed to be having an honest discussion and probably didn't need a crazed super-pathetic woman interrupting them, but common decency was too far down my list of priorities. They both stared at me as my bare feet slapped into the kitchen. "Have you seen Priest? I mean Matthew—er, Priest." I corrected, and corrected again, when I thought changing his address would make our intimate relationship too obvious—not that running around after him like a madwoman was keeping it obscure.

"Slow down, baby," Devin drawled. "Good morning to you too."

"Is he here?" I squealed, tears welling in my eyes.

"I think so. The Tahoe is still here." Devin stood and engulfed me in a hug. "What is wrong with you this morning? What did he do to you?"

"What's wrong with her?" Haden came in from the laundry room and crossed behind us.

"I was just determining that. She wants to know where Matthew is."

"He's out in the front yard," Haden answered like it was a stupid question. My body sagged in relief and Devin looked at me with a knowing smile. "Damn fool's been out there for over an hour twirling around like the sound of fuckin' music," Haden continued.

"There now, Lenore. No reason to get in a tizzy. Your lover's outside."

I stared blankly at Devin. I felt like I had been caught doing drugs by my father. "You didn't..." My eyes darted over his, searching for the answer so I didn't have to ask it.

He laughed at my reaction. "Haden said he wasn't on the couch early this morning when she went down to grab me another ice pack. We assumed the rest, which of course you just confirmed." Devin bit his lip trying to control his grin.

"If he's not going to sleep on the couch, we should really get back to a rotation," Haden said diplomatically.

"Am I seriously the only one in this house, not getting laid?" Ian griped from the table.

"Yes, yes you are," Devin said with a little more malice than he probably intended. He squeezed my shoulders and went back to his chair. "Haden's making breakfast. You want some?"

I didn't bother answering before slipping out the side door to get to the front yard. I ran through the soggy grass toward Priest. He was indeed looking to the heavens and spinning, like Julie Andrews minus the singing.

The cloudy day had parted just enough to offer streams of light where he was standing. He seemed to be bathing in the sunlight.

The closer I got to him, the more I slowed. When I reached the well-defined circle of luminance he was standing in, I stopped. I shouldn't have been afraid, but part of me wondered if stepping over the threshold would cause my skin to erupt in blisters.

I took a deep breath and stepped inside. To my relief it was only slightly warmer, not scalding. I moved to Priest, and watched him mutter silently to himself, eyes closed to the sky. His lips parted just enough to mouth the words, but not enough to read what he was saying. I didn't want to interrupt him, but I also wanted so much to touch him and make sure this private moment wasn't him having second thoughts about being in a relationship with me instead of exclusively pursuing his commitment to God.

Rather than scare the crap out of him by touching him, I whispered as quietly as I could. "Pr—Matthew."

He drew in a breath and smiled. Slowly he opened his eyes and looked over at me. There was more love in that look than any I had received from other men. "Good morning." He lowered his arms and turned to me. He perked his brow. "Aren't you going to rush into my arms like we both know you want to? I know I want you to."

I smiled and ran into his arms. He lifted me up and spun me around before setting me down and kissing me. It probably looked about as shameless as a Hollywood camera spin around a kissing couple, but it felt good to be unabashedly affectionate with him.

"You haven't said good morning yet, but I'll forgive you since you remembered to use my given name." He smiled at me and I buried my face shyly against his chest. "Are you blushing?"

I nodded into his chest.

"My, my, and even after all those ungentlemanly things I did to you last night." I giggled. "And all those unladylike sounds I extracted from those not-so-innocent lips."

I looked up at him, grinning. "I heard some rather uncouth sounds coming from you as well, *Matthew*."

He smiled at his name again. "Those weren't uncouth sounds. Those were animalistic." He winked at me.

"Care to make them again?" I asked with intent.

"Yes, Lenore, I have every intention of making those sounds with you again and again, but I need to finish what I'm doing here. Then we can *run to town*." He made air quotes.

"What exactly are you doing here?" I asked, looking up at the sky.

"I'm praying, but it is a particularly good day for it, so I can't run away with you just yet."

I glanced up at the parted clouds and wondered what was particularly good about today. I didn't want to be an unsupportive pest, though. I smiled and withdrew from him. He caught my hand and kissed it. "I'm not going anywhere, okay?" he said firmly.

I nodded and offered him a more sincere smile before leaving him to his *work*.

More Good News

I WENT BACK INSIDE, shutting the kitchen door quietly in hopes that I might be able to keep my presence unobtrusive to the meal that could no longer be reasonably called breakfast or brunch.

"What the hell is he doing?" Haden asked, peeking up from her cornflakes.

"Praying," I said simply. I expected her to give me a smartass remark or at least a grimace, but she didn't.

I stepped up to the counter, but found the coffee pot empty. I settled for juice rather than make an entire pot for myself. It wasn't caffeinated, but I would be running on dopamine for a while anyway.

"Is she really crystalline?" Haden asked as I sat down at the table across from her, next to Ian. I glanced at Devin, who seemed intent to hear the answer as well. Despite hearing the answer yesterday morning, they still needed to hear it from me.

"Yes," I said with a nod. "Priest was hiding it, and I suspect Garrett knew about it. I've reburied her a couple times already." I didn't bother making an excuse for not telling them. They understood why I didn't, and on some level they probably wished they still didn't know.

"What does that mean exactly?" Ian asked, feeling the tension in the room rise tenfold.

"For one, it proves we all have a chance to get back on God's good side," I said without the added "*bum bum bum*" it deserved. "For us, however, it means safeguarding the world from Adrian Dorn is not just a civil service, but possibly a favor to the Big Guy."

"Why would He care about one stray demon?" Ian shook his head in disbelief.

"He doesn't," Priest said as he came inside and shut the door behind him. "Adrian isn't the only demon we will face. He just happens to be the first." Priest headed to the coffee pot and found the same disappointing empty carafe. Rather than resorting to juice, he put his cup back in the cupboard. "Despite what some of you probably think," he said, pinning me with the responsibility of the *some* in his statement, "He did not leave us behind because He doesn't care about us. He left us behind for a purpose."

"He grounded us from heaven to teach us a lesson, we get it," Devin mumbled.

"No," Priest said, drawing all eyes to him. "The meek will never inherit the Earth, though I think Lenore may be the exception to that."

"Hey, I'm not meek." I objected to the statement on a number of levels.

"You're a work in progress," he conceded, but I still felt his critique was out of line. "All of us remaining here are sinners as much as saints. We are reckless, fearless, violent, and at appropriate times brutal. Who would you prefer to leave behind to stave off demon attacks on your people?" He looked to everyone individually, but no one spoke. "You were left behind to be soldiers of the apocalypse, because you aren't going to be hindered by religious morality or fickle stomachs. You will fight to keep claim on the Earth, and He doesn't care how you do it."

"How do you know that?" I asked—coincidentally—meekly.

Priest eyed me cautiously before answering. "He told me."

Hello Operator, Give Me Number One

I FOLLOWED PRIEST UPSTAIRS after he dropped his bomb and walked out. I found him unpacking his plastic tote into one of my dresser drawers. I paused to enjoy the view of him staking long term claim to my room—now our room.

"Priest?" I whispered and he whipped around to face me.

"Have you forgotten my name already?" The severity in his tone made me want to leave again, but I needed to get my answers before I did.

"You're talking to God again?"

"I never stopped talking to God. He stopped talking to me." He looked at the blazing sun shining through the window. "Until this morning." He looked at me and smiled. "Until you."

I narrowed my eyes. "Me? He started talking to you because we…"

"I'm sure it's because my love for you has focused me even further, but yes." He chuckled. "Oh, Lenore, you can't even imagine how elated I am. I don't have all the answers, but so much is clear to me now, including you. He's going to help us get through this."

I nodded and tried to find something supportive to say, but all I could think was, *"better late than never."* Also, the part of me that wanted Priest to relish his relationship with me instead of God was pitching a baby fit. "I'm happy for you both," I said and walked out.

I heard him cuss and stomp after me. I paused on the steps and waited for him to reach my bedroom door. He stopped there to glare at me, and I shrugged. "I don't know what to say, Priest."

He tipped his head in disbelief. "How can you shut me out, after last night?"

"I don't mean to, but I thought last night was about you and me getting closer. Not you and God."

"Oh, is that what you think I'm saying?" He smiled, albeit with narrowed eyes. He circled around to lean on the other side of the stairs and crossed his arms. "I thought I was saying that being with you was so magnificent that it opened my eyes and ears to God."

I licked my lips and fiddled with the stair rail, unable to hold his gaze without blushing. He stepped forward, uncrossing his arms but not touching me. "I'm not worthy of you, Lenore, but some-how, you loving me has made me worthy of Him. I don't know how to compliment you any higher than that. Now, I'm going back in your bedroom to finish moving in. If you want any more proof of my love, you need only say the magic word."

He slipped away and I leaned against the wall for support. I wasn't sure how he could claim to not be worthy of me, when clearly I was the puddle of goo at his feet every time he seduced me.

I tiptoed back into my room and shut the door. I moved in close behind him as he packed his claimed drawer. "Matthew," I whispered. My intent was to apologize for my behavior, but his name was apparently the magic word. He turned around and kissed me hard.

He pushed me back to the bed, undressing me as he went. I could barely respond except to relax my muscles so he could rip away my clothing and lay me against the mattress. "I just love you so much," I whispered as he removed his own clothing. "I don't want to share you with Him." He slowed his disrobing, and I thought I might have managed to ruin the moment. "I'm sorry. I know that makes me the most selfish person ever."

I frowned knowing I had for sure ruined the moment, and possibly the entire relationship. If he zipped his pants back up and walked out, I wouldn't have blamed anyone but myself.

Instead, he sat down beside me and looked me over. He drew his finger over my cheek. "Does a parent love their child?" he asked, pushing a tear away from my cheek. "Do you not love your friends as siblings? Do you not love the Earth and the beauty it provides?"

I nodded, feeling chastised. He drew his finger along my naked chest, stopping between my breasts.

"Does this heart not fill and break for many people?" I nodded and he drew his hand over my breast, cupping me as he pinned me with his eyes. "Does anyone but a lover touch you like this?"

"Not sober," I quipped and he offered me a conciliatory smile.

He glided his hand down and slipped his hand between my legs, making me inhale sharply. "I hope this remains the dominion of lovers." I couldn't answer, but I managed to nod. "You have many loves, Lenore, but I am your only lover. I may seek an audience with others, but I am still yours." He leaned forward and kissed my lips gently, and soon more urgently.

We spent the remainder of the afternoon coiled in each other's arms and legs, in and out of euphoria. Despite it being a very important question, I didn't ask him what God had revealed to him about me.

Penance

"DON'T MAKE ME KICK your ass, Matthew." Haden scowled at Priest from her spot at Devin's feet in front of the fire. I was in his arms on the couch trying not to smile at Haden's discomfort to his attention.

"Haden, sweetheart, it was meant to be a compliment." Priest was using his fatherly tone that reminded me of how personable he was when he wasn't fighting with me or banishing demons. Everyone had noticed that Haden was applying makeup even for our nights at home, but Priest was the only one brave enough to point it out. "Devin, don't you think she looks nice?"

"That she does." Devin gave her a coy smile and drew her hair back behind her ear. It felt gratifying to see them displaying their affections more conventionally, even if Haden was still uncomfortable with the PDA part of it.

"Can't you keep control of your man, Lenore?" Haden grumbled with less enthusiasm than she started.

"If you can't scare him into behaving, I doubt I'd have much of a chance to restrain him."

Priest's chest quaked with his bass laughter, but I had a sinking feeling he wasn't just laughing at my witty repartee. "We'll have to test that theory some time. Soon, perhaps."

I looked back to see what I was missing, but his attention had already shifted to Ian. He had been eyeballing Priest all night from his chair. I wasn't sure it was meant in malice, but the expression on Priest's face said otherwise. "Can I help you with something, Ian?"

Ian looked away and cleared his throat. "I was wondering if I could talk to you about something."

Priest's expression softened. "Of course." He pushed on my back and I leaned forward. He stood up and headed to the backdoor. Ian followed him out, shutting the door behind him. I knew it was meant to be a private conversation, but I couldn't help but wonder what it was about and why Priest was the only one privy to it.

Devin and Haden had the same look of curiosity on their faces, but they lost interest as soon as the two men were gone. I, however, watched the door for more than ten minutes waiting to see one or both of them return.

It wasn't until Ian screamed that I decided privacy was overrated.

I rushed out the door and found Ian some distance from the porch in the backyard. He was kneeling with his face upward to the sky. Priest's hands were pressed to his face as he chanted something nonsensical.

Ian was panting and tears were endlessly streaming down his cheeks. I ran to him, but Priest's power was too overwhelming. I stopped short of interjecting and backpedaled away from the tangible emotional overload. Despite the strength behind it, I knew it wasn't malicious, just impassioned.

When the connection broke, Ian fell abjectly against Priest. He patted the back of Ian's head, comforting him like a child. Unsure of what to do, but sympathetic of the emotions that must have been colliding in Ian's mind, I knelt down next to him and held him from behind.

He broke from Priest and looked at me. He glanced up at Priest and he smiled down at him, like they were sharing an inside joke. Ian turned and touched my shoulder. He dragged the touch down my arm. It wasn't intended to be a caress, but rather exploratory. When he had established I was in fact flesh and blood, he locked eyes with me.

"Are you okay?" I asked.

"Yeah, Chief, I'm good. I'm real good." He chucked my shoulder, got up, and walked away like nothing had happened.

"What the hell was that?" I asked Priest after everyone else had gone back inside. I was surprised Devin and Haden hadn't stuck around for the interrogation, but everyone was getting used to the weird shit that came with knowing Priest.

He helped me up and tugged me through the yard. "He needed to confess his sins. I listened."

"That was more than a confession," I snarled, pulling back slightly on him.

"Yes, that part was forgiveness and penance." Priest pulled me behind the garage and pushed me against the wall. He tried to undo my pants, but I stopped him.

"Don't change the subject, Matthew."

He smiled at me and started to unbuckle his own pants, but I pressed my hands to stop that as well. He gave up momentarily and leaned on the wall behind me.

"Why did he look at me like that?"

"Because, for a moment, he could see what I see in you."

"What do you see in me?"

"It's just a glow, really. A strong aura, some might call it. I saw it the first time I met you, and randomly after that. When you aren't hiding it."

"Hiding it?"

"I know you don't want to be the hero, Lenore, but... that's only because you aren't supposed to want to be."

"What the hell does that mean?" I protested at what sounded like a passive-aggressive way of calling me a coward.

He tapped my forehead. "Your instincts are hardwired to protect you. You do that by running and hiding. The only time you've run headlong into battle was at your competition, with that demon. Something about him made you forget to hide your true self."

"What exactly is my true self?"

Priest chuckled and looked me over longingly. "You *are* a hero... a warrior, a guardian. I don't care what you call it, Lenore. You are not a frail, cowardly, little woman. That's just your disguise."

"You're saying Lenore doesn't even exist."

"You are definitely Lenore, but you have a longer backstory than you realize."

"Tell me what I am."

He leaned his forehead against mine. "You're the only woman I've ever been in love with, and I knew it the first moment I laid eyes on you. That's all that matters right now. The battle we've all been waiting for... It's coming and it's going to be a challenge for all of us."

"Ah, hello, if you have insider information on me or the big battle, don't you think you should be sharing it?"

"I don't know details. Besides, when did knowing the truth do anyone any good?"

"But..."

He persisted to tug open my pants. "I don't care about all that right now. All I care about is what's right in front of me." He leaned in slowly, asking and begging for me to give in.

"Am I going to die?" The words were out of my mouth before I knew they were a question. He froze and stared at me. "August... Isn't that what the hero does? Dies to save the people she loves?"

Priest shook his head, but something told me it was only a denial to the second question. "I have no knowledge of one particular life or death. I only know that battles are not without casualties. I also know I will be by your side, to support you, protect you, and love you."

I nodded and pulled him closer so I could re-initiate the al fresco tryst. I was more than happy to christen yet another part of our home—albeit the back of the garage—but I couldn't help but wonder if the reason he couldn't get enough of me was because there wasn't much time left to get it.

Rat Trap

"**I**AN." I FINALLY SPOKE.

Ian glanced between the highway and me. He had been avoiding me the last few days. I wasn't sure if it was because of what he saw in me, or because he knew I would persist to make him talk about it.

When he announced he had an errand to run, I offered my help. He accepted, but only after a moment's pause to non-verbally confer with Priest. I wasn't sure what had transpired between them, but I was happy to see them on better terms. Even if it did leave me feeling like the odd man out.

"What is it?" he asked with increasing irritation.

"What are we doing again?" I asked, chickening out on my primary motive.

"Well, if I'm going to be fighting the good fight with all of you, I might as well give up my day job. I need to make some adjustments to my grim trap."

"Yeah, but what exactly—?"

"Why don't you just ask me what you really want to ask me?" he interrupted, barely leaving my head attached.

"I'm trying to give you your privacy, but..."

"I asked Matthew to absolve me."

"Yeah, he said that. It seemed pretty intense." He didn't respond except to tighten his grip on the steering wheel. "Afterward, you seemed to see something. Priest said you saw my aura." Ian scoffed. "Do you mind telling me what you saw?"

"I would if I knew. That's twice I've seen your insides, and honestly... you're kind of scary."

I held his gaze as long as his driving allowed it. "Oh." I didn't have a better response. I still couldn't put my body with the character everyone was talking about. August saw it, Priest saw it, and now Ian, but I couldn't see it and I was the one supposedly wearing it. "I don't suppose you can give me a little more insight than *scary*? I'm kind of missing a few pieces to my puzzle here."

"Your... aura is... big."

"Big?" I asked as he pulled onto a narrow blacktop road.

"Yeah, big." He didn't elaborate and I didn't push because he seemed to be uncomfortable with the topic.

He pulled the van through a checkpoint, and up a steep hill. I recognized the location as the town's garbage dump. There was a building at the very top of the hill containing a compactor.

"You'll want to keep your bow with you, just in case," he said.

We rounded the corner and backed the van under the roof of the garbage depository. I got out of the van with my bow in hand. I could hear the feral growls of grim and I nocked an arrow. I headed to the cement gully that crushed the massive amounts of waste my small town used to produce on a regular basis.

There were eight not-so-agile grim stumbling over the garbage at the bottom of the pit. They were young enough to let themselves fall for such a guileless trap, but even with their growing coordination they weren't able to jump the ten feet necessary to climb out of the compactor.

"So, this is your rat trap? Clever."

Ian popped out from around the other side of the van. "Thanks."

"What draws them in?"

"Bait." He perked his brow as if he were having a private joke, but even as his quiet smirk waned, I could see his jaw clench and his eyes darken.

It was the muffled string of insults that drew my eyes up to the so-called bait. Bound, gagged, and hung on the building's rafters above the chasm, was a live man—a very angry live man.

Revenge

I HELPED IAN DRAG the man onto the platform, after he had lowered the mechanical hook pulley holding him over the pit. He smelled so strongly of feces and urine that my eyes watered. I waited for Ian to explain, but he didn't seem to be bothered by the inhumane state the man was in. Nor was he distraught by the endless stream of cusswords still escaping through the cotton socks lashed in the man's mouth. I, however, was bothered by it and continued to seek my answers with a healthy amount of staring.

"Hello Milton," Ian said, staring down the man.

I was appalled he knew the man by name, but I said nothing. I wanted to give him the benefit of the doubt. I knew what was in his heart. If this man had received this punishment, he must have wronged Ian terribly.

Milton stopped cussing and started talking—for all the good it did, since it was more mumbled than the cusswords. Ian grabbed a bottle of water from the stash in his van and I carefully removed Milton's gag. I expected him to yell at me or bite me, but his attention was entirely on Ian.

"Who's this, your girlfriend?" Milton asked with a raspy voice.

"Yup," Ian answered, not bothering to waste breath for the correct relationship status. He shoved the bottle into the man's mouth and Milton guzzled all the water down with ease.

"She's cute. A little old for me though, you know?" Milton managed to smile and snarl at the same time. He looked to be in his fifties or early sixties with his graying beard.

"Yeah, I know," Ian said. He grabbed another bottle of water, but this time he drank it himself.

"Did you bring her here to prove something? Why don't you give me a show before you go? Go on, don't be shy, Ian. Show her what I taught you." Ian ripped the bottle from his lips and stuffed it in Milton's mouth, letting him drink the last of the water.

When he was through, Ian faced off with him, glaring eye to eye with the man. "You know, I came here to serve my penance. I came here to free you, but I don't think I can do that. At least not the kind of freedom that involves walking away."

Milton frowned. "What are you—?"

Ian pushed the man slightly on the chest and he stumbled back, toward the gulley. He did it again. Milton tried to push back, but he was too weak and tired from his days or weeks—hopefully not months—as bait. The third push sent Milton swinging over the garbage pit.

"Ian!" Milton yelled. "Put me back up."

"You aren't going up, you sick fuck. You're going down. I came here to free you from your captivity and I will. I will release you into hell."

Ian moved to the controls on the wall to lower Milton into the ravenous mob below. They were already leaping at his feet, trying to get a foothold on his body. I knew this was revenge pure and simple, but I couldn't help feel for what the man was about to face. The grim would rip him apart. Not metaphorically either. It was old-school quartering and evisceration.

I reached out to Milton's mind. The images that flashed before me were of a pedophile. His tastes were directed at young pre-teen boys, a taste he developed from his own experiences with a pedophile as a young man.

Milton was definitely worthy of the exceptional torture Ian had bestowed on him, but I wasn't sure that such a death was revenge or Ian's way of continuing the cycle of violence. He was already a trained killer. That couldn't have been a coincidence.

I raised my bow and put an arrow into Milton's eye socket just as his legs reached the grim. I knew Ian wouldn't be pleased with my mercy killing, but I hadn't expected him to tackle me to the ground.

Mercy

"WHAT THE FUCK DID you do that for?" Ian's hands were wound so tightly into my shirt I was practically out of it. He had instinctively clamped his legs around my thighs like a vise. He was crying, but only because there was liquid dripping from his eyes. Nothing about his actions were due to sadness. "Do you have any idea what kind of a man he was?" He shook me up and down, and all I could do was hold onto his biceps and wait for the rage to be filtered by reality. "He didn't deserve a quick death! He didn't deserve your mercy!"

"I didn't do it for him!" I yelled so he would hear me through his tantrum.

He pulled me up close and I could feel his hot breath on my face. For the first time since he had told me his occupation, I understood what that meant. Be it my special power or just seeing it up close, I recognized the glaze he put on the world before him, so he could make killing palpable.

There was a pain inside of him, not unlike the demon souls I felt inside of the grim. It demanded retribution, but also redemption. He put on a mask to hide the pain, and when one fell short, he'd pull out another. A personality for each person he met: the killer, the hero, the salesman.

Priest may have given him redemption to ease his pain, but his anger still demanded vengeance. Vengeance that I had stolen from him.

Ian stared down at me, eyes vacant and prepared to take his justice out on me. Despite our quick alliance—no doubt, another mask—I knew he could do it. He could snap my neck or strangle me with his bare hands and then go about his day. He would pocket any immediate regrets about the situation and place the long-lasting remorse behind a new mask, none the wiser of the damage it was doing to his soul.

To say I was frightened was an understatement. I fought grim all the time, but this was the first time I had been face to face with a live human on the verge of killing me with his bare hand—an intimacy that can't be overstated. I knew if my words didn't come out just right, I would be dead.

"I did it for you," I whispered.

His lip curled into a snarl and his fist tightened on my shirt, tucking it under my chin. I was so close to strangulation I couldn't even swallow.

"I know what he did to you and others like you. He's a child rapist and he deserves hell."

"He deserves to be ripped apart by demons, and I deserve to watch him being ripped apart!" Ian yelled and shook me viciously.

I could feel a few tears slip from my eyes. They matched his, but they were for very different reasons.

"I couldn't let you risk your own soul," I whispered.

"What?" he sneered.

"You aren't this man, Ian. You think you are, but you aren't. Milton didn't rip out your moral compass. You buried it."

Ian laid me back down. For a moment, I thought he was going to release me, but instead he pulled a knife from his ankle and rested the tip against my lowest rib. I pushed on his hand, but the angle was too awkward for me to do much good if he actually decided to push the knife in.

"Ian, please." I was beyond pathetic, blubbering through tears and snot. I wasn't sure what bothered me more: dying, or dying at the hands of a friend. I couldn't imagine anything worse than that. "Please don't do this."

I could see his eyes glaze over again, and I knew my life was in danger of being taken away. I stopped sniveling and reached for the thread within myself. I drew on the big scary aura that had quieted Ian once before. If anything, maybe a little light show would distract him enough for me to get away.

I don't know what there was for lights, but his body being thrown off me and into the van was a pretty good show for me.

Ta Da!

I SCRAMBLED ACROSS THE cement, putting my hands in all sorts of human refuse on the way. When I finally rose to my feet, Ian was coming back into the world sans birdies and stars. He looked me over and stood up.

"I'm sorry, but I'm not going to just let you kill me. We aren't that good of friends."

He offered a snort, but his eyes still looked dark. He wasn't going to snap out of it just because of a bop on the head and a good joke.

"I know you had about a thousand and one reasons to torture and kill that man, but if it's true we can win back our place in heaven, then I'm not going to let you jeopardize that by murdering him that way."

"I've killed more than a dozen men... and women." He added the specification to frighten me, but little did he know I was already horrified. "There is no hope for my soul."

"You killed them as part of your job, not because you enjoyed it."

"How do you know that for sure?" he smirked.

"Stop it!" I snapped. "You're not evil, Ian. You are undoubtedly pretty fucked up, but I don't think you're the only one to stake claim to that title."

"When the world went to shit, I wasn't surprised when I was still here. I also wasn't unhappy about it. As far as I was concerned, it was my chance to track down that asshole, and make him pay for fucking up my life."

"And you did."

"It wasn't enough."

"It's never enough, Ian. Do you think those grim will ever be satisfied after molesting and beating and ripping apart their victims? Do you think one day the broken souls inside will just pull themselves up out of hell and say, *I'm ready to be forgiven*?"

"You're starting to sound like Matthew."

I rolled my eyes reflexively, but he was probably right. I was starting to look at things differently. I wasn't sure if it was because of Priest or August or if I was just letting go of some of my own bitterness toward the Big Man.

"He knows what he's talking about and so do I... most of the time."

"It wasn't your call to make. Since when are you the designated soul protector?"

"I don't know, it could have something to do with my ability to free tortured souls, or hey, maybe it has something to do with me being your friend."

"If you were my friend, you would have let me kill him my way."

I nodded. "Maybe you're right, but I'm pretty sure friends don't try to murder their friends either."

He took in a deep breath and looked away. "I wouldn't have..." He trailed off, and I got the sense he wanted to believe that lie, but couldn't bring himself to try to make me believe it. For a moment, we stood there, waiting for the uncomfortable moment to go away, but when it was clear it wouldn't, I moved toward the van.

Ian tensed and shifted, gripping his knife. I noted the movement, but chose not to view it as a threat. At that point, we were both frightened animals, prepared to defend ourselves against any sudden movements or pin drops.

I opened the passenger side door and looked at him. "Take me home."

He at last holstered his knife and joined me in the van. He paused with his hand on the ignition. "You threw me off like I was a blow-up doll." He looked over at me. It sounded like an accusation, but his eyes flitted around the outskirts of my body, searching for something.

"Yeah, my emergency strength, I guess," I said, making light of yet another discovery. "Too bad I didn't have that little talent when I was training. Could have saved Garrett some time."

Ian looked back out the front window and gripped the steering wheel. "I really wanted to kill you."

"And now?" I asked, shifting closer to the door.

He chuckled. "I want to beat the crap out of someone, but it's not really specific to you. Anyone will do."

"Do you want to go kill some grim?" I said, half joking. "Free therapy."

"Yeah, I do," he said austerely.

Block Party

IAN SLASHED AND PUNCHED at the oncoming grim with more vigor than I had seen before. He might have been reliant on his gun in the big O, but he caught on to the quiet style of fighting easier than I expected. The middle-income neighborhood was filled with grim for the hunting, but one gunshot and we would be surrounded, outnumbered and dead.

I shot an arrow into the face of a sneak attack grim from my position on top of the van. I was more than willing to jump down into the street fight, but Ian didn't need nor want my assistance. This was stress relief, and quite possibly the only reason I wasn't going to wake up to a knife in my chest.

Three more grim came out of the neighboring houses, tripping over fences, sprinklers, and tricycles to get to the impromptu battle. I took out two and left the third for Ian, who was ready just in time to slam his brass knuckles into her face. I couldn't help but think he found more pleasure in dispatching grim, since she looked a little like me. I brushed away the thought and killed two more, leaving the street empty. We were out of line of sight with the other houses. Unless we went deeper in, or made noise, we were done for the day.

Ian panted, sweating from his exertion. Despite the brass protecting his knuckles, they were bloody. His face was already forming bruises from the hits he hadn't blocked.

"Feeling better?" I asked, slipping to the edge of the van roof.

"Yeah," he answered before helping me down. He kept his hands around my waist after I was down. He still looked angry, but he at least looked exhausted by the anger.

All of a sudden, he pulled me into a hug. His breathing stuttered at my ear, and he struggled to find the right grip around me, as if he was frustrated that I wasn't simply absorbing into him.

He pulled me back and gripped my face. For a split second, I thought he was going to kiss me, but he only stared into my face. "I'm sorry, Lenore." His tears flooded his cheeks. "I'm so fucking sorry." He grimaced, squeezing my face.

"I know," I said, trying to touch his face or arms in some way to convey my empathy.

He pulled me back into the hug and his knees collapsed, taking me with him. We knelt together, my body crushed against him while he despondently begged for forgiveness from me.

Just like at the dump, my power took hold without my summoning it and Ian's grief filled me with his personal experiences. I saw his pain first hand, and the pain he had caused others. It was overwhelming, and I couldn't help but join him in his suffering.

Somewhere between his pain and my pain I screamed, or howled, or wailed. The sound was inhuman and very unladylike, but after I did it, I felt strong again. Strong enough to absorb Ian's pain. Strong enough to quell his anger. And, most of all, strong enough to defeat the two dozen or so grim I had stupidly just announced our presence to.

179

Calling All Grim

"WHAT THE HELL WAS that?" Ian asked, looking me over.

"I don't know, but it got a lot of attention." I nodded to the approaching grim.

"Oh, shit." Ian stood up, practically lifting me along with him. "Come on, let's drive. I'm not up for that much of a fight."

"Yeah," I said, mesmerized by the onslaught of grim running, marching, and wobbling toward us.

"Come on!" Ian yelled, shutting his driver's side door. The engine was still going, but he shifted into gear and moved forward slightly to get a view of me in his side mirror. "Lenore?"

I couldn't help but be inspired by my runaway senses. I had grabbed onto two minds without even trying. I wondered what else I could do.

I reached out to the grim minds, tethering myself to my soul as tightly as a human ever could. As I suspected, they were easy to grab onto. The minds were similar, broken records of carnage. They all had different stories and different motives, but they were the same angry, bitter, pained souls on the inside. The tiny fragments of light within were all but snuffed out. At best, they were embers hidden under gray ash, but not enough to spark a flame; not without help, anyway.

I focused on the tiny souls, even as the grim barreled down on me. I should have protected myself, but I couldn't do both. When the first grim reached me, Ian had returned to my aid and his fist shattered its jaw. The remaining body flew into a mailbox. He cussed at my brazen stupidity, before proceeding to hammer two more arriving grim.

I tugged on the remaining souls that could still be considered human. The remaining six were too annihilated by evil's grasp to be saved by me. They belonged to hell and there was no distinguishing between them and the soulless demons that unhappily resided there.

The energy that burst from the grim was brilliant and energizing. It was enough to put Ian and me on our asses, but luckily it did the same for the last attacking grim. We both got to our feet and waited for the grim to revive, but they all appeared to be empty.

"Shit," I said without any more ceremony than it needed.

"I take it you did that?" Ian stared at me.

"Yeah. I..." I wobbled a little, and Ian moved a little closer in case he needed to hold me up. "That was a little bit cool."

Ian laughed and grabbed me into an impromptu hug. He pulled back and kissed me partly on the lips, but mostly on the cheek. "I think it's about time we got you a cape, hero."

I groaned. "Ah, damn it."

Hero's Welcome

I SLIPPED MY ARM into the crook of Ian's elbow as we approached the house. He glanced down at the familiarity and smiled. "Does that mean you forgive me?"

"No, that means I need you to help me stay up, because I'm about to lose all muscle control and fall down." His smile slipped away. "And yes, I have forgiven you," I added. "However, if you wanted to drop an 'I love you' to reassure me you aren't going to kill me in the night, that would be super."

Ian chuckled and shook his head. "Oh, come on, you don't want yet another man emotionally driveling at your feet, do you?"

"Don't underestimate my neediness. Why do you think I don't want to be the hero? I excel at *damsel in distress.*"

"Could have fooled me." He stopped at the backdoor and looked at me. "I don't suppose I have to tell you my history with Milton is private."

"Oh, yeah, of course. I wouldn't dream of it."

"Hmm, that's another secret you'll be keeping for me. I can see why you'd be worried for your life." He smirked.

"Yeah, still not to the funny stage yet." I frowned as he helped me inside.

Aside from inadvertently slipping deeper into the hero role, there was one more thing in line to ruin my day.

I stared at the scene Ian and I had walked in on. Haden and Devin were sharing a chair by the fireplace—him on the chair, her on the arm. Priest sat on one end of the couch, and my ex on the other.

"Garrett," I spat out instead of a hello. I must have gripped Ian a little harder, because he took it as a signal to play up the intimate position we were in. He wrapped his arm around my shoulder and put on his deep voice.

"Garrett Smith. I've heard a lot about you."

Priest shifted into a more relaxed position on the couch. He observed our interaction with bemused quizzical fascination, but so far he didn't seem annoyed. He either trusted me, or he didn't want to play the jealous boyfriend part in front of everyone.

"I don't believe I've heard about you." Garrett looked between Priest and me, no doubt trying to ascertain if this was a normal interaction.

"I'm Ian." He squeezed my shoulder. "The *new* guy." Ian smiled, finding his own amusement with the tension in the room, as well as the confusion on Garrett's face.

I knew I should have been moving away from Ian, but he really was holding me up. Even if I did move, where would I go? Devin was officially off limits. The only open seat was either the chair next to Garrett or between Garrett and Priest—which seemed wrong on many levels. Instead, I stood frozen and baffled by social graces.

"Ian's a good fighter," Devin said, giving him a respectful nod. "He's offered his services, and we are lucky to have him."

"He's here for the storm, just like the rest of us," I added.

"Where have you two been?" Haden's nose scrunched up. "You stink."

I looked down at myself as if I might see a banana peel hanging from my clothes.

"We were just getting a little dirty." Ian gave her a wink I didn't approve of, but could hardly kick him for, since I had officially lost feeling in my feet.

I glanced at Priest, silently begging him to retrieve me, but his introspective position seemed to be his way of disguising the smirk behind his hand. He was apparently amused by my discomfort of seeing my current and ex-boyfriends in the same room.

"We were at the dump," I specified.

"What, did you roll around in it?" Haden added.

"Well..." Ian took the bait for another innuendo.

"We..." I opened my mouth to explain, but I couldn't very well say Ian tried to kill me. "We were attacked by some grim." I looked to Ian, imparting a little guilt on him for the small lie. "I should go shower."

"I'll help you," Ian said, in reference to assisting my ascent, not the actual shower, but his previous innuendos left little room for a different interpretation.

Priest gave us both an emphatic glare, but I didn't bother responding. I moved toward the stairs. Ian was doing his best not to reveal my malady, which I was grateful for, since it meant avoiding an interrogation from the others. However, with Ian supporting my every step, it became obvious I was no longer a bipedal all-star.

"What's wrong?" Garrett asked, before anyone else could.

"She's pretty smashed up from the fight. I'm going to walk her up." Ian answered Garrett, but it was Priest he looked at.

"Let me." Garrett stood and approached us.

Ian and I exchanged comically shocked glances. He wasn't sure if he should let Garrett take over, and neither was I. Had I not lost all feeling up to my thighs I would have forced myself to walk, just to avoid any perceived relationship faux pas.

Ian let go of me so Garrett could take over, but neither man realized how weak I really was. The moment I was released I slumped to the floor on my knees. There was a belated leap from both of them, but the short distance didn't allow for a dramatic catch.

Priest finally stood to retrieve me, but before he could reach me, Garrett scooped me into his arms. "I know you're happy to see me again, Lenore, but there is no reason to get weak in the knees," Garrett joked.

"Ha. Ha," I said rather than try to feign a smile.

As he carried me upstairs, I watched Priest let me go, without complaint, interjection, or even following. I knew I had hardcore abandonment issues that skewed my interpretation of relationships, but somehow, seeing my lover stand by silently while another man carried me away, made me sad.

Numb

"Y ou can't feel that?" Garrett poked my legs with his pocketknife while I sat on the bed. "Seriously. That can't be good."

"I used some of my specialness on the grim today. I guess it was too much too fast. I don't think it's permanent."

"Yeah, but…" Garrett poked my leg again, this time with his finger. "Tell me when the feeling starts." He traced his finger up my leg, but I couldn't feel anything. He started back on the side of my knee and slowly traced his finger up my inner thigh.

"How's your wife?" I asked before his finger found the area of my lower body that still had feeling.

Garrett drew back his finger and smiled. "She's seeing someone else."

"Oh, I'm sorry." I shook my head. "You must hate me for sending you back to her."

"No, I don't. Funny thing was, she was seeing him while I was seeing you. When I came back to work on things, she thought it was only temporary. When she realized I intended to stay, she told me about him."

"Shit." I chuckled, mostly out of discomfort.

"It's better this way," he said. I frowned at his silver-lining interpretation. "No, really, it is. We love each other so much, but trying to stay together through this... It would destroy us. Someday we'll die, be reunited with our children, and then we'll be together. But not here. Not now."

He touched my hand, stroking his thumb over the soft ticklish skin. "What about you? Is Ian your new man?"

I chuckled, thinking about my almost-murder. "No, Ian and I are buddies. He's loyal, but I'm pretty sure he only likes blondes."

"And Matthew? Has he finally figured out what to do when a beautiful woman is madly in love with him?"

I opened my mouth to answer, but I wasn't sure how to respond since Garrett seemed to have figured out my feelings long ago. I nodded and he retracted his hand. I shrugged apologetically.

"I shouldn't have left." He shook his head somberly.

"I made you leave, Garrett."

"No, I mean the first time," he whispered. "I should have tied you to the bed with that damn night gown and made love to you until the others came back."

I gulped. It sounded appealing, but in a *those were the days* kind of way.

I glanced at the door, but Priest was not standing outside monitoring our conversation. I was in my bedroom with my former lover and he was content with catching up on his reading downstairs.

"I would have liked that very much... at the time, but even if it changed who would lie in my bed, it still wouldn't change my heart. As much as I love you, I'm drawn to Priest—Matthew. I don't know... insert any lame gushy love song here."

Garrett smiled warmly, and tucked my hair behind my ear. "So, you're a romantic after all. Well, thanks for letting me down easy." He leaned in slowly, tipping my chin up for a kiss.

Again, I wasn't sure what the protocol was on this. Garrett was once someone of great importance to me, and still was, so ripping my face away could hardly be considered proper etiquette. I didn't hear the scuffle on the stairs until his lips were pressed to mine. It wasn't a romantic kiss, but it was intimate, and from anyone's perspective, meaningful. The difference between *hello* and *goodbye* is pretty vague when it comes to kissing.

"What's going on, Lenore?" Haden came crashing through the partially open door, interrupting our innocent dalliance. She barely blinked at the scene, since she had no intention of stopping her rampage for the likes of a soap opera.

Of the three men following her, Priest was the one to catch my guilty retreat. He looked between us, but didn't say anything. He didn't look angry or hurt, just bitterly observant. Garrett moved off the bed as Ian came crashing down beside me.

I was about to yell at him for the rudeness, but he shoved a container of nuts in my face and I instantly realized I was famished. Whatever I had achieved that afternoon took a lot of energy to do. "Oh, God, yes," I said, snatching the peanuts from him.

"Not in your bed more than a few seconds, and I already got you begging for more," Ian joked. "Beat that preacher man." Ian pointed a finger at Priest.

"It's not God she's calling for when she's with me," Priest joked right back, only he wasn't really kidding. The heated look he gave me from his spot against the dresser made my mouth go dry—or perhaps it was the peanuts. Either way, my moisture was no longer being reserved for my mouth.

"Will you two shut up," Haden interrupted the antics, and I blushed, ducking myself a little lower in the bed. "Lenore, what happened this afternoon? Ian said you took out like two dozen grim."

I glanced at Ian and we both did a quick calculation of which grim he hit, and which ones collapsed. "I think it was eighteen."

"Holy shit," Devin whispered.

"Wait, what?" Garrett drew himself away from the window. "You mean like what you did at the tournament?"

"No, I..." I glanced at Priest, but I wasn't sure why, since he didn't know any more than I did. At least not the details. "At the tournament, I killed the demon inside the grim."

"You killed it, not just kicked it out?" Garrett clarified.

"Right, but I figured out I can also release the soul inside the demon, inside the grim."

"Release the soul. What soul?"

"Oh, crap, you're that far back," I mumbled.

"Demons," Priest thankfully interjected, "is a general term. There are different schools of thought on them, but what seems to inhabit the grim is tortured souls, human souls that have been residing in hell. They could be considered demons, but what we are really concerned about is Adrian Dorn. Whatever is inside of him, is a real demon, born and bred as a servant of the devil."

"So, you don't think he *is* the devil?" I asked, since Priest was on the teaching circuit anyway.

"No."

"How do you know that?" Devin asked.

"Because I was able to remove him from the body. If he were a higher-ranking member of the demon hierarchy he would have laughed in my face."

"Yeah, but you have... Him," I said.

Priest looked away.

"Wait, wait!" Garrett flailed his arms. "What did Lenore do?"

"She reached inside eighteen grim simultaneously." Ian demonstrated with an overdramatized hand display. If I had been ripping their hearts out, it probably would have been a pretty accurate presentation. "And ripped out their souls."

"No wonder you're paralyzed," Garrett said.

"Paralyzed?" Priest's face was wrought with worry, but he still didn't move to my side. I knew he was probably keeping his distance so he didn't flaunt our relationship in front of Garrett, but the distance was starting to piss me off.

"Not paralyzed, just numb," I clarified. "And hungry." I grabbed another handful of nuts.

"Eighteen." Haden paced at the end of my bed. "Was it hard? Did you pass out? How long did it take you?"

"No, no, and... less than a minute."

"She can also push an attacker off with Herculean strength." Ian and I exchanged a glance.

"An attacker?" Priest asked, looking us over suspiciously. "As opposed to a grim?"

"Including grim." Ian lowered his voice and gave Priest a look that probably meant *mind your own business*, but that wasn't likely to happen.

"You really are becoming the person my sister thought you could be." Garrett stared at me with awed fascination. I swallowed my peanuts and opened my mouth to object, but the whole room was looking at me the same way. Some were a little more bitter than others—thank you Haden—but they were all proud and relieved to see I wasn't a screw-up who inherited shoes too big to fill. I was finally starting to look like the hero to them.

Damn it!

Beta Male

AFTER MY SNACK AND a long discussion about the potential ramifications of releasing or killing the puppet masters behind the grim, I passed out from extreme fatigue. When I woke several hours later, it was starting to get dark out.

I slipped downstairs in time for a cold dinner. Garrett and Ian were playing a game on the Xbox that involved just as much melee as we dealt with in real life. Apparently, the game was a stress reliever. Neither one of them paid much attention to me, but in their defense, they were very busy.

Haden was on the couch with her feet propped on the coffee table, painting her toenails. It wasn't completely abnormal, but the little feminine touches were coming more frequently.

Devin called me into the kitchen for my cold dinner, but I told him to save it for me while I talked with Priest. He pointed to the backdoor and I slipped outside.

I found Priest on the west side of the house watching the last tendrils of sunlight disappear behind the horizon. I expected it to be a beautiful sunset, with as much attention as he paid it, but it wasn't really. The smears of clouds should have looked purple, but they were mostly gray, and the oranges and pinks that usually accompanied the sunsets were a blend of muted yellow. I wondered if it had looked more appealing earlier.

I kept my approach quiet, in case his observance was more meditation than stargazing. I leaned on the white plastic corral-style fence that had once served to outline the official lawn and waited for him to open himself to conversation. After an eternal moment of silence standing in his periphery, I decided to climb the fence and sit on the upper plank. Tragically, the fence was as cheap as it was useless.

The hollow plastic panel snapped and I careened over into the tall grasses behind it with a yelp. After a half second, Priest appeared above me with a grimace that quickly turned into a smirk. "It's good you aren't letting this hero talk go to your head, Lenore." I rolled my eyes and let him pull me back out of the tangle of weeds that were demanding I pay homage to them by spreading their seeds.

Once I was up and facing Priest, I glanced at the sunset that was nothing more than the afterglow of the day. "Sorry," I mumbled.

"For what?"

"I didn't mean to disturb your... session."

"My session?" Priest pulled a long twig from my hair. "It's the sun, honey, it's not exclusively mine."

"Oh, I thought you might be... you know."

"Praying?" He perked a brow and tipped his head. I could feel the scold coming even before he spoke. "Lenore, I appreciate that you are willing to give me space to be who I am, but that's exactly what it feels like—space."

"Huh?"

Priest took in a deep breath and looked up as if he was begging for strength. "I know this is all so uncomfortable for you—"

"I'm not uncomfortable." I huffed, crossing my arms. "I can't explain it. I get it. I do. I know you love me, but you have this special connection I can barely comprehend, let alone participate in. I just feel like the odd man out in a threesome with you and *Him*." I couldn't help but snarl the word.

Priest thankfully chuckled. "You're jealous?" He lost his smile and stared me down. "Imagine how I feel sharing you with three other men."

I let my mouth drop open in preparation for my defense, but today was not the best day for my loyal girlfriend performance.

Priest raised his hands in defense. "I'm sorry, that was out of line. I promised myself I wouldn't play the part of the domineering boyfriend." He strolled away, pulling leaves from random branches and ripping them up.

I followed behind him, pulling up a few dandelions on the way to make an ugly bouquet. "Why not?"

"Because you're not a doll I can manipulate and govern," he said, looking back to pin me with his gaze.

"Oh, right," I mumbled.

He turned away again and kept walking. "You're disappointed?" he asked. I shrugged even though he couldn't see me. "Do you prefer that I pee on your leg?"

I crumpled my nose. "Apparently," I grumbled sarcastically.

"Or do you just prefer an alpha male." He stopped and waited for my answer. "Perhaps you prefer me to beat my chest and roar at any male that comes near you." He turned slowly, revealing the scowl that had trespassed on his face earlier that day.

I frowned and started popping off the heads of my dandelions. "No," I lied. I did want him to be territorial. Not because it was a turn-on—although I'd be lying to say it wasn't—but because I needed to know where I stood with him. I needed to know I was his, and by the rule of reciprocity, that he was mine.

"Would it make you feel better to know that you have made me very jealous today?" He crossed his arms and stepped closer to me. I preferred the anger directed at the usurping men, but it was probably more appropriate this way. I was the one playing the dimwitted damsel.

"Ian was only joking. He—"

"Ian likes to instigate chaos and put people on edge whenever he can. Especially men," he added, and my eyes widened; I wondered how much he knew about Ian's past. I decided it didn't matter either way, since I had already promised my silence to him.

"Yeah. I suppose you weren't happy about Garrett taking me upstairs."

"It didn't upset me as much as you think. Garrett has far more experience caring for your injuries than I do. Plus, I knew you two needed some time to talk." He stepped forward again, moving his hands to his hips. "I was expecting you to be using your lips for talking and not kissing, though."

I froze under his glare and for a moment, I thought that was it. He was going to break up with me and storm off in a huff. I waited for his anger to turn bitter, but instead he reached his finger up to my face, making me flinch. He touched my lips, tracing his finger over them.

"I can tolerate the coltish kisses Devin gives you, but if you ask me to share your lips with Garrett, then you'll be sweeping my heart off the floor." Although he started off with a firm reproachful tone, his ending statement was pained and pleading. He wasn't demanding anything from me other than to be cautious with his heart.

I pushed past his finger and kissed him hard on the lips. I didn't want there to be any confusion about whose lips I wanted on mine. He grunted in surprise, but I didn't relax my fervor until he could meet my intensity. We stood in the yard kissing until the mosquitoes herded us back into the safety of our bedroom.

Familiar Strangers

I WOKE FROM A deep sleep to August whispering my name. I grumbled at the interruption to my slumber, but she insisted I come downstairs to talk to her. She tiptoed away while I rolled my feet off the bed and slipped them into my slippers.

I was surprised by the near four a.m. awakening. The population of the grim had been significantly reduced since the mayor was collecting all the animated ones. The upside, aside from not being randomly attacked the minute you walked into commercial areas, was limiting our watches to late night movies and early-rising coffee drinkers. The few hours in between the two didn't concern us much, especially with a house full of a half dozen people.

I wasn't sure why August was waking me up at such a strange hour.

Especially since she was *dead*!

My body broke into a cold sweat and I bolted upright, turning my instantly awake eyes to the partially open bedroom door. I always shut it at night. It wasn't just a dream.

My mind reeled with a thousand thoughts, but it was really only one repeating.

Please God, not a ghost. I could handle zombified corpses that wanted to brutalize me and kill me, but an incorporeal manifestation of a previously living person? Oh, *hell* no!

I was terrified, but the only physical response my body could activate was a 500-million-year-old defense of puffing up my *fur* to look bigger. I ignored the prickling sensation of every hair on my body rising in preparation for what was to come and I stood up.

I forced my feet to move, putting one in front of the other until I was out my door and at the top of the stairs. I could see the kitchen light was on, and I knew it could have just as easily been left on as turned on, but that was my rational mind getting in the way of my modern reality.

I went down the stairs, determined to face my fears. I stopped at the base of the steps and let my peripheral vision scare the hell out of me. I could make out the dark hair and the pink robe that neither Haden nor I had the heart to throw away. It always hung on the back of the bathroom door.

Always, until now.

I forcefully turned myself and walked to the kitchen. As determined as I was to know for certain, my eyes watered and my legs became shaky and slow. The body before me was familiar, but I couldn't see the face—until she turned.

Familiar strangers.

That's what the grim always were to me. I had killed a hundred and then some. They all looked the same to me: A man who might have sold me my car insurance, a woman who might have delivered my mail once upon a time, or even someone with a name I should have known, but chose not to try too hard to remember.

This grim was not a familiar stranger. She wasn't even familiar. She was intimate. She was my friend, my family, and at one time... my everything.

August smiled at me and it took me a long moment to get a grip on reality. Her desiccated features stared back at me and the fearful tears in my eyes turned painful. She was still beautiful. As beautiful as the day she died in my arms.

This was not August. This was just another puppeteering demon, and I killed puppeteering demons. I hardened my heart and scowled at her. I took a step forward to wring the offensive creature from her.

"Lenore," she said, stopping me in my tracks. It was *her* voice. It shouldn't have been. By all laws of our post-apocalyptic world, it shouldn't have been, but it was. "I wouldn't do that if I were you."

"How do you know my name?"

She smiled and offered me the chair across from her at the table. "Sit, Lenore, we need to talk."

"Who the fuck are you?" I ground out.

Her demeanor shifted slightly into annoyance, but her coy smile returned. "I'm the one who just walked into this house and stood over your bedside without stabbing a knife into your chest. I can't say I offered that privilege to the others. Did you even check your lover before you came down?"

My mouth dropped and I whipped around, prepared to race back up the stairs to check on my friends. My eyes had only just left August before they arrived back on her behind me. I intended to barrel through her, but she tossed me easily to the linoleum floor, where I lay gaping at her inhuman movement.

I remembered the rumors of the big-city grim that were as fast as the mythical vampire, but I had never seen one. Even the one I had killed in the arena was not that fast. I stood and tried to move to the other side of the island, but she was on me again.

"Sit down, Lenore. I want you to imagine what I might have done to all of them while you were sleeping."

I looked to the stairs once more, but I let my logic takeover. If she was going to kill us all, I especially would have been included. There would be no time for chit-chat. Not to mention, if she had killed them all, she would want me to see, so I would be helpless and hopeless.

"What do you want?" I asked, retrieving my backup weapon of anger.

"I want you... *to sit... down.*"

I ripped out the chair she had offered earlier and plopped down. As she sat down across from me, I reached for her mind the way I had the other grim.

"Stop." She waved her hand over her face and my fledgling connection snapped like a cobweb. "Your talents have been growing, haven't they?" She leaned over toward me. "I know you've been freeing souls." I frowned and leaned back in my chair to get more distance from her. "You should have stayed hidden. That's the only thing you do really well, Lenore. From the minute you trespassed onto this Earth, you were in a perfect camouflage. I never would have guessed—and I didn't. When I saw you the first time across the stadium, I sensed strength, but I had no idea how much."

"Adrian," I snarled.

August raised her hands to present her revealed identity. "In truth, that's just a name too, but let's not bother with formalities. I hate it when people get hung up on labels."

"You mean like demon or asshole?"

August snickered. "No, I mean like evil." She licked her lips. "There is a battle coming."

I snorted. "Like I haven't heard that before. Are you sure you don't still have a little of August in there?"

She shifted back in her chair, already showing annoyance at my inability to take my grave situation seriously. It made me chuckle again, because it was also what August would have done. I was apparently an equal opportunity pain in the ass.

"Yes, I imagine she warned you about that, but are you sure you're on the right side?"

"I'm on the side that isn't evil."

"There's that word again. Evil. Do you really want to fight for a god that has left you behind?"

"I'm not fighting for Him. I'm fighting for the human race and our claim on the Earth."

She chuckled. "You have no chance of reclaiming the Earth. And as far as the human race is concerned... extinction is the only future they have."

I gritted my teeth and shook my head. "We'll see."

August tipped her head to look me over. "You do realize you have no chance, don't you? Even if you survive this battle, you will be squashed in the war."

"We are prepared for war."

August giggled and sighed. "No, Lenore, the war is not between humans and demons. The war is between angels and demons." She smiled, barely able to contain her amusement at my apparent ignorance. "You're just the trees we're burning down to make room for it."

Burning Down the Trees

I T FELT STRANGE TO be strangling my best friend, from the moment my fingers wrapped around her throat, I no longer saw her. The sickening black form housed inside of her was strong. Stronger than me, but I didn't let that stop me. I was surprising myself left and right this week. I might as well try giving the big bad a run for his money *before* the climax.

I could feel my ethereal hands wrapping around the darkness within August and I focused my mind on ripping it apart. I thought I was making leeway, but my mind was dragged in like quicksand. The darkness inside of her crawled inside of me, tainting my heart the way looking into hell had.

I threw myself back, away from August, and landed on the floor by the stove. I looked at my shaking hands, and saw vines of black streaming under my skin like blood poisoning. I clenched my hands into tight fists as the anger inside of me threatened to take me over. The harder I fought it, the worse it became. Finally, I let go.

The pain and anger absorbed into my body, claiming my mind and heart. For a moment, I was blind with unfounded rage. When I turned it on my enemy, I found August's face.

There were at least a few reasons to still be mad at her. She brought me into this whole mess. She was ridiculously enigmatic, leaving me unprepared for the future. She had greatly underestimated the learning curve I required. She died and left me alone to deal with it all!

I stared at my enemy's mask and I let it all go. There were always reasons to be angry, but there was only one reason not to be angry, and it conquered them all. Love.

I loved August and, more importantly, I trusted in her. That meant she had to be right about me. I was more than a nuisance tree, and I wasn't going to be burned down by the fires of hell, no matter how hot they were!

I felt myself grip onto the determination that had brought me this far on my journey. It was the same determination that had been misinterpreted over and over again as cowardice, stubbornness, and foolishness. In the end, it wasn't any of them. It was a compulsion. Something inside me had a very specific purpose and goal. Despite the training, and my gaining abilities, it still only reared its head when it wanted to. Every step I took toward being who I was meant to be was paced for a reason. A battle was indeed coming and for the first time I could feel it, because I was feeling stronger than I ever had.

August watched the anger dissipate from my face as she prepared for my rabid attack. She looked disappointed, but also surprised. "How the hell did you do that?"

"I never was much good at being mad at August." I stood up and she joined me, squaring off her hips. "I guess John was right: 'all you need is love.'" I chuckled in amusement and smirked as the rage that was supposed to be inside of me lit her face.

"You'll need a lot more than that, sweetheart." August was on me before my mind had even registered the movement. I was bent over the stove face first with my arms pinned behind my back. "I am still stronger than you in this form. Don't forget who you are speaking to."

"How could I forget? Standing within three feet of you makes me want to rip my skin off just to rid myself of the creepy crawly feeling I get from you," I sassed. I probably should have stowed the sarcasm, since my shoulder was about to be dislocated.

"I know you hate me, Lenore, but rest assured, it's no small gesture on my part to reduce my magnetism." August leaned over, pressing her body against my back to whisper in my ear. "I wouldn't want to upset you, by drawing you to *this* body."

I frowned, remembering how easily Adrian drew me in at the party. Even then, I considered myself strong, but he still twisted my libido around his finger and tugged me behind him.

"Actually, this might be working for me. I just need you to shift me to the left over the oven dial," I said a little too arrogantly.

She slammed my face down against the electric burner. "I think it's time to remind you that this isn't a joke." She turned on the dial and I immediately felt the warmth press into my cheek. "If you scream, they'll come to help you. If they come to help you, I'll kill them all."

I was already starting to smell my hair singing, and my face hurting, but I was relieved at the insinuation that my friends were alive upstairs. That alone gave me the strength to bite back my screams as my face sautéed on the stove.

Burn in Hell

"WHY DID YOU DO that?" I asked from behind my makeshift ice pack of peas. My cheek was already blistering, and I couldn't stop crying salty tears, so there was no hope of alleviating my pain. That, however, wasn't going to prevent me from getting some answers.

"You needed to learn a lesson. I don't like being defied. Plus, it was fun."

"No, I mean why were you trying to impregnate me? Were you trying to make a cambion?"

"Mmm, sounds like somebody has been learning from their priest. Tell me, does it bother you to fuck a man of the cloth?"

"Not really. The Thorn Birds is one of my favorite movies." August scoffed. "What, not a Richard Chamberlain fan?" I flinched as she reached for my hand, which made her smile.

"I was going to use our offspring as a mortal vessel, as many of my dominion will to gain a foothold on the Earth."

"Why? Why not just stay free to move about in any vessel you want?"

"Because I would be stronger in a vessel conceived in darkness. I'm not going to clatter around glass dolls and old bones like an amateur. I do have standards."

"You can't inhabit the Earth without a vessel, can you?" I asked, but I wasn't really expecting an answer. "You can't claim the Earth without one and you can't fight your war without one. Why do you even want the Earth? If it is as you say, the humans will be gone and you will have no one to torment."

August shook her head and stared at me, curiously annoyed—apparently my ignorance was showing again. "The humans were the only thing protecting the Earth from us. And trust me, there aren't enough of you left to keep us from taking it. The sooner you acclimate to that idea, the less disappointed you'll be at watching your friends die for a futile cause."

I didn't want to let her statement hurt me, but I couldn't help fearing for my friends. Somehow, I felt more compelled than ever to give my life to save the world, but I wasn't sure I could ask my friends to do the same. "If you wanted to spawn so badly, why did you give up?" I quickly changed the subject.

"Who says I've given up?"

"Well, the dreams are gone. Kind of a difficult undertaking to begin with, I suppose. Let alone when people keep kicking you out of your body."

"I wouldn't worry too much about that. I have plenty of bodies to choose from for now." She motioned to herself.

"How *did* you manage that? I've been drenching her with holy water since I found out about her."

She rolled her eyes. "Do you really think holy water will keep me out, when a free-thinking human mind can't?"

"You must be very powerful."

"As are you."

I nodded. I wasn't sure I would have agreed when I first sat down, but I could almost sense a shift in myself. Either my ego was getting more brazen, or Adrian wasn't as strong as he claimed.

"When I saw you destroy that grim..." August sucked in a deep breath and shuddered. I cringed, wondering what pleasure Adrian was receiving from that memory. "I knew you were something special. I assumed your priest had imbued you with some heavenly power. Completely against the rules, of course."

"There are rules?"

"Oh yes, Lenore, very strict rules, and you will be disappointed to find that none of them are for humanity's benefit. As I said, this war is between angels and demons."

"What sort of rules?"

"Your priest hasn't told you yet. I imagine he doesn't want to put his god in a negative light. But at this point, who really cares? I mean there's not a one of you left He gives a damn about."

I smiled and pointed at her. "He gave a damn about August. She's crystalline, or did you forget to check the mirror on the way in?"

"That's true, but she was always a believer. She always trusted in her god. Can you say the same? Can you say you trust Him, even after He betrayed you?"

I shrugged. "If it took a reaping to enlighten us all, so be it."

"I don't mean that betrayal! I mean the one against you. His first betrayal."

I stared at her, not understanding which *one* she was talking about. I didn't want to reveal too much, but my confusion was written all over my face. August tipped her head to examine me. She was annoyed again.

"Oh, you poor, stupid girl." Her features shifted into sympathy. "You really aren't faking this, are you?" She laughed and bit her lip. Particles of her lip fell to the table as she did. "That is precious. Oh, so fucking precious. And here I came to tell you that revealing yourself to me by freeing those souls was a grave mistake. Little did I know, you still haven't revealed yourself to yourself." August laughed heartily.

My anger renewed, but it was purely my own. I let it fuel me as I found my tether to strengthen me. I reached across the table and struck August in the chest with more than my own strength. Distracted by her own humor, she didn't defend herself. Her body flew back and shattered against the fridge.

I gasped and stared at the millions of little pieces of August's former body lying on the floor with her pink robe. I had never been a devoted fan of destroying grim, but for once in my life, I regretted it entirely.

Not only had I cut short what might have been a more revealing conversation with Adrian. I devastated my best friend's beautiful body.

The Rest in Pieces

I SCRAPED TOGETHER THE shattered remains of my friend and immediately took them back to her gravesite. I sprinkled the pieces over the freshly overturned ground and mixed the soil. I couldn't help but wonder if it wouldn't have been better to dismantle her body the minute I discovered she was a potential grim. Then again, I had no idea holy water was useless against higher-level demons.

By the time I made it back to the house, the sun was up. As I approached the backdoor, I could hear Devin inside yelling. "What do you mean she isn't here?" Judging by the commotion it was no wonder no one heard the ATV approach.

"She wasn't in bed when I woke up," Priest said, nearly frantic. "I've looked everywhere." I probably shouldn't have been pleased to hear the fear in his voice, but I was glad he wasn't being rationally calm.

"You guys," Ian said quietly.

"The four-wheeler is gone too," Garrett reported.

"You guys," Ian said more sing-song.

"Where the fuck would she go?" Haden interjected more as a complaint than any design of deductive reasoning.

When I turned the knob and pushed open the door. Priest, Garrett, and Devin looked over at me with paused surprise and concern. Haden snorted on the couch and got up—probably to head back to bed, but once she was in view of my burnt face she paused, showing the same concern.

"Lenore!" Priest snapped out of his trance and lifted me into a tight hug. "Where did you go? What happened?" He put me down and examined my face. He raised his hand to touch my face, but I flinched.

"Don't, it still hurts."

"I know. I'm going to take the pain." He moved to touch me again, but again I pulled away.

"No, then you'll hurt," I objected.

"If you three would have shut up, I could have told you the four-wheeler just pulled in," Ian said, leaning back on the couch.

"You heard her pull in and didn't say anything?" Garrett glared at Ian. "Do you think this is some kind of a joke?"

Ian shrugged. "I didn't know she was injured. You okay, Chief?" Ian nodded his chin to me.

I knew his haphazard attitude irritated everyone, but I couldn't help but appreciate the small humor he forced into my otherwise serious life. "Yeah, Ian, I'm good."

"I told you, there's no pilot light on an electric stove. Stop looking for it." He smirked and I smirked back, even though it hurt my face.

Garrett, however, did not find his humor amusing at all. He lunged at Ian. Since Garrett had not gotten the background on Ian, he wasn't prepared for his response.

Ian was up from the couch in a microsecond, and flipped Garrett into the coffee table, which broke under his muscular weight.

Devin tried to grab Ian, presumably to settle things down, but Ian pulled a knife from behind his back and flashed the metal along with a bright maniacal smile. "Ian!" I scolded, but he was no longer in his right mind.

The sound of Haden cocking her gun did grab his attention. He stared over at her, wondering the same thing we were all wondering. Would she shoot him? Garrett recovered from his *fall* and joined the ranks of glaring faces.

Priest started to puff his chest and I knew he was going to force the calm back into the room. I knew he could do it, and in many ways, I would have been proud to watch him squelch the temper tantrums with his ominous power, but I knew that wasn't what my team needed at that moment. They needed August, but I had just put her to rest once and for all—in more ways than one.

I touched Priest's chest and he understood instantly to stand down. I loved him for that. He was really the ultimate power in our group with his beeline to God, but he was willing to step aside and let me lead. It said a lot for his rehabilitation from pride addiction.

I stepped into the center of my friends and turned to examine them all. They each wore expressions of anger and irritation. It wasn't the same anger that tried to suffuse itself to my mind and heart hours earlier. It was only human anger, but it was a seed. A seed that planted ideas. Ideas that could grow into evil.

"I know you're all angry, and right now anyone saying the wrong thing at the wrong time is liable to cause broken furniture and brandished weapons. I get that." I looked to Garrett. "But what you have to understand is that you're afraid." I looked to Ian. "There's a battle coming and it's coming soon." I looked to Devin. "I know I haven't been the leader August was, but that's going to change, starting right now."

I looked to Haden and sighed. "I'm sorry it's taken me so long to figure this out." I looked back to Garrett again. I could see pain creeping in on the edge of his already sour mood. It barely took the mention of his sister to pain him, but he especially needed to believe I could live up to her expectations. "I may not have every detail yet, but I understand one very important thing now."

I glanced at everyone, pausing for a moment on Priest. "I am surrounded by the bravest, most capable warriors God could ever give me. I know August believed I was special, and that I would lead you all through some great battle against a great evil, but... the truth is, you are the special ones. You have all stood by me, nurtured me, taught me, pushed me, and loved me. Without all of you, I would have nothing: no family, no purpose, and no hope." I could see everyone easing back the reins on their weapons and fists.

"The Earth may be forfeit, and humanity may be on the brink of extinction, but I don't care. I'm done running. I can finally feel the battle approaching and I'm going to face it as August intended." I hardened my gaze on each of them. "I would rather *fight*... my last moments beside each one of you, than *survive* a single day without you. But..." I let the word hang as I watched their faces rise to meet mine. "If any of you wish to leave, or decline the honor of fighting for the last vestiges of humanity, then I will understand."

Devin and Haden glanced at each other in shock. My most notable vice had apparently also gone through rehab. Instead of clinging to my friends for dear life, I was setting them free. I only had to wait to see if they would fly away or settle in for the long haul.

"No one's going anywhere, Lenore," Devin said resolutely. "August isn't the only one who thought you were special. Even if I didn't love you with every inch of my heart, which I do, I would still follow you into battle. We've always downplayed what we thought of you, because August wanted us to." Devin glanced at Haden, who looked chagrined at this revelation. "You brought us hope as well, Lenore."

Haden stepped over to Devin and wrapped her arm around his waist. "He's right. It was different once you were around. Whatever *magic* courses through you, it is as enthralling as Adrian Dorn is repellent. We are here to fight with you, because we want to, not because August told us to."

I took a deep breath, allowing those words to satisfy and bolster my resolve. "If that's true, of all of you"—I pinned everyone with motherly glares—"then this bickering and fighting is done; no more broken furniture, no more weapons drawn at each other. We are a team, and we have a mission and it doesn't include competition between each other. Understood?" I got a few sheepish nods, a salute from Ian, and a smile from Priest. I wanted to smile back at him, but somehow I knew that as proud as he was of my newfound bravado, he wasn't going to like what I did with it next.

Sovereign

"I AM NOT HAVING this conversation in front of everyone," Priest mumbled to me from the couch, while Garrett knelt before my chair by the fireplace, tending to my injured face. He seemed a little uncomfortable being between Priest and me while we pretended not to be arguing, but he was deeply concerned about infection. My cheek had unfortunately started to fester and despite my best efforts I wasn't managing to stay still long enough for anyone to properly assess and treat it.

"You need to cough up every last bit of information the Big-and-Mighty has given you since you started having regular conversations, and I mean *now*." I raised my voice enough to let him know I was serious.

Everyone else was still maneuvering around the living room and kitchen, trying not to be extremely interested in what Priest's answer might be.

"Hold still or I'll pin you down," Garrett threatened under his breath.

"You'd try," I snapped back. His eyes met with mine and I could see the shock. He was probably dead serious about holding me down, but I was just as serious in my statement. He seemed to understand he could no longer bully me around. I was not his lesser, nor even his equal anymore. I was not the same Lenore he knew when he left. Even if he still had fleeting thoughts about being with me, they dissolved instantly in that moment.

I tamed my expression and leaned back so he could properly attend to me. I may not have wanted to be bullied by him anymore, but I did appreciate his medical care.

"Yeah, Matthew." Ian shuffled a deck of cards dexterously in the chair next to the couch. "What is the word from the Big Man? We've heard all about Dorn's recent visit. What's *your* player got up his sleeve?"

"I don't have any information that would be useful at this time," Priest insisted.

"But—" I started to interject, but Garrett took over.

"You do have information though," he said as he dabbed my face.

Devin and Haden had been putting away dishes in the kitchen, but their noise stopped in anticipation of the answer.

Priest groaned and threw up his hands. "I know what you all want. Details! I don't *have* details! It's not like He's communicating via text message. I can get responses to my questions, positive or negative. He exudes and implies many things, but in the end I am only offered a general understanding of His purpose." Priest stared me down. "I understand your frustration, but I think it was made abundantly clear today that some revelations take time. Don't ask me to offer up information that has been specifically designated for a certain time."

I pursed my lips, which made my cheek hurt. "Don't give me that crap, Priest. Adrian said you would know what the rules are. He also implied that I haven't revealed myself yet. I know you know what that means."

Priest's gaze hardened and I felt his energy pressing on me, even before he spoke. "It means that you are still you, until you are not, and I am not going to push for you to become someone else until it is absolutely necessary." He stood up and paused by my chair to lean into my face. "And my name is Matthew!" he yelled in my face, and I resisted the urge to retaliate as he stomped upstairs.

Everyone pretended to go on with their menial tasks. I, meanwhile, contaminated Garrett's hard work with fresh tears. He gave me a somber smile and squeezed my hand. I knew that conversation wasn't going to be easy, but somehow I thought approaching him in front of everyone would force him to out his secrets.

Healing Injuries

"**I** DON'T LIKE SURPRISES," Priest blurted out when he slipped into bed beside me that night. "You shouldn't have called me out like I was a traitor to our team." He stared at the ceiling. "And you called me Priest again." He mumbled like it was an afterthought, but I knew it was the main reason he was so mad.

"It just slipped out. I'm used to yelling at you with your nickname." I smiled, but he wasn't looking at me anyway. "What did He tell you about me?" I stared at him, waiting for him to speak, but he didn't. "Why won't you tell me? Matthew, please."

He rolled over to face me and propped his head up on his elbow. "You know how coma victims lose their memories? The doctors tell you not to try to push the memories. They will come back on their own with or without help. Well, you, my dear, are like that. One day you are going to remember... everything you need to know."

"And then what?"

"And then... we all live happily ever after." He smiled sarcastically, but I could tell there was pain in his eyes.

"Why can't we push it a little? Surely a hint isn't going to blow my brain."

He reached over to touch my face and I flinched away. "Hold still."

"Stop it, no, it doesn't hurt... that much."

"Lenore, hold still," he said gently and he held his hand over my face, not touching, just hovering. He closed his eyes and I felt a wave of relief come over me like a warm fuzzy blanket. After a minute or so, the warmth ended and Priest returned to staring at the ceiling.

"I told you not to take my pain. I don't see any reason—"

"I didn't."

"Why does it feel better?" I touched my face and felt soft smooth skin. I jumped out of bed and checked the mirror. "Holy crap!" I yelled. I heard a scuffle outside the door. "I'm okay!" I quickly amended, touching my face all over. "Why didn't you do that earlier?" I asked, returning to bed.

"Before or after you played Brutus to my Caesar?" he grumbled.

"Clearly you missed the roll call this morning. I said no more bickering. Just answer me, once and for all. I will accept your willingness to avoid revealing the rules of battle, if that somehow puts us at risk. I will even respect your choice to keep a coma victim out of the know. But tell me *why* you won't tell me."

"Because I love you!" He spat the words at me and for a moment, all I could do was hold my tongue. It wasn't the type of professed adoration that required a response. "Don't you see, Lenore?" he whispered. "I'm in love with the amnesia girl and she's in love with me. Someday you'll remember... who knows what happens then? Maybe I'm not your Matthew anymore. Maybe I'm just Priest again."

I pushed myself under his arm and snuggled into his chest. "I can't imagine any woman not wanting you, and if remembering makes me forget how much I love you, then I'll put myself back in a coma."

He scoffed and smiled slightly.

"You really are afraid of losing me, aren't you?" I sat up and looked down on him. I wanted to ask why. I wanted to know, even more, what would cause such unrest in an otherwise confident man, but I couldn't bring myself to ask him. Instead, I shut off the bedside lamp and kissed him until he was no longer doubting my love for him.

The Glowing Graveyard

Sometime after midnight, I heard the third bedroom door close. Priest had exhausted himself trying to savor every last moment with me. His earnest concern that our time together was limited to my awareness should have tamped out my curiosity, but it didn't. I was more determined than ever to get answers. The tournament was only days away, and I didn't have time to acclimatize to my discoveries.

I slipped out of the bedroom and dressed in the hall before sneaking downstairs and out the door. I threw my quiver and bow in the back of the truck and jumped into the cab. After I started the engine, Devin's head popped into the open window, making me jump.

"What the hell are you doing?" He reached in and grabbed my wrist before I could roll up the window. "Don't even think about it."

I rolled my eyes, trying not to smile. "Devin, I'm not running away. I just need to check on something."

"Alone?" He glared at me.

I glanced at the house. I had considered taking Ian with me. We already had a few secrets between us, so there was no reason not to add one more. In the end, I decided I would be safer on my own, but it was going to be very hard to convince Devin of that.

"Look, Devin, this is about me. You don't have to come with me."

"Team, right?" He opened the door and slid me across the seat before climbing in and shifting into gear. Before he could accelerate there was a *thunk* in the truck bed, followed by Haden opening the passenger side door.

"Move," she groused before pushing herself into the passenger seat and forcing me back to the middle. Devin didn't flinch at her arrival and took off slowly so we didn't disturb the others.

After a forty-minute drive, we arrived at a small cemetery north of town, not far from our previous house. Beyond a big black metal gate, a short paved road cut through the center of the graveyard. Devin stopped the truck a few feet in and shut off the engine, leaving the headlights pointing straight down the narrow road.

"What are we doing here?" Haden asked before getting out and slamming the door behind her.

"Looking for answers," I said. Devin helped me out of his side and held my hand a moment before moving to circle the property. He disappeared over the hill of tall tombstones.

"How are old bones going to help you?" Haden asked, loading shells into her shotgun and shoving more than one gun under her belt.

"It's not the bones I want. It's what moves those bones."

"Could you give me a straight damn answer, for once?" Haden rested the shotgun on her shoulder and started walking with me down the road.

"When I spoke with Adrian, he said something that sparked my memory. He said I was trespassing on this Earth. When I first spoke with the marionette corpse angels, they called me a trespasser. I thought they just meant we were trespassing on their land, but I started wondering if they didn't know the same thing Adrian does."

"Which is what?"

"Why I'm so damn special." I stepped off the road and into the grassy lawn around the burial plots.

"Still looking for your backstory, huh?"

"Yeah, I guess." I tripped over my own feet and Haden nearly shot my foot off. "Easy, Haden, I don't think we have anything to be afraid of here."

"Right, because walking through a cemetery, at night, after the apocalypse is likely to turn out fine."

"Strangely enough, yes." I sat down on the shrine that commemorated Jesus and the Virgin Mary. I looked up at the white statue of the virgin and shook my head. "You really put the bar high, M. Gotta love a religion that condemns women for perpetuating the species through sex."

Haden snickered and sat down beside me. "Do you really think they'll show up?"

"Not sure. Took them a while to show up before, but this has to be where they got their corpses from."

"Why would they choose here?"

"I get the impression angels and demons are staking claim to lands all over the world. They are setting the battle lines. If there is a war coming, it's not just here."

"No, I mean Earth." Haden frowned. "I get the demons rising from hell to take over the Earth. Hell sucks. But angels live in heaven; heaven's great. Why would they want the Earth? Or are they fighting to give it back to us?"

I could see Haden was still hoping for a happy ending. I wanted, more than anything, to offer her the reassurance that everything was going to be okay, but I knew she would rather have the brutal truth. Disappointment she could handle; it was hope that wore on her nerves.

"I don't think so, Haden. I think God put us on a beautiful stage to watch us dance, and now the show's over. They're just fighting over the real estate."

"If the Earth and humans are doomed, why did He leave us here to fight for them?"

I smiled. It was the same question I had yet to get an answer for. It was easy to say that we were left to fight as warriors of the apocalypse, but to what end? Clearly we were outgunned. Was it just our last chance to prove our worth to God? Was this our penance and punishment?

"I think we're the finale," I answered. "That's why He left the best of us behind; better entertainment." I winked at her.

She didn't find as much amusement in the jest as I had hoped, but I could see the rest of the questions knitting her brow fade away. Except one. "Why do they call this the glowing graveyard?"

"Supposedly one of the gravestones glows in the full moon," I answered blandly. "I've never seen it though."

"That's it? Not really scary."

"Mmm, no, not really. Although there was a tale going around that the lonely grave in the southwest corner holds a serial killer. I was told there used to be a ball, engraved with the names of his victims on top of his gravestone."

"What happened to it?"

I shrugged. "What always happens when you try to offer the public a meaningful display; some dipshit teenager vandalizes it."

"Oh, come on, you could have made that so much scarier."

"Okay, his grave swallowed it up," I caved to the new plot twist.

"Not you. Devin." Haden motioned behind me. "The zombie walk was good, but without the moaning, it lacks something."

I turned to see Devin's arrival. His eyes were glassy and his shoulders were up in a high shrug, as if he was hanging by marionette strings. "Devin," I whispered, barely audible, and waited for him to respond, or break character. "Say something, Devin. I'm not kidding."

Haden chuckled, but she wasn't sensing the tangible shift in the air. I stood and stepped toward Devin's half-standing, half-hanging body. I was almost certain he was being manipulated by an angel. What I wasn't certain about was whether or not they had killed him to do it.

I reached for his wrist to check his pulse, and the being behind him revealed itself in technicolor. Unlike the last time, when it was shades of wispy white, this one was tangible and warm with gold highlights.

"What the hell is wrong with you?" I heard Haden say behind me before her too-tight grasp landed on my upper arm.

The instant she touched me, the light of the summer sun times ten blinded my vision.

Let There Be Light

T HE WARM HEAT WAS soothing to my body. The headstones that dotted the ground were gone, and replaced by perfect grass, tall trees, and kempt flowerbeds. It was iridescent beyond the capability of the Earth's yellow sun—or maybe just beyond the capability of land this far from the equator.

There was only one logical conclusion to be reached, and Haden was gracious enough to say it aloud. "Oh, shit. We're dead!"

I blinked away my eye-gasm and turned to look at her. She was still holding on to my arm as she grazed the landscape with a watchful eye. I was about to add to her comment when I noticed the aura of color surrounding her body. The bright red refracted the imagery around her, making it look like she was on fire.

I wasn't sure what the color signified, but I was certain it fit Haden to a tee. "Haden, you're beautiful."

Haden whipped her head back to look at me. The scowl on her face took the place of the face slap she wanted to give me, but it quickly faded as she saw me. Her eyes traced around my outline. "Why do you look like that?" she asked, as if I was the one making it happen.

"You look different too." I smiled. "You're red. What color am I?"

"You're just... it's.... black."

"Black?" I frowned. That didn't sound good.

"Are either of you going to tell me what the hell is going on?" Devin groused beside me. My hand was still on his wrist, and I didn't dare let go, lest this beautiful vision be interrupted. "I can't move," he said, revealing a tinge of anxiety in his voice. He was still hung up on something, but to my surprise the creature holding him was even less visible than before. His wispy-white-turned-gold highlights were blending into the sun-filled day, making him nearly transparent.

"He's blue," Haden pointed out.

I took in the deep blue that faded to a lustrous turquoise as it bloomed away from Devin's body. I couldn't help but grin at him.

"What the hell is wrong with you two? Help me."

"Okay, okay. Haden, let go, I need to speak with Geppetto."

"What?" She grimaced.

"Look at what's holding him up," I said, nodding above and behind Devin.

Her eyes scanned through his blue haze, and stopped on something. I could see the fear translate into defensive anger and her red glowed even brighter. "What the fuck is that?"

"That..." I looked back at the creature myself, "...is an angel."

"It's ugly," she spat. She tried to reach for her gun, which was there, but somehow out of phase enough that she couldn't actually grab it.

"Yeah, they are kind of birdlike."

"Hello, still waiting for my rescue," Devin reminded us.

"Okay, Haden, let—" I didn't finish my sentence before she let me go.

The lights went out and the world was cool again. Everything was as it was supposed to be, except for the addition of the angel holding up an unconscious Devin. I wanted to know why he wasn't unconscious in the other vision, but that was far from vital, so I let it go.

"Seraphim," I said to the creature that stood an incredible nine feet high.

His mouth frowned and his winged brow deepened to glower at me. "Submit, trespasser." He spoke in an audible voice, which was deep and rumbling.

I gasped, feeling the power of the words hit me with gravity I couldn't ignore. My body shook, and my knees begged to keel to his will, but I fought against it. "No!" I said, forcing power into my voice from my tether.

The angel took in a deep breath and yelled the words again. "Submit, trespasser!"

I could feel the authority he was aiming at me, but instead of fighting against it, I took it in and released it, like the anger Adrian foisted on me the night before. It wasn't so much fighting hate with love as ignoring the taunts of a bully.

"You have no authority over me, angel," I said, even-tempered and proud.

His eyes danced over me, analyzing me. His glossy green eyes may well have been carved from emeralds, the way they glowed. They settled on my own boring hazel eyes and he released the scowl on his face. "Why have you returned to the territory of the eldest?"

"I want answers." I glanced at Devin. I probably should have demanded he release my friend, but I could feel Devin's steady pulse, and I didn't want to break the connection that was allowing me to communicate verbally instead of mentally. I could sense Haden behind me, but she was wisely staying quiet for my perceived one-sided conversation.

"I have knowledge beyond the depths of known time. I was the first, long before the Earth, and man."

"Clearly!" I jumped in before the sermon put me out right along with Devin. "You understand more about me than I do, and I want to know what you know about me."

"You are a traitor to God."

Traitor? That was new.

"I betrayed God?" I frowned. "I thought He betrayed me," I said gingerly, knowing full well I couldn't consider the source of my information reliable.

"You are fallen," he said, offering the sole explanation as all I should need to understand.

"What do you mean by that?" I asked, shaking my head.

"You are fallen," he said again.

"Have a little sympathy on a human brain, feather-face. What do you mean by that?"

"You are not human." He looked me over as if I had put on the flesh and bone as a costume—and a cheap one at that.

"Then what am I?" I demanded.

"You are fallen."

"Yes! What was I before I was fallen?" It was probably obvious, but I still needed to hear it.

"You were an angel of the second sphere. Raised and guided by the Lord of the heavens, until you conspired to kill another."

"Angel?" I stood frozen, trying to wrap my mind around the word *angel*. There were literal interpretations, but since I didn't have any wings, I was searching for a metaphorical one. "An angel like you?"

"You are nothing like me! I am the first!"

"Okay, okay, first-born, got it. No resentment there," I murmured. "Wait, who did I conspire to kill?"

"A malakhim. Young and stupid, but he managed to defend himself." The angel nodded to me and my so-called appendix scar started to itch.

"Oh," I said, touching the scar on my right side. I wondered if I should mention that I killed the asshole that put that scar there, but I wasn't sure successfully murdering him was going to help my case. "What happened to him, after I almost killed him?" I asked as an afterthought.

"He is fallen as well."

"Really? And I fell for trying to kill him?"

"You were banished."

"So, I didn't fall, I was pushed. Who banished me?"

"The Lord of the heavens."

"Sounds like a strict punishment for *attempted* murder."

"The banishment was not for murder. The banishment was for accusing the Lord of telling you to do it."

"I claimed that God told me to kill him? So, schizophrenia is frowned upon even in heaven," I quipped, even though I knew the joke would be lost on him. I could sense the creature's disinterest and I prepared to make my demand for Devin's release, but Haden's question popped into my mind. "Why are you fighting over the Earth? What do angels have to gain on Earth that they don't have in heaven?"

"Earth is the median of heaven and hell. The water's drawn back by the Lord to stop the war. So it began, so it shall continue. Humans are no longer here to balance the tide of good and evil."

"If humans were the moderators preventing war, then why did he remove us?"

"Those are the rules, set forth from Earth's creation. Your time is up. The war is upon us again. He's offered clemency to the risen and condemned the fallen."

"He didn't condemn us; He commandeered us. We are His new army. We will protect the Earth."

"And who will protect you?"

I tried to think of a sarcastic comeback, but he released Devin and his image was gone. Devin slumped to the ground, still unconscious. Haden rushed over to check him while I scanned the empty graveyard.

I had the answer I was seeking. Unfortunately, it didn't really make me feel any better. I had just gone from reluctant hero to unemployed angel.

Angel

H ADEN AND I SAT in silence most of the way home. Devin was still passed out by the passenger door, and I was stuck in the middle while she drove. I could see from her discontent that she had heard enough of the one-sided conversation to understand what the angel was telling me. She was taking it pretty well, I thought.

As she slowed to turn into our driveway, she shut off the headlights, since this wasn't a pre-approved outing. When she shifted into park and shut off the engine, we both sat for a moment, elongating the silence further.

"Please say something," I said finally.

"What do you want me to say?"

"Get angry. Yell at me for... something."

"Reach over into the glove box and grab Devin's flask."

I pulled the flask out and she took a sip before handing it to me. The whiskey was harsh, but a nice nightcap since I probably wouldn't be sleeping anytime soon.

After I handed it back to her, she splashed a little on Devin, to make him smell drunk. Once again she was thinking about the reaction to our late-night excursion.

She took another swig and tapped her thumb on the steering wheel. "Angel?" she clarified.

"Yup."

"That explains why you're such a pussy." She scoffed.

I dipped my brow and started to defend myself, but then I realized she was only doing what I asked her to do.

"That explains the archery too. You were probably a chubby-cheeked cherub spreading love."

I scoffed and chuckled. "Whatever you need to tell yourself, Haden."

She looked at me. Really *looked* at me. She probably expected to see the faint outline of my broken halo or the tattered remains of broken wings, but I was still me. No matter what the fate of the world was to be, I would always be me.

I was pretty sure there was a huge moral lesson in that revelation. Something about being good to others so you could tolerate yourself, but I didn't have time to stitch it on a pillow.

Haden's eyes settled on mine and she shook her head. "His loss, our gain, as far as I'm concerned," she said quickly, and left the truck before the consoling could cross the border of mushy.

And Haden would always be Haden.

Angels and Aunt Jemima

GARRETT WAS MANNING THE grill when I woke up the next morning. Ian and Devin were side by side, competitively hammering down pancakes, while Priest and Haden sipped on coffee. Without room for a fifth at the table, I hung back to sip my coffee and steal a pancake from the grill. Garrett mockingly swatted my hand with the spatula before smiling at me.

I enjoyed the moment for a little while before doing what any sane human being wouldn't do. I told the unabashed truth about myself.

"So, I guess I'm an angel," I blurted out.

Haden and Priest looked up at me with paralleled scouring looks. Ian and Devin offered a glance, but didn't bother to empty their mouths to speak.

"Why? What did you do?" Garrett asked. His face wasn't wrought with any concern. He was wondering what task I had completed to dub me the new namesake.

"Nothing. Well, I imagine I had some duties. Angels do stuff, don't they?"

Garrett turned away from the grill to give me his full attention. "What do you mean, angels?"

"Angels," Ian said over his overstuffed mouth. Devin had joined the ranks of the shocked, but Ian didn't seem affected by it yet. "You know; feathered wings, halos, moral superiority."

"Moral superiority?" I objected. "How many angels have you met?"

"Just you."

"What? How are you the only one not shocked by this?" I asked, almost insulted he wasn't giving my grand announcement the pomp and circumstance it deserved.

"I was a little thrown off the first time I saw that display in the church, but I got a pretty good glimpse of it the night Matthew did his thing."

"So, you knew and you didn't tell me?"

"I assumed you knew and were just hiding it from everyone." Ian shrugged and returned to his pancakes.

Priest stood and started to walk out. I knew he was going to be upset by my new discovery, especially since I went behind his back to get it, but I couldn't believe he was going to walk away. "Leaving already? I guess I should be glad you stayed this long."

He stopped and turned back to me. "I was going to grab some books that might help everyone, including yourself, understand what you are." He was mad. I could see it, but all I could do was look chagrined and hope my foot was as easy to get out of my mouth as it got in.

"Are you all serious?" Devin said.

"Yes," I said and moved over to flip Garrett's pancakes before they burned. He looked me over the same way Haden had the night before. I crossed my eyes and stuck out my tongue at him. He smirked and brought his hand up to brush down my bedhead hair.

"Oh man, I could've fucked an angel," Devin said more to himself.

I scoffed and laughed at his brutal assessment of the situation. Haden kicked him under the table. Garrett gave me a knowing smile and let his hand slide down my cheek before returning to breakfast. "Sit, I'll get you a plate," he murmured.

I moved to sit in Priest's spot beside Haden, across from Ian. He didn't offer me the furtive glances the others did while I ate my pancakes. By the time Priest returned, he had several books under his arm, and a folding chair. He didn't bother to ask me if I was finished before shoving my plate over to lay his books down.

"Angels and demons have a hierarchy much like humans, only it's not based on income, and you don't exactly get to climb the ranks. Each type of angel has a job to do. The Seraphim, as you know, are the highest order. They are essentially God's attendants and guardians. You don't get much closer to God than that."

I frowned. I hadn't even begun to tell everyone what the angel had accused me of, but it already seemed that I wasn't going to be overruling an elitist angel.

"The Cherubim are—" Priest paused while Haden got her laughter under control. I hid my smirk behind my hand, refusing to feed her amusement. "The cherubim are the second highest. They are generally symbolic of God's glory, but the information is limited. Some Christians believe they continually praise God."

"Wow, suck-up angels," Ian said as he nudged me under the table with his foot. "That's definitely not your posse."

"Are you still an angel?" Devin asked.

I was about to offer more information, but Priest's rise in volume signaled that he was not done.

"The Thrones are the angels of peace and submission."

It was Garrett's turn to snicker. He didn't bother to express his reasoning. I could about imagine what he was thinking. That title might have fit when he first met me, but not anymore.

"Dominions are angels of leadership." Priest glanced at me; he must have thought this title fit me pretty well, but I didn't agree. Even if I was here to lead, it didn't mean I was a good leader—just the one with the sixth sense.

"Virtues control the elements. They control the seasons and provide miracles. The Powers are warrior angels. They defend the cosmos and humans. They fight evil spirits." Priest glanced at me again. This must have been another possible label.

I wondered if he already knew I was fallen. I assumed that was obvious, since I was physically human, but perhaps he thought I was wearing a costume. That was probably why he avoided the discovery so long. He assumed the minute I found out my backstory, I would burst from my flesh and take flight.

So far, I didn't feel the need for heights.

"The Archangels are leading angels. They are like generals. They tend to be a little more famous, since they get all the fanfare during critical times. The Principalities are described as hostile to God sometimes, but they are also referred to as the guardians of the Earth."

"That sounds about right," Ian interjected. "Save the Earth."

I smiled, though I couldn't agree. It was becoming increasingly obvious that the Earth was not going to be saved. It pained me, because I really did believe humans had a right to it, but apparently our lease was up, and no one was going to listen to our appeal.

"There are lower-level angels that aren't really given names. Every book has another interpretation, but hopefully that helps."

"Helps how?" Devin glanced between us. "Why are you here instead of up there?"

I looked to Priest, but he seemed reluctant to say anything. He must have known a bit about my past, but didn't want to be the one to say it. "I tried to kill a fellow angel. The grim at the tournament was inhabited by him. A fallen angel too, I guess. Anyway, when I was questioned about the incident, I accused the Big Man Himself of setting me up. That didn't go too well, so they kicked me to the curb."

I glanced around the table. Haden had already offered her condolences on this front, but the others seemed sympathetic, albeit perplexed. Priest rested his hand on mine, not demanding anything, but I gripped it. It wasn't the apology I owed him, but not every fight required make-up sex.

"Is that why you were so dark in that other realm?" Devin asked. He hadn't mentioned it at the time, but he *was* being hung out to dry.

I shrugged. "Sounds about right."

"What does this change?" Garrett asked. "I mean, aside from shock value, and a greater understanding of why my sister was drawn to you. What does this change in our tactic?"

"Nothing," I said, frowning. "We are still going to the finale. I'm compelled to be there more than ever. I'm still not sure what it will have in store for us, but I agree with August's ultimate goal. That is where we need to be." I was surprised not to hear any contention at the statement. We were essentially walking into a trap without any further tactical plan than *it feels right*. Adrian was right. The chances of surviving in the crosshairs of a dimensional war were vanishingly small, but the coming battle was going to be our only chance to make a stand and we needed to do it. If not for our lives, then at least for our souls.

Angel of Darkness

L ATER THAT EVENING, PRIEST stared at me across the living room from the couch. He was poised and ready to answer the thousand and one questions that were percolating in my mind and brimming on my face. I had chosen to sit in the chair by the fire, away from everyone. I was getting so many furtive glances I thought it would be easier to give them an open view so they didn't hurt their necks. I knew they expected me to sprout wings, or don an inexplicable crown of luminescence, but so far, I had no halos nor feathers.

Garrett had been on kitchen duty and for the most part left me alone, but I knew that was only because he wasn't as easily driven by curiosity. Devin and Haden, on the other hand, seemed more interested in me than the movie they were watching. Ian offered me just as many glances, but he wasn't really interested in hiding them from me. He offered me a wink or a kiss when I would catch him gawking extra hard.

While they were trying to decipher the mystery of how a majestic angel had fallen to Earth and turned into a scrawny little girl from the sticks, I was trying to put together all the information I had gleaned from my opposing sources.

I understood from Avery that some of the grim were legitimate demons, while others were tortured souls. I presumed from my experiences with the tiny fiery cores that the difference between a tortured soul and a demon was only a matter of time and hope. The demon grim that wanted to eat our souls only wanted to replace what they had charred useless after a millennium in hell. I wasn't even sure that was possible. Was it a fruitless pursuit, drawn from desperation and instinct, like a moth to a flame? Or could they actually consume a soul?

I wasn't even sure what a soul was, exactly. Most people considered it to be the essence of the person: memory and personality. If that were the case, then wouldn't a soul be specific to each person? Were the grim so despairing for their former humanity that they would seek to wear another's mind?

By my own definition, the soul had a tether to God. If that were really the case, then it was obvious why the grim would be uncontrollably drawn to seek another. Hell must have been unbearable torture, but to lose that tether, the only hope of salvation... What wouldn't you do to get it back? And what happened to the current holder of the soul if you did?

I had freed the souls of eighteen grim already. I had felt the release, and even the relief in that. I knew I had sent them to heaven. Whether or not God wanted them seemed irrelevant at the time. I was certain there was absolutely no chance of rehabilitating a blackened soul, but I was now questioning if I had the right to bypass God and shove the shriveled souls into heaven without permission. However, if I had no right to do that, why could I? And why did some part of me still hate the idea of abolishing the grim.

I rubbed my face, trying to get a stranglehold on my thoughts before I drove myself insane. Before I could, though, a cup of hot tea appeared beside me. I looked up at my waiter and found Garrett. He didn't even offer me a smile or verbal explanation. He was playing the part of the medic, just in a different way. I took the cup and he left. I glanced at Priest as if to ask permission to drink the tea.

He was still staring at me. I should have been unnerved, but the truth was I was smitten enough with him that I enjoyed having his eyes on me. When I felt the warm fuzzy blanket wrap around me I closed my eyes and absorbed it. He was several feet away and yet I could feel him right beside me. When I opened my eyes again, he was smirking at me. I wasn't sure what thought was running through his mind, but I got the impression he was pleased with himself. I sat back to sip my tea and revel in relaxation, but not too long into my mental softness, a new series of thoughts popped into my head.

I understood from the angel that the Earth was a barrier between heaven and hell. Humans were the embodiment of a treaty that held back an infinite war. The moralities of men were as mercurial as the emotions that welled within them, but if the good and evil in man remained balanced, the truce would stand. We were essentially the wall between light and dark, not allowing one to contaminate the purity of the other. Now the balance of humans was gone. Light and dark were spilling through the cracks in the wall of truce, the dark seeking to extinguish the light and the light seeking to illuminate the dark.

Was it as simple as that though? The inhabitants of two opposing ethereal realms were breaking through to a corporeal one so they could bash each other's brains in. What was once a wall protecting them would now become the ruined battleground for a fight that—even in the most expanded construal—could never have a resolution.

Why use the Earth as a frontline anyway? It's not as if these beings needed a physical location to have their battle. The war started long before the existence of the Earth. Couldn't they just bypass the planet altogether and leave the pathetic humans alone? Or were we the doorway as much as the wall?

"If you scrunch your face any harder, you're going to wrinkle prematurely," Ian said from his spot on the chair next to the couch. He looked thoroughly casual, but I could sense he was as interested in the cause of my consternation as everyone else was.

"How will the angels fight?" I asked without specifying who should answer.

"What do you mean?" Priest asked. Haden and Devin turned down the television and Garrett came in from the kitchen to hear the conversation.

I looked over them all, hoping I was asking my question based on lack of information and not lack of understanding of the information at hand. "The lesser demons, the lost soul demons, are taking over the silver saints. The true demons like Adrian Dorn are jumping into active minds, and with some effort, they will eventually create new permanent bodies for themselves. They need vessels to inhabit the Earth, but how will the angels wage a war on Earth without physical bodies?"

Everyone turned to Priest for the answer to this. To my relief he didn't seem annoyed or puzzled by the question. "There are many stories in the Bible of angels coming to Earth. The archangels especially have visited during pinnacle moments in history. The Earth may not be their domain of origin, but I'm sure being on God's team comes with certain privileges."

"Then how come we can't see them then?" Haden asked, twisting to face Priest so she could use Devin's chest to brace her back.

"I saw them when I touched their puppets," I added, "but they were still just ghosts."

"I think angels possess the ability to be corporeal or not. In Lenore's case, I think since she was banished from heaven, the only form she possesses is the corporeal one, but she is far from human."

I dipped my brow. "Why does that sound so insulting to me?"

Priest smiled. "Trust me, it's not."

"But if she's still an angel..." Haden trailed off and looked back at Devin. He shook his head slightly.

"Go on," Priest urged her.

She glanced at me, already remorseful for what she was about to say. I offered her a crooked smile and shrugged. I saw no reason for her to start tiptoeing over my feelings now. "When we were at the graveyard, the angel holding Devin was bright, so bright that it was practically invisible in the light. But Lenore... her aura, or whatever... was black. If she is still an angel, why isn't she a glowing beacon of light?"

Priest looked at me curiously, letting his eyes skirt my silhouette. He looked to Ian to confirm his suspicions.

"She looked pretty freaking beacon-y to me," Ian said with a shrug.

Priest turned back to Haden. "I think what you were seeing is just as you said—an aura of her. You are not seeing her essence. I assume because of my connection with God, I have been able to see this aspect of her on occasion."

"Yeah, but still." Haden grimaced. "Why would an angel have a black aura? Is that because she is fallen?"

"Perhaps, or it could be part of her defensive technique," Priest suggested.

"Black auras can signify long-term un-forgiveness," Garrett added. "Past life hurts." I looked at him, surprised by his contribution. "My wife's into all that crap," he admitted sheepishly. I wasn't sure if he was embarrassed more from mentioning his wife, or because he actually retained the knowledge well enough to share it.

"In any case," Priest said, "we would all be wise to remember that angels are not gentle beings designated to be human guardians. They are creatures of great power, designed to serve God and actuate his will. Having Lenore and her power available to us for the finale tournament is very fortuitous, but it is by the grace of God that she has remained hidden for so long. Had she not, more than a few of us in this room would not be breathing for our indiscretions against her."

I stared at Priest, trying to decide whether he was insulting me or complimenting me.

"Well, I, for one," Devin said, standing abruptly, "can honestly say, I've always been on Lenore's side." He pulled out his cigarettes and shifted it so he could draw one out with his lips. "Not always the position I was aiming for, but what can you do?"

I smiled shamelessly at his flirtation and he winked at me before heading out onto the back porch. I didn't bother looking to Priest to see what he thought of the exchange. Devin's flirtations were above reproach as far as I was concerned.

My happy thoughts of Devin fled my mind, and a painful shiver ran down my spine, as if someone were knocking their knuckles along each one of my vertebrae. Instinctively, I gripped my thread and my mind reached out, touching my friends in turn. Ian, Priest, Haden, Garrett... Devin's mind was not there. In his absence, however, I did find two dozen additional ravenous, sadistic minds, begging me to come outside and play.

Come Out, Come Out, Where Ever You Are

"**D**EVIN!" I SHOT OUT of my chair and grabbed the door in one step, which was an amazing feat of memory lapse, since it should have taken at least five steps to reach the door.

Regardless of my safety, I burst onto the porch and scanned the backyard for him. I couldn't see him, but in amongst the shadows, outbuildings, and tall grasses, were moonlit, glittering faces. They were all standing stock-still, eyes piercing mine as I sneered at each one of them, silently demanding my friend back. I could only count a dozen in my line of sight, but I assumed the remainder were around the front of the house, blocking our escape.

Haden and Garrett popped out on either side of me holding guns at the ready. They must have taken in the scene as quickly as I had, because they forwent their usual *shoot first* modus operandi in exchange for gawking at the scattered threat around us.

"Where is he?" Haden hissed, sounding more concerned than angry, despite her intent.

"I don't know, but these are old grim, so don't be stupid."

"Just do your thing!" she seethed between gritted teeth.

"Not until I know where he is."

"We're surrounded," Ian announced when he joined us on the tiny porch. Priest didn't speak, but I could feel his ominous presence at my back as well. Had he not been on my side, I might have felt compelled to defend myself. As it was, I shifted away from him.

"Where is he?" I yelled when the lack of movement finally sparked my fear into forced anger.

I heard a clicking tongue and Adrian Dorn—in his original body—stepped from behind the garage. A slow clap might have matched his leisurely saunter, but he kept his hands linked behind his back as he made his approach. He stopped half way to the porch and offered me a genuinely pleasant smile—albeit loaded with the promise of pain.

"Hello again, Lenore. Our conversation was cut a little short the other night, so I thought I would stop by *in person* to speak with you."

"Why bother? I would have seen you at the tournament."

"Mmm, yes, I don't think you are going to make it to the games this time." I frowned, glancing at the simultaneous shift in the grim. It was only one small step, but it broadcasted the threat before us. Not only were these grim going to be fast; they were going to be forestalling our every move. Adrian must have sensed my unease because his smile tipped the scales to smugness. "Don't you just hate it when the heroes of the story are wholly unprepared for the villains, yet they still think they can win without casualties?" he drawled, tipping his head to one side.

My jaw clenched and I felt my body thrum with anxious energy. Garrett and Haden glanced at me and took a step away. Apparently I was a little scary at close proximity as well. "If you've hurt him I'll—"

"You'll what?" he snapped. "Continue to flaunt your impudence against an army that could crush you one-handed?"

"If you're so damn strong," Haden snarled, "why haven't you done it already?"

Adrian turned his disinterested gaze on her. "I've been batting at a nuisance fly until now. I thought killing August would stifle your little band of misfit toy soldiers, but when I discovered Lenore's little secret, I knew it would require more attention. So, here I am... flyswatter in hand."

"You son of a bitch!" Garrett hissed and leapt off the porch. His dramatic attack was cut short by two grim appearing next to him, each with a firm grip on his neck. His gun was knocked to the ground in the scuffle. He clawed at the flaking hands choking him, to no gain.

Adrian tipped his head, watching the struggle curiously. "How weak you all—"

Two shots rang out next to me and Garrett's attackers fell limply to the ground, their shattered faces spilling into the lawn. Garrett coughed and wheezed. Priest joined him off the porch to attend to him.

Haden turned her gun on Adrian. "You were saying?" she vaunted.

Adrian chuckled and shook his head. "Oh, Haden. You should have never given up the needle. Sobriety has not improved your social skills."

"Fuck you!"

"If you'd like, I can arrange that," Adrian purred.

"I'd rather—"

"Don't!" I barked. I wasn't sure what Haden was about to say, but I knew saying anything disparaging against herself could be taken as an invitation to Adrian. I knew this with a certainty, just as I knew accepting his ownership of me in my dreams was unwise.

Adrian huffed in amusement. "You're ruining my fun, Lenore. No bother. I have other methods of influence." His hand rose, pointing a finger at Haden. With a slow, shaky effort, he twisted his finger back toward himself.

Haden grunted and I looked over at her. Her gun-toting hand trembled as she fought Adrian's internal demand. I grabbed her wrist to stop her movement, but the motion that defied her muscle strength wasn't hindered by mine either.

"Rules, Adrian," Priest hollered at him.

"I am following the rules. She was threatening me," Adrian crooned.

"Haden, drop the gun!" Priest called over to us.

I tried to rip the gun from her grasp, but it wouldn't move. "She can't. It's stuck."

"Yes, she can!" Priest insisted. "Haden, you must surrender the gun yourself."

"Better be quick," Adrian sang as his pointed finger twitched to draw in his imaginary trigger.

"Haden!" Priest yelled.

Haden groaned and screamed before releasing the gun to drop to the porch. She panted and leered in disgust. She directed it at Adrian, but I imagined it was meant for herself. Giving up her gun was far more demeaning to her than being shot by it.

"What do you mean by 'rules'?" I asked Priest. I noticed all three men had lined up in front of the porch. They were prepared to fight the grim, which had moved closer, clustering around Adrian. Over a dozen stolen faces stared at us through glazed eyes.

"He cannot hurt humans unless they present themselves as a threat," Priest clarified.

Adrian's head lolled back and he groaned in annoyance. "Must I be deferred because of your lack of candidness?"

"He hurts *me* just fine," I said without thinking.

"You aren't human," Haden grumbled and I frowned, embarrassed that I had somehow forgotten that little character flaw.

"Happily though," Adrian's eyes narrowed and he motioned to his surrounding entourage, "*they* don't have to follow that rule."

I was hoping for more witty banter and leaked information, but it seemed that Adrian was not interested in another sit-down with me. He had come for blood.

Blood Lust

THE ATTACKS WERE SIMULTANEOUS and fast. I hadn't even realized the battle had begun until I was lying on the wood planks of the porch wrestling against two grim. Shots rang out left and right. I knew Haden had gotten to her gun, but I heard an angry shriek and it dropped to her feet again.

I punched one of my attackers, but he ducked out of the path. My lazy human hustle was not enough to reach the target. However, I was once again forgetting I was not human. I jabbed at my two grim as they tried to strangle me and rip open my gut with their bare hands. It took several tries, but I managed to reach the blurry speed I had achieved with my less infamous and now deceased archenemy.

After several blows, I found myself gripping the black entities beyond where my physical hands could reach. My mind sought the soul within, but the damned creatures had nothing worth saving. They were already dripping with so much anger and pain that there was no distinction between their existence and the viral hunger that fed from them. I gripped tighter with my wraithlike hands. The drive and raw emotion that could barely be defined as a being imploded in my grip.

I pushed the inanimate bodies off me and crawled to help Haden fight off the three grim that were trying to fit her bloodied head through the five-inch space in the porch posts. I could see the struggle between the men and their attackers just off the porch. Garrett was faring well enough with his brute strength as the sidekick to his gun, but Ian was taking more than a few head shots. His gun had apparently been lost early on.

Priest should have been surrounded by a thickening layer of empty grim, but only moments after they fell they were back on their feet again. These puppeteers were not so easily banished. I could see more grim arriving from the front of the house, prepared to tip the scales of the already insurmountable battle.

I wasn't sure if I could destroy this many strong demons at once, but I reached out for the demons behind the grim. My ever-expanding powers easily bloomed to encompass the minds of the fourteen remaining grim and, regrettably, Adrian.

My head whipped back and my spine arched as he reciprocated my invasion. I screamed as he latched onto my mind, but it was a weak, pitiful damsel-in-distress cry for help. The pain faded into the background along with my connection to my physical body. My link offered a brief read of Adrian, but I was barely able to discern it before my mind succumbed to the visions he was feeding me.

Adrian pulled me into his psyche, taunting me with images of carnage and sex. The carnal delirium took the front row seat and my nightmares were reborn. I found myself naked on his lap, fiercely riding him into a bloody painful ecstasy. No less painful than a knife stabbing into my body, and no less pleasurable than a riptide of multiple orgasms crushing my most basic instinct of self-preservation. The scene was real and tangible, as if I had stepped from the porch right into his bed.

"Come to me, Lenore," Adrian's voice demanded inside my mind, from the mouth of his apparition, and from somewhere exterior to my body.

I couldn't believe it when my legs stood. I could barely feel them, but I was uncontrollably drawn to his voice. I was nothing to his power. I couldn't understand why I had fought so hard, only for it to amount to so little.

Adrian's imagery conveniently overlapped my real life visual as I passed Priest. It offered me a close-up view of his stunned face as I passed by him to surrender myself to Adrian. I could see his fear for my safety and anger because he couldn't get away from the grim to save me. I wondered when the pity and disappointment would seep in. When would he feel the betrayal of his weak heroine?

To add insult to injury, the pleasure side of my torment increased as I passed him. It wasn't until I reached Adrian that the pain stopped. A culmination of pleasure overwhelmed my senses before it too released. I fell against him, exhausted by the intrusive connection. My tears spilled against his chest as he wrapped me in a cold, creepy embrace. I wanted to dust him off like cobwebs with a potential tag-along spider.

"Now then, that's better," he lulled, freely groping my body. Much to my dismay, I couldn't move to stop him. From anyone else's perspective, I was probably happy to receive his attentions since my only visible expression was a blank-faced stare.

Ian collapsed under his attackers, but thankfully they didn't kill him. Haden was dragged, nearly unconscious, from the porch and lain next to him. Priest was shoved to his knees by two grim that held his arms in a poetically ironic crucified pose.

Garrett was still fighting hard, but without Priest to give him a break from some of his attackers, they forced him flat on the ground, crushing his head into the grass with more than one foot on his back, neck, and head. He roared viciously, until he saw me draped against Adrian. "Lenore! Fight him!"

"I am," I was allowed to say. The spoken words ripped at my heart because even I had anticipated being a greater threat than this.

"Oh, she is indeed." Adrian sucked my earlobe. "Tell me, Lenore, what would horrify you more? Watching me kill one of your sidekicks..." I frowned at the reference to sidekicks more than the threat of killing. I knew he planned to kill everyone, but I was insulted he considered putting any of them beneath hero status. "...or watching your priest's face as I fuck you right in front of him?"

Priest's face darkened and I could feel the energy of his rage touching my skin, eliciting goose bumps. Adrian clucked his tongue. "Now, now, priest. Rules, remember?"

"What—?" I started to ask as Adrian shoved—or perhaps in my state, dropped—me to the ground.

"Your priest is, in effect, an extension of God's hands," Adrian said as he knelt down between my legs. "He can no more use the Lord's power against me than I can hurt a human. However, there are no bylaws forbidding me from hurting angels, former or otherwise. That would kind of defeat the purpose of a war between us." Adrian pulled a knife from behind his back and I gasped. He looked at my position and then the knife. "Oh, no, Lenore. I'm not going to fuck you with this. I have every intention of letting you enjoy this." He looked at Priest. "I'm not sure what's making me harder right now: The thought of sinking this cock into you, or watching your lover rage impotently on the sidelines."

Priest bucked against his captors and I could only wish I had the strength to fight that hard. My will was so far gone I was certain Adrian could have been strangling me, and I would only watch him do it. He was just too strong.

"Settle down, Matthew, or I'll do this the other way around." Adrian blew him a kiss as he lowered the knife to cut open my pants for access. I could see dried blood on the blade and I looked around the grounds for the victim of a laceration.

"Devin," I whispered, spearing Adrian with my eyes as he tugged the rent in my denim open. He pushed two fingers through the fabric, feeling my wetness.

"If you insist. As I've said, the names are irrelevant."

"Where is he, asshole?" I growled, no longer concerned and barely aware of the stimulation he was offering. He withdrew his fingers and glanced at the bloodied knife before stabbing it into the dirt beside me. The movement would have made me jump if I had more control of my faculties.

"Devin is dead," Adrian said loudly to make sure everyone heard him.

My eyes widened in disbelief and I shook my head. "No."

Haden revived with a string of screamed cusses that should have been followed by tears, but she didn't get that far before she was knocked unconscious.

I felt Priest's power reach out forcefully. Every last grim fell to the ground, vacant of demons. He and Garrett, freed of their confinement, were in a dead sprint before Adrian even realized Priest had gotten the upper hand.

Before they could reach him, though, they were propelled back with a wave of Adrian's hand. "You attack me, I attack you. Remember!" he yelled after they had landed. They would have come again, but the grim were already reanimating. I could see Adrian's drooped eyelids flicker as they each did. He was helping them return to the bodies.

"Devin can't be dead," I whispered definitively, but I hadn't felt his mind amongst the others when I reached out. I couldn't lose him. I couldn't lose anyone else.

"I wouldn't mourn too hard yet. I still have four more to go. But first let's see how many times I can make you cum before your lover breaks down into tears."

Deeper

ADRIAN RELEASED HIMSELF AND proceeded to debase me in front of my friends. As degrading as it was, I was happy it offered a stay of execution for the others. I turned away and saw Priest struggling violently against his captors. Up until that moment, he had avoided a heavy beating from the grim.

His beautiful glossy hair was matting with blood from fresh head wounds. His cheeks were starting to bruise and his sweet, kissable lips were cut and swollen.

I looked to the knife beside me, buried in the ground. It would have been easy to grab it. The strong hold Adrian had on me was slipping. He was more focused on keeping his grim active to hold the others while he raped me. Part of me wanted to grab it and cut off his dick, but I knew the Lorena Bobbitt offense wasn't going to hurt him. His connection to this body was only as palpable as he wanted it to be.

Staring at the blade reminded me of my so-called appendix scar. It was a lifetime ago, but even now I could feel it burn as my ire rose. I had been wounded by two that day: the angel I had been sent to kill and the God who told me to do it. I was finally beginning to understand. It was a wisp of a memory in the back of my mind that was linked to so many earthly emotions. The only thing I knew for sure: I was looking for strength in the wrong place.

I finally gave up on the thread I had been clinging to for nearly two years. Clearly, God wasn't going to be helping us in this predicament. I had only one hope left.

I went deeper. Deeper than I had ever gone. Beyond the buoyed tether, down to the reason for it. My essence. My soul.

The part of me that Priest shrank from. The part of me that fought to remain hidden, despite everyone's persistence to draw it out. The part of me that had been in the dark since the day I fell to this Earth.

I could feel the tingling icy hot pressure bleed across my body from the center out, but it wasn't until it reached my fingertips that Adrian stopped his ignominy. His stunned eyes rose to mine. I was leering at him sadistically. There was something satisfying about provoking so much alarm from a high-level demon.

"That's not possible," he whispered, more to himself.

My hand reached out to grab his throat and I could see the wispy outline of slender clawed fingers slightly out of sync with my physical body. His eyes widened as I latched onto his throat as well as the demon within.

"This can't be, you are fallen," he rasped through my grip.

I couldn't remember standing, but I did rise up, taking Adrian with me. I towered over him, and his eyes flickered over my new, enhanced form. I could feel and see tendrils of energy undulating around me, off me. I wondered if this was what Priest and Ian saw when they looked hard enough.

I opened my mouth to deride Adrian, but all that came out was a string of foreign words. I knew what they meant—in the sense that I understood the words I was using—but the litany was as comprehensible as tax law. I was speaking so fast I didn't have time to analyze it further.

Several lines of angelic smack talk later, Adrian started to fight back. Between the two of us, I was stronger, but I was still bound to my corporeal form. My humanity was my only weakness and he took his opportunity. He punched me in the face. It felt like a juvenile shove in this expanded form, but my earthly hand couldn't hold onto him.

His body dislodged and he sank down to grab the knife from the ground. He plunged it toward my side. Ironically, it would have been a mirror image of my other stab wound.

My hands moved imperceptibly, blocking his attack. Three more successive indiscernible hits later and Adrian's body was as bruised and bloody as Priest's. Time and energy expense no longer seemed to concern me.

Adrian's hands reached my throat, but strangulation was not the prevailing attack. He was lashing out at me from within. Anger, greed, lust, and a slew of other emotions tangled into my mind—which in the purest form were overwhelming and counterintuitive to human dignity.

The attack would have brought me to my knees weeping only minutes ago, but now it was once again pubescent. Adrian Dorn was throwing an emotional fit at me as his defense. The black tendrils of hate, albeit sticky, fell away when I let my mind push back against him. My power was nothing compared to what Priest could translate from God, but it still offered a subjugating pounding.

I pressed into his mind, and he stumbled back in retreat. He ripped at his body, trying to be rid of the grief, fear, and shame that were the foundation blocks of human morality, the compass that allowed us to know when something was inappropriate or malevolent.

I could feel the tiny smothered soul still within the human body he inhabited. He was not a good man. If he had been, he wouldn't have been so easily taken by a demon. He was, however, not cruel or sadistic, and he didn't deserve to be punished for Adrian's murderous intent.

In this form, I merely thought about the human soul and it aligned itself with me, begging for forgiveness even as I ripped it from the body that harbored it. The recoil of a living soul was more energizing than eighteen fragmented embers and I was thrown back from the impact.

Adrian's body had also been leveled to the ground some distance away. He righted himself just as I did and I eyed his skin's new luster. He, likewise, discovered his human body was now crystallized. He was puppeteering a grim instead of his Cadillac Ken doll.

He shook his head in disbelief and sneered at me as he gave the order. "Kill them!"

Adrian's request pushed me over the line between humanity and angelic revenge. I reached out for the grim souls and with little more than a sweep of my hand ripped them from the bodies. The crystallized minions all fell at once, just as they did when Priest removed them, but with the energy of the demon souls now in the palm of my dual hand, they wouldn't be reanimating any time soon.

I stared down at the tiny orbs that only existed to spread hell into the hearts and minds of others. Parasites to ignorant minds, and provocateurs to weak hearts. There wasn't a worthy soul among them. I closed my ethereal/corporeal hand and tamped out the last vestiges of a cruel existence. It was as much an act of kindness as violence.

Adrian's consciousness invaded my mind again and demanded my compliance. I sloughed off the attack like satin sheets. His frustration ignited another childish fit and he charged me. His physical offense was wasted, because I was apparently no longer restrained by my corporeal form. With only a slight push he fell to the ground.

I sensed more than knew that my body and essence had merged. The angel part of me had taken over the driver's seat, allowing me to be stronger and faster. I picked up Adrian by his neck again. I tipped my head, seeing the power that held him to hell, but also supplied him with the power he needed to carry out his evil deeds. It was not unlike my own tether, but his was nothing short of cocaine to an addict. It provided pleasure, but only as much as was required to keep his allegiance.

Garrett and Priest had shifted positions to assist me if need be, but so far I had Adrian right where I wanted him, so they hung back and watched the show.

"The darkness will rise to consume the Earth!" Adrian spoke clearly through my grip. If desiccated vocal cords couldn't stop the voice, why should throttling? "The humans who aren't crushed in the advent of our war will be enslaved!"

I reached within to extinguish his life, but the slippery blackened residue was gripped hard by the fires of hell and it burned my mind to be so close to the connection. I recoiled from the connection and so did Adrian.

The grim fell limp in my hands, vacant of the demon I desired to destroy. He would no doubt retreat to another body with a less than virtuous résumé. It wouldn't be the last time I encountered him, and if Priest was right, there would be plenty more of his type in my future.

I tossed the Ken-doll grim to the ground, reducing it to a sandy pile at my feet. Gone or not, I didn't want to see that face any longer. I knelt down to look at the remains. The adrenaline still pumping through my human body wanted revenge. Sweet, dark, painful revenge.

"Lenore?" Priest might have said my name a few times before I heard him. I looked up and saw the concern on his face. "Are you okay?"

I paused, thinking about how I felt. I was, as near as I could tell, back to normal. My wispy extensions had gone, leaving me with one set of hands. I was amazingly still conscious and able to walk. I might have considered lifting a truck to check for certain, but I remembered something very vital that snapped me back into reality. "Devin!"

Parting Gifts

I RAN AROUND TO the back of the garage where Adrian had been and I found my worst nightmare come to fruition—again. One of my team was lying on the ground in a pool of blood.

I fell to Devin's side, touching his face and chest, avoiding the long gash across his neck that was deep enough to leave no doubt. His eyes were glassy, his skin already cooled, and the only heartbeat I could feel was the one thumping with outrage in my chest.

My beloved, beautiful Devin was gone.

Where were my sixteen seconds?

My hands were shaking and repeating the same three actions over and over. Priest arrived and knelt down on the other side of Devin. I did the round again. I touched his face, his chest, and squeezed his hand. I was seconds from screaming, crying, and cursing God for yet another abandonment.

"Oh, shit," I heard Garrett whisper behind me.

Priest looked up at him and jerked his head back toward the house. "Don't let her see him like this."

I heard the movement, and Garrett murmured something around the corner of the garage. Haden was conscious again and asking why she couldn't see Devin. I couldn't hear what Garrett said next, but I did hear Haden demand that he move. After a pause I heard her yell her command. Her screams turned irate and tearful, but her voice became muffled by the distance Garrett was no doubt forcing on her.

Ian crouched behind me and reached around to check for a pulse on Devin's wrist, even though it was obvious. He sighed and exchanged a look with Priest as I continued on my round of unnecessary contact with shaky hands. "Chief." Ian pressed his hand over mine as I touched Devin's chest. "Matthew's got some last rites to give."

I must have shaken my head.

"He's gone," Ian whispered in my ear, before wrapping his other hand around my waist. His intent was perhaps to pull me away kicking and screaming just as Garrett had Haden, but I stalled him with my words.

"Heal him." I stared down Priest with my earnest request.

His brow dipped deeper into sympathy. "Lenore, he's gone. I can't put him back."

"He's not gone yet. Not completely. I can get him back, but he won't stay if the body isn't healed." I didn't know what I was saying, but it felt right, and I was willing to try anything.

Priest shook his head remorsefully. "He won't let you do that. Devin belongs to Him now."

"The hell he does! I'm not letting him go!"

"He—"

"He owes me this!" I yelled with an echoing voice that was not entirely my own.

Ian let go of me and though Priest didn't retreat from my severity he looked like a deer in headlights. He seemed to glean that I was not to be reasoned with, and looked to Ian for a sane mediated opinion.

I doubted there was anything he could have said to change my mind, but I'm not sure that was what Priest intended.

"If there's a chance, you better take it. We can't afford to lose anyone," Ian said diplomatically.

Priest seemed satisfied that the vote was unanimous and lifted his hands over Devin's bleeding throat. Warmth ebbed off him in waves. With each surge, the warmth became more profound and powerful. Ian returned his grip to my waist, tighter than before. He might have been doing it out of gallant defense, but more than likely the deity's intensity made him want to hug a teddy bear until the stuffing came out.

I didn't fight the power as I had in the past. I lay my head back against Ian's shoulder and absorbed it like sunlight. Despite the bare-wire, teeth-chattering strength behind it, there was something predominantly peaceful about it.

It was the one true balance in nature. The happy medium between loving someone enough to die for them, and loving someone enough to kill for them. It was the line between fighting for what you believe in and fighting because that's all you believe in.

Somewhere in that brilliance was the so-called darker half, that when properly managed could create the passion that drives every man, woman, and child: to hope, dream, strive, and love, beyond the limits of predetermined rules, boundaries, and taboos. Based on that equilibrium, humanity was indeed created in God's own image.

Some of us just weren't as good at balancing it.

When the bulk of the power subsided and Devin's neck was free of injury, Priest sat back, breathing heavily. I disengaged from Ian and reached for him, fearful that I had exchanged one life for another, but he waved me off. "Just harder than I expected."

I nodded and noted that the blood that had pooled around Devin was gone as well. If I wasn't mistaken about my abilities, Devin would come back good as new.

I held my hands to Devin's chest and found his soul. Just as I suspected, it was still there, just dislodged. The lasso that reined him to the Earth was weakening and the tether drawing him to heaven was strengthening.

I drew his soul into my hand and I felt him—the honesty and goodness that I loved beyond the bond of blood or even sex. He was the most beautiful man I had ever met, and his soul was no less perfect. I sensed his flaws and the challenges he had barely overcome in life, but unlike the souls that I had freed or vanquished, Devin was strong and alight with the fire of humanity.

Part of me felt compelled to release him to heaven. He would have been a nice addition and I wanted him to be a part of that so much. Yet the part of me that was still just an unbalanced, selfish human wanted him back. I slipped his soul back into place, and it locked in like a puzzle piece.

I wasn't surprised when Devin's eyes snapped open and he took a lung-popping breath, but I was surprised that I didn't have time to celebrate his return before vomiting slightly to his left.

Recovering

I SAT ON THE bed in my pajamas, staring at my hands. I was crying, or at least my eyes were. I was too exhausted to sob and sniffle. I was finished being sick, and freshly showered to remove every last memory of Adrian's touch. I was sore and a little wobbly on my feet, but otherwise I had come out of the battle with little more than a few scrapes.

Priest was finishing up his rounds—healing Garrett and Ian. Devin was fine and if I wasn't mistaken was enduring, *thank-God-you're-alive* sex with Haden. I was disappointed I wasn't getting the chance to express my own joy at his revival, but I understood Haden's state of mind. She wasn't the best at expressing simple sentiments, let alone capacious ones. She would translate her feelings better in bed.

I went over the events of the battle in my head. I was pleased to see my powers were becoming easier to wield, but frustrated that Adrian had just walked onto my property and killed my friend without even a tinge of warning from my sixth sense.

I probably should have expected Adrian would try this. I *should* have known a lot of things, but everything I had figured out since the very beginning had been parceled out so desperately close to the time I needed it, that people were at risk.

I lost August because my instincts were too late. I almost lost Devin because my instincts were too late. How many more would die because I wasn't quite quick enough?

I jumped when I felt a hand on my back. I turned and saw Priest leaning over the bed. His eyes were bloodshot and the skin beneath them looked sallow, but his own bruises and cuts were mostly healed. He looked at me with more than concern. He looked uneasy. He was afraid of me. I had officially turned into a winged monster.

I looked away and shrank down, letting the sniffling finally come out. He knelt on the bed and pulled me back into an embrace. I shook my head. "Don't," I whispered.

"Don't what, Lenore? Are you hurt?"

"No. Don't pretend you want to be near me."

"What?" He pushed the hair from my face, as if seeing my lips speak the words might make them more comprehensible. "What are you talking about?"

"Isn't this what you were afraid of? I'm a freaking angel."

"Yes, I always sensed that, but why would I not want to be near you?"

"I'm the biggest reject of all. He didn't invite any of you to the party, but I got kicked out of the party." Priest didn't seem to know what to say to that, so he just pulled me closer. I sniffled and sucked in a few hastened breaths before speaking again. "I'll understand if you don't want to be with me. I know this isn't quite what you signed up for."

Priest started to speak, but stopped. He dragged me up to the head of the bed and spread out beside me, pulling me to his chest. "I want you to stop talking for a while. You're upset and I know you don't realize it, but you are breaking my heart." He kissed my head.

I was feeling a good number of emotions, each of which I deemed important enough to be vocalized, but I was overwrought and couldn't distinguish between protecting my heart and ripping out his. I did as he asked and didn't speak.

It was at least twenty minutes later when the sound of another round of *thank-God-I'm-alive-sex* inspired me to force another uncomfortable conversation.

"Matthew?"

"Yes, Lenore."

"Do you think I was wrong to bring Devin back?"

Priest chuckled. "I think Devin is very happy to be here, or can't you hear?"

With some effort, I sat myself up and looked at him. "But he would have gone to heaven. I know it."

"And he will again, if he should be so rude as to die without your permission." He smiled at the small levity, but I couldn't join him.

I played with the metal pendant at his neck. "Do you understand what I'm saying though?" I asked, trying to avoid eye contact. "I could... give you all to heaven. Direct passage, you know. I did it for the grim. I did it for Adrian's host and he was still alive. I could..." I paused as tears welled in my eyes. I pushed myself back on the bed before he could console me and shush my statement away. "I could save all of you."

"Save us?" He shook his head.

"I could save you all from this miserable war. You don't have to be here. I could release you to God. To heaven." I pinched my lips back. "Isn't that what you want? What everyone wants?"

Priest furrowed his brow. "Oh, Lenore, the answer to that question is so complicated now. Do I want to go to heaven? Of course. Right now? No." He sat up and scooted closer to me. "You've spent so much of your life hiding who you really are, I'm not sure you can even recognize when you've been found."

It was my turn to be confused. He took my hand and kissed it. "We have all found you. We are not leaving you. Nothing short of death will keep us from fighting at your side—and apparently not even that." He bobbed his head in the direction of the noisy couple in the other room.

"But—"

He put his finger on my lips. "Are you really okay? Did he hurt you?"

I shook my head. I didn't elaborate that I had far worse experiences with him in my nightmares. His display tonight was just annoying.

"Good." He pulled me onto his lap. He kissed me gently on my lips, but didn't press to go any farther. We sank down into the covers and held each other for the rest of the night. His internal warmth spread over me, calming my overactive thoughts. For the time being, I let go of my self-doubt, and ignored the dread that was looming over the near future.

The Eve of Battle

"**C**AN I TAKE THE blindfold off yet?" I asked as Priest steered me indoors... somewhere. I had been blindfolded since we left the house. I wasn't a big fan of it, since it made my claustrophobia flare, but he was insistent I keep it on.

"Not yet," he said, gripping my shoulders tightly to guide me. I could tell he was excited about the surprise he had for me.

I had wanted to spend the evening with everyone, since it was our last night before the tournament. Our plan was thus far reliant on the guise that everyone, except Priest and Ian, would be competing in the event. We assumed the ultimate plan would be revealed once we got there. Everyone was probably hoping I would have a sudden enlightenment, but with or without wings, I was bound to a human brain.

My stupid, stupid, human brain.

"Okay, now," he said, untying the scarf on my head.

It took a moment for my eyes to adjust to the dim candlelight, but I could have guessed the location by the smell of incense. The church was yet another I had not deigned to enter pre-apocalypse, let alone post. It luckily wasn't the one I had been almost exorcized in.

I understood now why that priest had tried to *save* me, but now I wondered what exactly would have happened if he succeeded in releasing my possessor. Would I have died? Would the human body remain and become someone else? Was I the angel, or the human, or both?

Or perhaps I would have just kicked his ass and gone back to being myself again.

"What's wrong?" Priest asked.

I must have frowned at the surprise. I quickly put a smile on my face and looked at him. "It's beautiful," I said, nodding to the fifty-plus candles that had been arranged carefully at the head of the church. It *was* beautiful, but candlelight made everything look good.

Priest looked me over, seeing right through my lie.

"I'm sorry." I shook my head. "I should have known you would want to spend the evening in prayer."

His mouth turned upward in a devious smirk. "I don't want to spend the evening praying. However, I would like to get a few "oh, God's" out of you before the night is through."

Despite having spent many nights in Priest's arms, my body tingled with anticipation and I felt my cheeks bloom red from his blunt roguish flirtation. I chuckled and grimaced. "Um, you want to do that here?" I was definitely putty in his hands by now, but the idea of reliving his days at the old white church seemed a little presumptuous.

He glanced back at the altar and looked at me, mortified. "No, Lenore. I have someplace else in mind for that." He smiled briefly and then he sobered again. He looked me over, memorizing my face.

I touched his arm when no words came from him. His seriousness was starting to make me uncomfortable. "What is it? Is something wrong?"

"Nothing is wrong. I brought you here to prove I will never leave you."

"If this is about what I said last night... I was just upset by the encounter. It's not every day you experience angelic roid rage."

"I know, but your reaction to it reminded me that you are still a woman."

"What did you think I was?" I joked and feigned a frightened face.

His reserved adoring smile pushed through his stoic façade. "I thought you were... an angel."

I shrugged and glanced over my shoulders to be sure I hadn't sprouted any wings. "No feathers yet. I think I'm a mutt."

Priest chuckled and touched my cheek. "I love you, Lenore. Human, angel, or mutt, I love you. With all of my heart."

My eyes watered with the sentiment. He had said it many times before, but the earnestness in his voice pulled at the very core of me. Not only could I hear his love and see his love, but at that moment I could feel it emanating from him. It was pure, unselfish, and it was all for me.

"I didn't bring you here to make love to you. However, regardless of what your answer is, I will be doing that soon." I crinkled my brow as he knelt down before me. "I brought you here because I would like to marry you tonight." He pulled a small black box from his pants pocket and opened it before displaying it to me.

The petite silver band held an oblong diamond. It was perfect: delicate and feminine, but not so outlandish that it would feel out of place on my hand.

My face crumpled and I sputtered out tears. It was not the reaction he wanted, I was sure, but the gesture was so sweet and so out of place for this new world. The Earth was about to be turned into a warzone, the human race was officially an endangered species, and tomorrow I had to lead my friends into a battle that would most likely result in us being squashed like bugs. Yet my lover was down on one knee, proposing.

Priest waited patiently for me to return my attention to him. I nodded to him, but he raised his chin and brow, waiting for the words. I sucked up a stuttered breath and found my vocal cords. "Yes, I will marry you."

I collapsed to my knees and hugged him tightly. He pulled me away long enough to kiss me and place the ring on my finger. I would have held on all night, but he hadn't asked me to marry him. He had asked me to marry him *tonight*. Apparently, there were preparations to be made.

White Knights on White Horses with White Dresses

"I HOPE YOU DON'T mind that I picked something for you." Priest led me into the vestry where three white wedding dresses hung on display for me. "I wasn't sure which one you would like."

I smiled at his selection. They were all beautiful, and tastefully adorned. I had never imagined what my wedding dress would look like, because frankly I had never really thought much about marriage, but much like the ring, they were just modest enough that I wouldn't feel like I was living vicariously.

"I'll be waiting. Take as much time as you need," Priest whispered and kissed me on the cheek. He was gone before I realized I hadn't offered him any thanks or compliment to his choice.

I tried on each dress—just to be sure I chose the best one. The first was a slim dress designed for a taller woman. In the proper heels, it would have been perfect, but without them, the dress dragged. The second dress, though beautiful, had a plunging neckline. Not that Priest would disapprove, but I wanted him to be focused on my eyes. When I slipped into the third dress, I felt like Cinderella—minus the glass slippers; glass wasn't going near my feet anymore.

The skirt that I thought at first too puffy, draped gracefully around my hips. The long sleeves and high bodice balanced out my bare shoulders and back. I slipped off my bra and let the girls fend for themselves. I didn't have high heels, but Priest had gone so far as to bring my strappy blue sandals from home. Something blue. Cute.

I checked myself in the mirror and discovered I had no hope of looking my best without a full makeup kit, but to my surprise a small bag of supplies lay on the table below it. I did my best to piece together my look without hurting the dress. I even had enough bobby pins to do a pinup do.

When I was finished, I had to admit I looked good. It was generally a rule that a woman in a wedding dress was always beautiful, but I was surprised it applied to me.

With butterflies in my stomach and my cares for tomorrow in the back seat of my mind, I headed to my wedding.

Dearly Beloved

"**H**EY GORGEOUS." DEVIN'S SMILING eyes surprised me from the behind the door.

My mouth dropped and I peeked out to find Haden, Ian, and Garrett in the front pew. Priest was not around. "Oh my… you all knew?"

"He just told us today." Devin drew my arm around his. "I've been invited to give you away. Of course, now that I see you, I don't think I can part with you." I beamed stupidly at Devin, and he chuckled and towed me from the dressing room.

He stopped me at the first pew and Haden stepped forward. Everyone was dressed nicely, and for a change Haden was wearing slacks and an ornate shirt that didn't belong to an eighteen-year-old's closet. She pulled the long pearl necklace she was wearing over her head and double-wrapped it around my neck. It offered just the right touch to complement my bare skin.

"Something borrowed," was all she said before she sat down again.

Ian seemed to be next on deck. He stood and brought over a small tattered-looking box. He smirked at me before opening the box. Inside was a jeweled hair comb. The creases where the glue had aged were yellow, but it was stunning and timeless. Ian took a moment to strategize my hairdo, but he found a satisfactory angle for the comb and stood back to check.

"Something old." He poked my nose and sat down again. Priest had planned this more thoroughly than I thought.

To my surprise, Garrett was the next to step forward. I wondered what he thought of all this. Was he bitter or angry? The smile he offered me seemed peaceful enough, but I knew no matter what his face displayed, it had to suck to be attending his ex's wedding.

He pulled a box from his pocket and opened it. Two round pearl earrings sat inside. He offered them to me and I placed them on my ears. He looked as if he wanted to say something more than his designated line, but he followed suit with the others instead.

"Something new." He smiled.

I mouthed thank you so I didn't disrupt the theme, and then Devin pulled me to the back of the church. We stopped by the doors. He glanced forward to the altar. When he looked back at me, his face was alight with a mischievous smirk. "I got something for you too," he whispered and knelt down in front of me. "Don't tell Matthew where you got it."

He pulled a garter from his pocket and twirled it around his finger. He raised his eyebrows and beckoned for my leg. I lifted my leg and raised the skirt slightly.

Aside from a few furtive glances to the sanctuary, Devin took his sweet time moving the garter up my leg. He smirked as he reached my thigh. He pretended to keep going even after the garter had been abandoned, but at the last second, he squeezed my leg and withdrew, as I knew he would.

He stood and shook his head at me. "Last chance, baby. We can jet out those doors and run away together. We'd make beautiful babies together."

I grinned wider, if that was possible, since I already couldn't feel my cheeks. "You'd make beautiful babies with a Sasquatch."

"It would have to be very cold," he said seriously. I giggled and his smile returned. Time stopped for a moment, and we just stared at each other.

"I..." My eyes began to water and he quickly pulled a tissue from his other pocket and dabbed me before the flood began.

"Shush, don't cry. This is a happy day."

"It's..." I blinked away more tears. "It's the happiest day of my life. I just love you all so much. I... I've always felt apart from the world. With good reason, apparently." I rolled my eyes. "But right now, I feel... whole."

"Are you saying I complete you?"

I chuckled and shook my head. "I'm saying I was broken and lonely long before the apocalypse and you guys brought me to life."

Devin's smile waned and his jaw clenched. He cupped my face and I could see he wasn't going to be able to offer much of a verbal counter to my compliment. Instead, he leaned forward and offered me the sweetest, most gentle kiss... on my forehead.

When he leaned back, he straightened my comb, tugged a few stray hairs into place, and repositioned my arm around his. He stood up straight and looked to the front of the church. When I turned to look as well, everyone was standing up waiting for me, including Priest.

Given to You

PRIEST LOOKED MAGNIFICENT IN his suit. Instead of his bow tie, he wore only the necklace I had made for him. I nearly cried again looking at the mentally-challenged-looking creation. What man would persist to wear such an awful thing? Apparently, one who loved me enough to marry me.

When I arrived to Priest at the sanctuary, I was no longer the grinning fool I was when I left him. I was nervous, self-conscious, and on the verge of blubbering. I offered him a small smile, so he would know my tears were not from disapproval. He seemed to know the difference already. His gaze never left mine as he extended his hand.

Devin placed my hand in Priest's. Before he could draw me away, Devin grabbed his wrist insistently. Priest broke his gaze with me to look at Devin. Neither of them said a word, but Priest nodded, acknowledging the undertaking of securing my heart.

Devin sat down in the front pew, while Priest led me to the altar. We both knelt, facing each other in front of it. I expected he might provide a litany for the occasion, but instead he gripped my hands and I felt his warmth enfold me.

For once, I didn't question it or doubt his intentions, I just let him do whatever he thought was appropriate for the ceremony. We exchanged impromptu vows with the usual foundation of *I love yous*. We skipped the bulk of the formalities, but he did open the floor for anyone to question the sanctity of our union.

I looked to everyone, trying not to focus on Garrett. I wasn't sure if this was Priest's way of rubbing it in his face, but I hoped it was a gentlemanly gesture to offer him one more chance, if he truly felt enough to fight for me.

When no declarations were made, Priest spoke the traditional "I take thee" speech from memory. On my turn, he whispered the words to me so I could say them back.

"From this day forth, in the eyes of God, as witnessed by our friends, we shall be united as partners in love and life," he said simply to conclude. I was glad he skipped the *till death do you part* clause.

When he kissed me, I felt the warmth he usually bundled me in, but I also felt a strength in it that I hadn't experienced before. I wasn't sure if it was just more of himself he was offering me, or simply the pull of our marital bond. Whatever it was, it made me feel safe.

Dinner and a Show

I T DIDN'T SURPRISE ME that Priest had arranged a meal for us at a local abandoned bed and breakfast. I *was* surprised he had invited everyone. The food was surprisingly delicious, and after Ian and Haden served everyone, they sat down for their own.

We all chatted about anything other than tomorrow. More back-stories were revealed that evening than in our entire time together. After cake, Priest suggested we move into the other room to enjoy our show.

The movie he chose was one of my favorites, "The Princess Bride." We all shouted out our favorite lines and threw popcorn at the screen whenever Prince Humperdinck came on screen.

At several points in the movie, I turned to Priest to see if he was enjoying it as much as me, but I found him watching me instead. I tried to kiss him, but each time he moved to the side, only allowing me to peck his cheek.

The denial of his lips did precisely what I assumed he wanted it to: I wanted them all the more. I resisted the urge to beg him for more, and endeavored to finish the movie.

When the last popcorn was thrown and the final *"as you wish"* spoken. My friends yawned, stretched, and started for the door, like a choreographed dance number. I walked them to the door and kissed each of them goodnight—much to Haden's dismay.

Garrett reminded me to lock the door behind them, and Ian and Devin both gave me hugs that might have broken my ribs, had I held my breath. When the door was secured, I turned around to thank Priest for including them in the evening, but he was nowhere to be seen.

I went upstairs, following the sound of music and running water. In a far back bedroom that might have once been a master bedroom before the house was converted to a business, I found candles, flowers, and the radio that was playing the soft satin tones of a piano.

The smell of lilac drew me into the master bathroom where Priest was drawing me a bath. I had hoped the tub would fit two, but I was not that fortunate. He shut off the water, drew his fingers through the bubbly water, and looked up at me.

The candles surrounding the room lit his face just enough for me to recognize more of that love he held for me. I didn't understand it, or deserve it. By all rights, if the reckoning hadn't brought us to this point, I never would have had a chance with him. Since this was probably our last night on Earth together, I wasn't going to waste time trying to dissect our connection.

Even before he asked, I removed my dress. His eyes widened slightly in surprise, before he inhaled and enjoyed the show. I slipped off my blue sandals and tossed them aside. With care I removed the necklace, earrings, and comb and placed them on the vanity. I removed every last bobby pin and let my hair fall as it may, disheveled but honest.

When I was completely naked in front of him, I bolstered my bravado to let his eyes openly gaze at me. I could see him gulp as his scrutiny weakened his confidence.

He reached out his hand and helped me into the tub, which was warm and silky with bubbles. I didn't want to break the trance he had on me, but I had to ask him a question.

"Tonight, wasn't just about us, was it?" I whispered.

He pushed back my hair and shook his head. Tears rose in his eyes, and I matched them with my own.

"Thank you," I said as mine rolled down my cheeks. "Thank you for making tonight so perfect."

He nodded, and wiped away his tears before they could fall.

"If things don't go well tomorrow—" I started.

"Shhh." He pressed his finger to my lips, but I pulled it away.

"I have to say this." I licked away the tears gathering at my mouth, and steeled my resolve. "If the worst should happen. I want you to know that you are a beautiful soul and you never should have been left here with us heathens and betrayers." He looked away from me, but I pulled his face back to me. "But I am so glad that you were." I shrugged and frowned. I was ashamed to admit the selfish sentiment, but it was true.

"Lenore," he croaked over hidden emotion. "I would follow you through the gates of hell to be with you." He kissed me hard.

When he pulled back, I took in a stuttered breath. "You might have already." I smiled.

He smiled at my not-so-funny joke, and kissed me again, softer.

The night continued as any honeymoon should, but with the additional adoration of a couple who knows they may never get to repeat it.

More Conversations with Dead People

I STARED INTO THE fire that was crackling hypnotically before me. A long while ago I had sat before this same fire with August waiting for a grim to speak words to me. The grim was gone, but August was there. She was sitting across from me on a log, poking at the fire with her sword to breathe new life into it and offer more heat.

I gazed at my former guru, relishing the dream before me. However, my assessment quickly changed as another possibility occurred to me. "Oh crap, I'm dead," I said, more exasperated than disappointed.

"No, not yet."

I sighed and leaned into the fire for more warmth. I wasn't really cold, but the air was definitely more hospitable near the fire. "We're going into battle tomorrow." I decided to bypass the long list of *where am I, why are you here* questions since it didn't really matter.

"I know." She nodded. "Are you ready?"

I chuckled. "No."

"Why do you say that? Haven't you seen how powerful you are? I recognized it the minute I saw you."

"Fat lot of good it does me when I can't keep myself conscious or my cookies in my stomach after I use it."

"The human body wasn't meant to contain the power of an angel. Certainly not one of your distinction." I looked away from the fire and locked eyes with her. She was somber, which was to be expected, I suppose, but I would have preferred to see her smiling. "Aren't you even going to ask?"

"Ask what?"

"Anything. I can see your gears turning. Don't you want me to tell you who you are? Or are you still hiding from it?"

I looked away. My heart was racing. I felt trapped despite the open surroundings. I wanted to offer a scathing sarcastic retort to defend my bravado. Moreover though, I wanted to plug my ears and refuse to listen to her.

"Do you remember the day we met?" she asked.

"Of course," I snapped. It was the most important day of my life. How could she think I would forget such a thing?

"All of it?" she whispered.

I looked at her and shrugged. "I passed out, so no."

"What about before you passed out?" I furrowed my brow trying to figure out how being strangled by a grim was also supposed to have slipped my mind. "I doubt Haden and Devin ever told you. When it was clear you had no idea what had happened, I made them promise not to tell you."

"Tell me what?"

"That I wasn't the one who saved you that day." I frowned and shook my head. I remembered looking up at August after... something happened to the grim that was strangling me. I couldn't remember what exactly, but I had just lost a lot of important inhalations and exhalations, not to mention blood flow. "We happened upon you, though I had been searching for something since we left Chicago. I knew you were what I was looking for the moment I saw you.

"The light was dancing around you so high that we saw you from a mile away. Devin sped toward you and there you were, being strangled by a grim on the verge of death. You weren't afraid, though. You were speaking in tongues. I didn't know what it meant at the time. I ran to rescue you, but I no sooner reached you than a wave of... energy swept me off my feet. You were barely conscious when I got to you. All you remembered was me standing over you. The light you thought was coming off me, was actually you." I took in a deep breath, not sure if I should be affected by this news. I already knew what I was. Angel for hire, right? There wasn't anything more shocking than that.

"There was a good long debate about what to do with you." August smiled when she saw the concerned look on my face. "We didn't mean to do you harm, but frankly, after seeing and feeling what you could do, we weren't sure if you were a safe asset to have around. Haden was vehemently against you joining. Devin was torn between the two of us. In the end, though, they both deferred to me. My sixth sense had helped us on more than one occasion, so they couldn't deny me the determining vote."

"No wonder Haden was so offish to me those first few days."

"It didn't take long for us to realize you were as docile as you seemed, and then she had a different reason to be mad."

"Did Garrett know?" I asked out of curiosity.

"I told him, but as you might imagine, he took my description with a grain of salt. I think he pushed you so hard because he wanted to see it himself. Since he never did, I think he figured it was my imagination." August took my hand and I was surprised that I could feel it. It wasn't a ghostly numb touch. It was her warm, soft, yet calloused hands. "I never understood why you couldn't repeat that talent, especially after Garrett. Now I know it takes very dire circumstances to bring it out. You have to fear for the life of people you love or be near death yourself, though it appears you are getting more skilled at tapping into it as needed."

I chuckled and squeezed her hand before pulling it away. I didn't want to let her go, but her touch was bringing up bad memories. "So..." I paused to rethink the question, but I asked it anyway. "Who am I?"

Once Upon a Lifetime Ago

"**Y**OU ARE NOT LIKE the other angels," August started.

"Of course not. I'm fallen," I said, hoping to speed things up.

August shook her head. "You are not fallen. You are embedded." I took a deep breath and shifted to a more comfortable storytelling position.

"You are not like other angels because you house within you all that is light and all that is dark."

I gulped, realizing it was as I had feared since I encountered my almost exorcism. I was evil, just wrapped in a shiny subservient paper. On some strange level I must have known; that was why I always ran from danger. I couldn't reveal my true identity if I never got into trouble. Maybe that was why I didn't have many friends before the apocalypse. Can't go berserk to defend your buds if you don't have any.

Or maybe I was just antisocial.

"I'm half demon, then?"

August poked the fire again. "Demons are cultivated in the darkness. You, like all humans, have the potential for both great acts of benevolence and horrific acts of violence. It is only through a delicate balance that you remain unconsumed by the darkness.

"You were not always this way. Once you were a leader among the Powers in the second sphere." She must have noticed I wasn't as well versed in the angel hierarchy as I should be, considering I was in it. "You were a warrior, and a good one. You fought on behalf of the Lord with unwavering commitment. You protected mankind from the constant influence of parasitic demons. And, when needed, you policed your own people. Prevented any disruption to your otherwise peaceful existence."

"I was a cop?" I grimaced so she would know I was joking with the rough interpretation. To my dismay she was still very much in story mode and didn't have time for my antics.

"Your devotion to God was unparalleled and He took advantage of it." August's eyes were sympathetic, as if she were apologizing on His behalf.

"What happened?" I asked, not wishing to be a third party to my own history.

"He bid you to kill one of your fellow angels. A Dominion of the second sphere. You didn't question Him. You simply chose your weapon and went to complete your duty. As you already know, you didn't finish that job. The angel fought you, and stabbed you with your own knife. When asked what your purpose was in attacking him was, you claimed God had sent you to do it."

"And He denied it," I finished for her. I broke a stick at my feet and added it to the fire. I had no clear memory of this event, but I could only imagine what it felt like to be so fully devoted to someone and have them betray you. You didn't need a dark side to know what that felt like. "That's why I was sent to Earth. A fallen angel destined for the boredom of humanity."

"Not fallen, Lenore." August smiled. "He tricked them. He tricked them all."

I frowned. "What do you mean?"

"Before He sent you to Earth, he demoted you." The smile playing on her lips finally made her look more like the August I knew. She looked so proud, and yet being demoted sounded like something to be ashamed of. "He gave you the darkness, a burden borne by the Principalities so they might transition between heaven and Earth with ease."

I nodded, seeing some advantage to that, but I still wasn't sure if I understood her. "I was banished. I lost all my memories when I came to Earth. I was born again as a child."

"But you didn't lose your power. You are still every ounce the warrior angel you were before, without the chains of God's will to control you."

I blinked away a handful of thoughts about loose cannons and rabid dogs. As if reading my mind, August continued. "You were a risk He was willing to take."

I swallowed hard, trying to remember what Priest had said about the Powers and Principalities. "A risk to do what, exactly?"

"Save the world, of course."

World Peace and Other Such Delusions

"WAIT, YOU MEAN THE human race."

"And the Earth. You can't have humans without the Earth."

"But everyone has been saying the Earth is forfeit!" I wasn't sure why I needed to use my squeaky oppressed teenager voice, but it was all I could manage. "I'm just trying to stay on the opposite side of dead and hopefully keep the human race from becoming breeders of permanent demon-puppets. I can't save the whole world."

"There are others that would rise up; they only need an example. They need to be inspired to fight. *Really* fight."

"But this is the end of days, we can't..." I shrank back and took a breath. August was always trying to put a positive spin on things. She was just trying to bolster my spirits. "August, if we can't create new life, then the human race will die off. I'm already willing to put up a good fight, to help save my friends' souls, but you can't possibly expect us to get anywhere in this."

"God has let go of the Earth, but that doesn't mean you have to. There are still three groups fighting for it. The angels and demons will fight for eternity and never make any more progress than they ever did. Humans are designed to balance them, but they can only do that if they have hope. Once you have hope, then children will be born again."

I was about to rebuke her for demanding hope in the new world, but the thought of returning to some spectrum of normal froze my mouth. I wasn't sure what I felt about life three seconds before that, but three seconds after, I was realizing how wonderful it would be to have babies and children around again.

Cooing, skipping, and arm farts. Peals of laughter powerful enough to infect any curmudgeon. That would be a wonderful addition to the new world. New souls that weren't sullied with guilt, sadness, anger, and a progressive depression.

"We could really have the Earth back?"

"I'm not saying it would be easy. It would be a constant battle against the demons and other humans and even the angels who didn't agree with your claim."

I chuckled. "So, this is just the beginning."

"It's the end of being alone in your fight."

"Why do this? Why end the world just to begin it again?"

"He couldn't very well flood the Earth again." She offered a sly smirk. "There are rules even in heaven. He's stretched those rules as far as He can, Lenore. It's up to you to bridge the gap." August stood. "Our time has run out, but there is one more thing you should know."

"What's that?" I stood with her even though I didn't exactly have a door to exit through.

"The day I found you. The day I first saw you use your power on that grim. You didn't kill it."

Send My Respects To the Decorator

I COULD FEEL THE vibration in my body even as I jumped out of the Tahoe and touched ground in the O. Something was different. Maybe it was the hope that my *dream* had inspired; maybe it was the impending doom that awaited me and my friends; or perhaps it was just the 10,000-plus people that were bustling around the stadium as if Mardi Gras, the Super Bowl, and New Year's Eve had landed on the same day.

The smell of fried food and spun sugar coated the back of my throat. The bizarre familiarity made my stomach growl, even while my throat threatened to convulse.

There were a good number of conflicting musicians, but the most audible to us as we entered the parking lot was a Japanese percussion group. The rhythmic beat provided drama to the people-driven, papier-mâché dragon that was shimmying and sinuating its way through the crowd. The powerful drums felt like a call to war and I had no doubt that at one point in the history they may well have done just that.

An elbow knocked into me in passing and I was nudged back. I glanced back to offer a glare to the man responsible for it, but the handsome face only offered me a coy smile. I reached for his mind to see if it was Adrian, but I only felt a glimpse of fleeting power before the shield of a dozen proximal minds crowded the read.

I let the minds slip away as I pushed forward to get through the melee with the others. Devin griped about something, and I could feel Priest pressing me to stay with him instead of lagging behind, but I couldn't find the focus I needed.

I couldn't stop thinking about the threats facing us at the tournament. Besides a fresh-faced Adrian and any number of demons that might be lurking in our midst, the pseudo capital, at last count, contained more grim than people.

My eyes drifted over the small tents dotting the expansive party. Nearly everyone was dressed in brightly colored outfits or wearing masks. Some even donned Halloween makeup. The event hadn't even started yet, but the booze, drugs, and sex were already in full swing.

Far beyond the debauchery of fun was the not-so-gilded cage of Mayor Thompson's overpopulated pet grim. They lined the fence like an army in waiting, watching the festivities with an eerie serene stillness. Their numbers, though threatening enough, were not my primary concern. It was the fact that those captured grim were safely maturing behind the high fences.

This was likely where the trap would be sprung. The drunken residents and visitors would be swarmed and killed while we were inside fighting off a detractive grim attack. There was nothing to do to stop it though. There was no reasoning with them and even if I announced to the crowds that they were about to die, they wouldn't have left. Not whilst the party still had liquor and music.

"What is it?" Priest asked, sensing my change from stupefied gawking to intent staring.

I looked at him, observing that we hadn't made it much closer to the stadium. The path to the building was blocked several times over by semi-truck trailers that held television and stereo equipment. They planned to broadcast the finale to the thousands of people outside, as well as the hundreds of thousands who were still capable of receiving broadcasts. We were kind of a big deal.

"Ian!" I hollered ahead to the others. They were pushing through the crowd aggressively. They were eager to get checked in. I was not.

Ian glanced back and saw the concern on my face. His brow dipped as he plodded back to me. "What's up, Chief?"

"How many weapons did you bring?" He started to look over his body as if he were counting the hidden dangers under his clothes. "How many in the van?" I specified.

He looked at me suspiciously as if he were trying to decide how honest he should be. He glanced around at the passersby in case someone might actually be able to hear the private conversation over the din of music, laughter, and my beating heart. "Everything," he admitted.

The others started to see the intrigue between us and filtered back through the crowd to join us.

"How many grenades?" I asked.

He quirked an eyebrow. "They won't let you take those in."

"I know; I don't plan to, but you may need them out here." Ian narrowed his eyes on me. I glanced around at everyone. "If they release the grim on these people they won't have a chance. We need to even the odds a bit. At least give them a chance."

They each looked over at the fences holding the grim.

"Is that what all of this has been about? Lure the people here for the big event and close the trap?" Devin asked. "Or I should say, open the trap."

"I think so."

"Why would they kill so many people?" Haden asked. "Don't they want bodies?"

She was right, but I didn't have an answer. I glanced around at the television screens. "Maybe they just want an opening act," I suggested. "They'll be broadcasting this on radio and television as far as they can."

"So, this isn't so much a battle as a warning to the rest of the world," Garrett simplified.

"I suppose, but we can't let it be a massacre. They might see the demons rising up, but they need to see humans fighting back too."

"What do you want me to do, Chief?" Ian asked.

"The grim are living like cockroaches in those buildings behind the line. At the first hint of an uprising, I want you and Matthew—"

"Wait, what?" Priest interrupted. "I'm staying with you."

"You can't." I shook my head. "Ian—"

"The hell I can't." His face turned hard and I knew this wasn't going to be easy.

"You two are the only ones not expected to be in the tournament. You know as well as me that we are probably walking into the same damn trap in there as out here."

"So, let's just start the battle, right now," Ian proposed as he tickled the hilt of his gun under his leather vest.

I shook my head. "Let them reveal themselves first. Let the people see the truth of what we are facing, then attack. Thin out the numbers as best you can. Matthew can—"

"I need to be by your side," he argued.

"I understand that you want to protect me, but your first priority—"

"*You* are my first priority," Priest snapped. I could tell he wasn't comfortable with this conversation in front of everyone, but I could hardly excuse myself for a private moment. Everyone did their best to look invisible.

"This isn't the time to be overprotective. Even with his hoarded arsenal, Ian is going to need help."

His head shook slightly.

"Look around you. This tournament is the biggest thing since… well, ever, for this area. Tonight isn't about removing some nuisance humans. This is *the shot heard round the world*. And for once, that isn't an exaggeration. We are meant to be an example and a warning to the world. The demons are staking their claim right here. This is the front line."

"And you think that will convince me to leave your side?"

"How this goes down is going to determine whether the human race rises from the ashes, or if they get buried in them. You and the *man upstairs* are a big part of that outcome. These people need you now more than they ever did. You have to show them what you can do. Show them that God is still here."

Priest frowned and looked to the others. "There's something you should know." He turned back to me. "He will not help me in any offense. I can use my power on attacking grim, but I can't use Him as an extension to change the outcome of this battle. I can't interfere with the high-ranking demons."

I nodded and forcibly bit back a slew of cusswords I didn't want to come out.

"Un-fucking-believable!" Haden happily filled in for me. "We are left to fight on His behalf and He isn't even going to help."

"Those are the rules," Priest said with finality.

"The rules suck!" Haden snapped at him.

"Yes, they do," Priest surrendered to the agreement. "I will still be able to heal. I'm strong enough now; even the oldest grim shouldn't take much effort to dispel. The upside is that high-ranking demons like Adrian can't attack humans. The only threats to the people will be the grim, so long as they don't try to attack a true demon."

"Then it's settled," I chimed. "You will stay here."

Priest opened his mouth to protest, but stopped. "Here." He reached behind his neck and undid the cross necklace I made for him so long ago. He held it out to me and I blinked at it. "Take it."

"That's yours."

"I know, but I've blessed it more times than I can count. I want you to have it. Think of it as a good luck charm." I took the necklace and stuffed it in my pocket. "When this is all over, I want that back, Lenore... untarnished." I nodded.

"Ian," I said, "I would suggest making some fast friends to share your guns with."

Ian's face melted as if I'd asked him to give away his toys. "Alright, but the rocket launcher stays with me," he stipulated.

Several blank faces and open mouths joined my own. "You have a rocket launcher?"

He scoffed. "Yeah!"

I laughed and shook my head. "I knew there was a reason I liked you."

The Sands of Bad Times

I WALKED ONTO THE sandy floor of the arena with poise that was surprising even to me. I wasn't sure I could claim any commonality with the gladiators of Roman times who fought to their deaths in front of a live audience, but I was pretty sure I finally understood what bravery was. It really had nothing to do with strength of character or confidence. It was about accepting your fate and putting all your focus into your actions. Most of all, it was about relinquishing your hope for any future beyond that moment.

Looking over the arena audience, I saw the lukewarm leftovers that made up the remaining human population. The half-drunk, all-raucous crowd was primed for a battle, and they were about to get it. I couldn't help but pose the question that literature and B-movies had been asking for centuries.

Were they worth it? Was the human race worth the fight?

I jumped to the side as a particularly enthusiastic audience member vomited over the railing above me.

Perhaps not in the current form, but I had to start somewhere.

I surveyed the seats, looking for a familiar face, but I had destroyed that face. The mayor was sitting in his box, sipping champagne. I still wasn't sure if he was a key player or not, but either way he was not to be trusted. I didn't see any new faces in his entourage, but that didn't matter. Any weak-minded fool could be host to Adrian's demon.

"How you doing?" Devin sidled up next to me. Since he had won in the category of hand-to-hand combat he was not allowed a gun or sword with which to fight, but they did allow him the luxury of a knife. The ten-inch blade lashed to his calf probably wasn't what they had in mind, but we weren't exactly pocketknife kind of folks.

"Is it too late to run away together and have babies?" I asked, checking over my supply of arrows. It was limited, but once again, they weren't offering you enough to steal the show.

"Oh, *Earth Angel,* I'd love that, but we have some ass-kicking to do."

I chuckled at his nickname. "I can't believe you are turning down sex for fighting."

"Think of it as foreplay. Whoa, speaking of foreplay." His eyes turned to the center of the arena where the ringmaster was beginning her introductions.

"Ladies and gentlemen, you are in for a real treat tonight," the ringmaster started. She was in fine form. Her propriety-optional wardrobe was a half dress... literally. The half she did have on was a fully covering long black shimmering fabric that strategically strapped around her neck, waist, and hip to keep it in place. It draped in such a way through her legs, that it actually covered the v of her body. The half she was not wearing was only covered by the straps, and one well-placed pasty, which left her ass and the remainder of her breast free to the world. "Tonight, our first, second, and third rounds will determine the placement of our finalists. Our judges will base their evaluations on number of kills, speed, and accuracy." She waved to a panel of judges seated on one side of the arena at the midpoint.

Haden moved closer to me to speak as the ringmaster continued to rouse the audience. "How many arrows do you have?"

"Twenty, give or take, but I have my brass and a knife they didn't take away."

"Yeah, they left me a full clip. That's why guns are better."

"Why?" I asked, looking over her smug smile.

She leaned over to whisper in my ear. Her chest pressed into my arm, and I could feel something hard hidden beneath her shirt, tucked in her bra. "Bullets are easier to hide."

I smiled about more than the bullets pressing against my shoulder. Haden was a hard woman to know, and even harder to love, but given the choice of anyone to stand in battle with, I still would have chosen her. Whether she would choose me was still up for debate.

I glanced around at the many contenders who probably had no idea what was about to happen. The scattered competitors were listlessly enthralled by the announcements. The mayor bowed his head graciously at the praise being offered to him for the events. The rafters were completely empty of sharpshooters. They were no longer needed.

Behind me, I could see Cody Dodd, the young man who won the audience over with small explosives several months ago. He was still young, but his gaunt awkwardness had given way to a certain confidence that only came with popularity, respect, and consistent lays.

He caught me staring at him and offered me a chin thrust and an eyebrow tip. I decided to consider it a compliment, despite the fact that he probably had no idea who I was. I eased my way back to stand next to him. The smirk he gave me was certainly meant to be sexy, but his eyes were still too shy to pull it off completely.

"Hi," he drawled.

"Hi. You're the explosives guy, right?"

"Right. You're the "blitz" girl, right?"

"Blitz?" My brow dipped in confusion.

"Yeah, that's what they're calling you. You know the blitzkrieg? It means lightning war."

I scoffed. "Why would they call me that?"

"You're kidding, right?" I stared at him blankly, barely noticing that his goatee was shaved in the shape of a pot leaf—or perhaps it was meant to be an explosion. "You're, like, lightning fast. When you pummeled that grim at your competition, you were a maniac. I could barely see your arms moving toward the end."

"I'm not sure I'm comfortable being named after a German war tactic."

"How about I call you Lenore then?"

"That's—"

"Or Lenny," he eagerly offered.

"Lenore is fine. Listen, how many squibs did they leave you?"

Cody rolled his eyes. "Only a dozen. I don't know what they expect me to do when I run out. It sounds to me like they are sending in a bunch of grim at once."

"I'm sure they will. Cody, this is going to be kind of a strange request for such an early acquaintance, but I don't want you to use all your explosives on the grim."

Cody leaned his head back, disbelief on his face. I wasn't sure if it was because of my request or because I had elevated myself high enough to make the request. When there was no hope of a punchline coming up, he blinked away his confusion and shrugged. "Alright, what do you want me to do with them?"

Round One

THE SHRIEK OF THE first grim tore through the arena, signaling the oncoming attack.

Three, four, eight...teen.

I lost count as the shrieking, growling demon-puppets ran at us like angry bulls out of the gates. "Fall back!" I announced just before the other competitors started firing bullets, arrows, and other pointy objects. I didn't see any reason to actually try to win the tournament. We would have to let the others take the bulk of the fight so we could save our ammo for whatever Adrian had in mind.

More than a few grim got through, but Garrett and Devin handled them by sword and by fist, while Haden and I scanned the perimeter for any signs of a trap. Dutifully, albeit nervously, Cody Dodd joined us at the back of the arena to wait out the round.

"Ladies, as much as I'm enjoying this view, don't you think you are missing the point of the games?" a deep, familiar baritone voice yelled from behind me. I turned and looked at the box seats near one of the door alcoves. Jimmy the Card and his date—er—dates were watching the show.

"It's not a game anymore, Jimmy," I couldn't help retorting. He frowned at me and started to observe the perimeter as well.

After a barrage of bullets and clanging weaponry, the grim were down and the crowd was cheering. The announcer declared the winners of the round, with the most kills. Haden scoffed at the announcement. I should have known she would have trouble with this part of the plan.

"He's toying with us," Devin said when we reconvened. "Those grim couldn't have been more than a few months old. He has to have older ones."

"Yeah, I know. I think he's going to wait until round three to unleash them. He wouldn't dare ruin a perfectly horrific climax."

Round Two

WE STOOD ASIDE, PATENTLY waiting for the sideshows to finish. I had expected the usual, but tonight's performance was a flying trapeze exhibition. Since there was no net to catch the daring participants, the audience was on the edge of their seats gasping with each explosive leap, and cheering with every successful catch. I was almost surprised they didn't groan instead, since they were so thirsty for violence. Perhaps a shattered *human* skull was too much for them.

I watched the mayor from the sidelines. His gaze caught on mine and he gave me an easy smile. His cards were hidden well. So well that I still wasn't sure he was playing. It wasn't until round two that I knew he was definitely playing.

I lined up with the other competitors. The ones with guns were going to have to resort to fists. The ones using arrows and spears had retrieved what they could. Cody Dodd looked antsy, but he hung back with us, just as I had advised him to.

I could see the grim gathered on the other side of the gates, but I couldn't tell how many. I wouldn't know the maturity of them until I saw them move. I expected a quick rush of silvery bodies when the doors opened, but the slow-moving, wobbling attack was enough to make my heart thrum with adrenaline.

The audience's precursory cheers died off as quickly as they had risen. The competitors before me lowered their weapons slightly and looked to one another, baffled by this change of theme.

Two dozen silver-faced children lumbered toward us in stuttered steps. No one attacked, but I could see by the snarling faces on each of them that they would eventually give us no choice. We would have to slay the newly inhabited bodies. I wondered now if the war against the grim was starting to become unpalatable to everyone, as it always had been to me.

I looked up at the mayor. His feet were propped up on the rail of his box. His contented smirk made me sick. This was intentional. Dishonor the players by making them defile the bodies of former children. There would be no cheers for this round.

Emboldened by several layers of anger, I marched forward, away from my safety in the background and past the front line of panicked competitors. The children didn't seem to care who they went after, but my presence got their attention, and they corralled around me.

To everyone's surprise I didn't retrieve my bow to defend myself as their enthusiasm increased the speed of their hobbled approach. I reached within and found the power hidden deep inside. Though I was angry, the power didn't readily release to me. I assumed, as August said, that it was easier to access when someone I loved was in danger.

I felt a tangible tickle grow thick under my skin as the first grim child arrived. I ignored the lopsided blond braids, and the smear of something chocolate on her face. She was perhaps six years old. Yet somehow, the instant I touched her, I felt centuries of memories, old, new, and borrowed, flash through my mind.

I held the little girl's neck in my hands and focused on the demon holding her body hostage. I was surprised to find power not unlike Adrian's lurking in the depths. It must have taken strong demons to take over bodies that had previously been sanctioned immune.

She tried the same old tricks. The infection of anger was strong, but it sloughed off me. The offense of wrath was still no hope against someone who had love in her heart, and thanks to my friends I had plenty. Despite knowing this was probably a part of the trap, I reached out for the souls.

The multiplied power that bucked against me gripped onto my mind, trying to oppress me instead of the other way around. My claustrophobia flared, though I wasn't technically enclosed in a literal sense. For several seconds, I could feel the crushing weight of evil beckoning me, drowning me, and... igniting me.

Like smothered embers, the heat within grew until there was nothing for me to do but release it. It felt natural, and yet I knew it was too much. It would have easily destroyed the grim, but that wasn't what I wanted. I wanted to remove them without hurting the bodies. It was naïve to believe there was anything left of a child in these bodies, but it was important that the people didn't see me decimate them.

I grappled back the energy, trying to hold it in. It was the equivalent of throwing myself on a bomb. I yelled as the ballooning inferno burst. A tidal wave of emotion and unearthly energy released from me. The wave was enough to shatter the souls of the demons surrounding me. The grim children, now inanimate, were left mostly intact.

It took me a moment or two to realize that the power had also knocked the front line of competitors on their asses. Several of them were even crying, a result of who knows what slew of sentiments I had thrust upon them.

I was still holding the little girl in my hand. I wrapped my arms around her and set her down before turning my glare on the mayor. He frowned at me, but applauded. The audience slowly realized that I had saved them from a double-edged sword and they stood cheering for my victory.

As I made my way back to my group, the other competitors gave me a wide berth, especially those who were still grieving from the kickback of my attack. I tucked in close to Devin, and wrapped my arm around his back. He smiled at me and gave me a half hug. "Good job."

I shook my head.

"What's wrong?"

"That took a lot out of me." I didn't elaborate that what had taken so much energy was *not* using the full extent of my power. "I don't know if I can reproduce that anytime soon."

Garrett and Haden clustered around us. "That's what we're here for, remember?" Haden said, managing to sound sympathetic rather than admonishing.

I nodded. "Yeah, I remember. Be on your guard for the next round. He probably knows I'm weak. He's liable to pull out the *oldies but goodies* for this one.

"No, problem." Haden extended her hand. Both Garrett and Devin reached in the front of their pants. My brow crumpled as the two grown men fumbled in their underwear. When they each retrieved a clip of bullets for Haden, I laughed. Haden tipped her brow at me as she discreetly tucked them in her back pocket. "See? Guns *are* better."

Round Three

T HE GATES CLANGED OPEN and the audience paused in fascination when nothing came out. Everyone was fearing the worst, but for them the worst was only more child demons. My worst was speed and strength. Some of us were only human, after all.

I nodded to Cody as the final trumpet signaled the seconds remaining until the release. Unless fluffy pink bunnies came out of those cages we weren't going to take any chances of assuming this was going to be a fair fight. Really, what was fair at this point anyway?

The grim started to emerge, singularly, not bunched up like the overeager demons within usually demanded. One after another they stalked, sauntered, and sashayed onto the sand-covered arena. The competitors seemed baffled by this approach and didn't readily take aim to kill them.

When their numbers exceeded thirty, one brave archer sent an arrow at a leading grim. The female that was meant to be the victim snatched the arrow out of the air with an impossibly quick swipe. She brought the arrow back up with her manicured fingernails to examine it. She looked to the one responsible for the attack and snapped the shaft with a pinch of her fingers.

"Now!" I yelled to spur movement a millisecond before the grim charged.

The attack began on both ends. Grim and humans alike charged in. Fortunately, the grim were not as fast as I feared, but there were a few that shed easy blood with surreptitious attacks.

Haden hung back to protect Cody from any attackers that got past the line. Devin and Garrett followed me up to assist the others so they weren't killed for their efforts to win bragging rights.

I pushed through two attacking grim with a surprisingly graceful clothesline. Garret and Devin respectively stabbed and smashed their faces in behind me.

My easy movement caught the attention of several grim and they charged me. Since I didn't want to reveal my true self before a stadium of several thousand people, I had to rely on body-bound angel strength. Which, as it turned out, was enough to punch a hole straight through one of the grim. The audience cheered loudly at my achievement. Unfortunately, it was short lived, since the two remaining attackers lifted me by my neck and threw me back about twenty feet.

Garrett chopped both their heads off with a swift slash of his sword. To add to the spectacle, Devin threw one of the heads into the stands as a souvenir for the fans.

The competitors who had earned the right to be in the finale were doing better than I anticipated. Bodies shattered left and right. One man relying purely on brute strength ripped the arms off one grim and proceeded to beat it with its own appendages. Another, armed with a machete, was collecting heads at his feet. My presence, over-glorified as it was, was turning out to be even less necessary than I expected.

I pulled my bow and finished off several grim that were getting the better of their opponents. I couldn't say the competitors were all happy about my interference, but I ignored the bellyaching of the few objectors.

Haden finished off three more wounded but mobile grim, and everyone scanned the room for more attackers. The remains of the forty downed grim were already being dragged away by the event staff. The audience applauded the epic battle, but I was still waiting for it to start. I looked to Garrett and Devin, but they each shook their heads. We were predicting the trap, but it wasn't coming.

Cody Dodd ran up beside me once the ringmaster returned to make her announcements. "What the hell?" he griped. "I thought you said there was going to be a massive attack. Was this just a trick to keep me out of the competition?"

"No! I thought—"

"Whatever! I could have killed half those grim with one squib and won this competition. Now I'm dead last. Thanks a lot!"

"Cody I didn't..."

Cody stomped away before I could explain.

"What the hell?" Haden barked in my other ear, making me jump. "Where are the rest of them?" She scanned the audience, looking for the deception in the fans. "Is that it? The finale is over."

"It can't be." I looked over at the mayor's box, but he was already gone.

"Ladies and gentlemen, please remain seated as we collect the final tally and give you our finale winners."

Devin and Garrett moved back to us with the same baffled, almost disappointed faces. "Anything?" Devin asked.

"Any what?"

"Any feelings? Instincts?" His face was begging for an answer, but I didn't have one.

I shook my head. For once in my life, I thought I was right. I followed my instincts. I faced my fear, and nothing. The boogeyman was just a blanket over a chair. The shiver up my spine was only the breeze.

"Maybe he's releasing them outside first," I said, but the muted disappointment surrounding me was palpable.

"I don't hear any rocket launchers," Garrett retorted quietly.

"Well, I'm glad you decided to participate after all," Jimmy the Card's baritone voice announced behind us. We looked back as he strolled by with his dates on either arm. "Well done, ladies, and gentlemen." He nodded to the men as he passed to join the ringmaster for the announcements. I noticed the mayor had already joined her and was discussing the results.

"Our third-place overall winner is..." the ringmaster announced and drums sounded from the band section in the stands. "Albert Hanson!"

The audience cheered and the large man who was tearing the arms off grim came forward to accept his medal. They looped it over his neck and he stepped onto the lowest of three boxes that had been placed in the center of the arena. He threw up his fists proudly and the spectators roared with delight.

"Our second-place winner is..." Jimmy the Card announced like only he could. "Haden Summers!"

Haden looked to me, unsure of whether she should accept the honor. I shrugged and she went forward to take her medal. Jimmy took the honor of a cheek-to-cheek kiss before he released her to stand opposite Albert on the second-place block.

"And it is my great pleasure," Mayor Thompson announced, "to introduce our first place and grand prize winner of the tournaments... Lenore Evans!"

I stared blankly as my name was announced. The award seemed unwarranted, but the crowd was thrilled to hear my name. Perhaps it was just the enthusiasm for the event, or maybe they were thrilled with my magical display that knocked out two dozen children grim.

I moved forward, disinterested in the award or the honor of it. In part, I felt guilty. I knew Haden or Devin would have preferred the honor more than me. Had I trusted the tournament to be a fair competition, I might not have tried so hard.

I stepped up to the mayor and he draped the medal over my neck. "Congratulations, you have an interesting gift," he said. I stared at him, trying to get some feel for his character. I reached out with my mind, but it was only the lecherous alcoholic I had felt at the party. I thought I had felt something more, but it must have all been from Adrian.

"This way." He ushered me to the pedestal when I didn't move.

I stepped up to the highest block. The ringmaster instructed us to link hands and raise them up. We did, and confetti fell from the ceiling. I looked up for a potential attack to be sprung, but there were only buckets tipping shredded paper onto us. No sharpshooters shirking their duties. No vats of acid strategically balanced on the edge of the catwalk.

Nothing.

This was my grand battle. The good news was: I won. The bad news was: I lost my credibility.

Where Have All the Good Men Gone

"I'll be right back," I said to Haden after we stepped off the platforms. They were clearing space for a final gymnastic demonstration, but I wasn't interested in standing on the sidelines to "Ooo" and "Aah."

"Mayor Thompson." I caught up with the mayor and several of his entourage, including Jimmy the Card. "May I speak with you?"

The mayor looked me over. Despite the fact that he had met me several times and had just announced my name, he still seemed baffled by my identity. "Yes, what is it?"

"A moment alone, sir," I suggested delicately.

I smiled and he waved to his men to head up without him. Jimmy was apparently already in line to speak with him, but he shuffled off to one side to give us privacy. The mayor smiled cordially and bowed his head to instigate my conversation.

"I was wondering if you had seen Adrian Dorn."

"No, I'm afraid he's out of town," he answered quickly. "He was disappointed to miss the tournament. I know he was especially interested in competing with you again."

I tried to smile, but the mindless chit-chat could have been as much flattery as threat. This man was either a very well-hidden demon, or he was just a man.

"Well... thank you for your time. I appreciate the honor of the award tonight." I offered my hand to shake and he took it.

He frowned as he gripped my fingers for a tight jolt handshake. He looked down and turned my hand over. The barbed cross of Priest's necklace was hidden between my fingers. "Are you trying to cut me?"

"Oh, sorry, my good luck charm. Forgot I was still hanging onto it."

"Good day, Miss..."

"Evans," I said, annoyed that I was giving the man credit to collapse the world, when he couldn't even remember my name. He didn't even bother finishing his goodbye before he trudged through the sand back to his box seats.

"What a putz," Jimmy said, giving me a lopsided smile.

"Yeah, tell me about it. Asshole felt me up at his house and he still doesn't remember my name."

"Ouch." Jimmy sidled up beside me to watch the performance, which was yet another gravitational feat. This time, however, it had more fire and nudity. "Shame about Adrian, though. I thought you two might have had a thing, or was I mistaken?"

"Yes and no." I sighed. "In the end he was a putz too. What about you? Doublemint twins treating you alright?"

Jimmy chuckled and gave me a sidelong glance. "As a matter of fact, they treat me pretty good. Not that I'm not interested in new talent." He put on a lascivious smirk and it was my turn to laugh. He certainly wasn't my type, and fame never turned me on, but he did have a fine voice and he flirted well.

"I'm afraid I'm going to have to turn down that audition." I waved to Devin on the other side of the arena. He was concerned I hadn't returned, but I didn't want to cross in front of the show. If not for the sake of rudeness, then at least to avoid having beer thrown at me. "I'm happily married, as of yesterday." I showed off my ring.

"Ah, to the priest, I presume."

"Yeah." I paused and glanced at him. "I wasn't aware you knew about him."

"Well, I like to keep up on gossip."

"Sure." I kept my smile frozen to my face while I tried to calculate the number of events Priest and I had been intimately involved at, but I couldn't think of any. All of our relationship breakthroughs happened within the confines of my small town. "I should probably join my friends."

"The thing is, Lenore," Jimmy said, stalling the casualness of my exit. "I keep up with all the gossip and I heard you are responsible for Adrian not being here."

I stared at him, no longer able to maintain my façade. I reached out for his mind, but I was batted away like a fly. My eyes widened and he grinned. I started to back away.

"Stay." The word commanded me and without exposing my wispy angelic form I would have to abide. "I was mad at first. Mad that your little boy toy had disrupted my plans to impregnate you."

"Adrian?"

Jimmy snickered and shook his head. "No, it's still me. It's always been me, Lenore. The demon behind the man, behind the demon behind the man. Much to your disappointment, I'm sure. A pimply-faced nerd is the key to the destruction of the Earth? Well, maybe it's not that unheard of."

"How did you…?" My voice wavered.

"What? Get past your evil radar? Well, let's see… because you aren't as strong as me. I know, I know, this isn't your true form, but this isn't mine either. Truth be told, if it weren't for millennia-old sanctions preventing me from being on Earth in demon form, you would be pissing your pants right now."

"What do you want?"

"Oh, don't worry. I've long since given up any plots of impregnating you. As fun as it might be to bring back giants, I think we all have enough to deal with."

"So, what, we fight?" I stood my ground, reaching for my thread.

"Don't bother. I'm sure you would put up a good fight—futile, but good. However, I'm not interested in all that pomp and circumstance." He sighed and clapped for the final performance. I joined out of respect. While the clamber of applause gave us a break in conversation, I did my best to scream at my friends with my eyes. They were unfortunately distracted by the performers leaving the arena.

"You keep forgetting something very vital, Lenore." Jimmy stepped closer to me, leaning in so I could hear him over the continuing din of spectator chatter. "I know it's not your fault. Your friends have convinced you that you're the hero in this story, and in a way, maybe they're right. But you're also the villain."

I broke my attempt to contact my friends with waves of psychic screams and looked at him. He was serene in his monologue execution. He even had a sparkle in his eye. He was thrilled to have baited my attention.

"You see, Lenore, you *are* special." I almost rolled my eyes, but then I remembered this demon wasn't likely to appreciate my residual teenage rebellion. "You are a full-blooded angel. You aren't supposed to be here. You are supposed to be up there, but you're not."

"I know all that."

"Yes, but getting back to what you have forgotten about this war: The epic battle you and your friends have been preparing for isn't between humans and grim, or humans and demons. It's between demons and angels." I clenched my teeth so I didn't say something I would not live to regret. "I was mad at first that you were undoing my plans. Mad that you relocated one of my best soldiers. But then you revealed yourself, and I realized you were the key to my plans all along."

I shook my head. It was all I could do to combat his lies.

"You aren't just an angel in human form. You're an angel *stuck* in human form. Unlike your brethren, you can't freely move on and off the Earth." He moved closer, letting his words breathe into my face. "I have the opposite problem: I have no form. I have to borrow others, and getting into those minds is very difficult, but there is a way to make it easier. A way to open a real portal to hell. Do you know what it takes to do that?"

He smiled as he gazed over my face. "Angel's blood." The movement was slight, and the pain was minimal, but it grew with time. He had unsheathed the emergency knife attached to my belt and stabbed it into my back. It was low, into my kidneys. The pain, though exquisite, seemed far away. "It's hard to come by. Most angels aren't stupid enough to interact with a demon in human form."

I lost my enthusiasm for his discourse and looked over at my friends. They were conversing amongst themselves, and hadn't noticed my murder yet. I should have been screaming and shouting for help, but I felt ashamed. If I could have dragged my broken body away and died alone, I would have. I couldn't face them. I couldn't reveal yet another epic failure. At least it was only me getting hurt this time.

As if Murphy's Law hadn't offered enough humor to my life, the ground started to tremble beneath my feet.

And Where Are All the Gods?

J IMMY TWISTED THE KNIFE and yanked it from my back. I turned and saw my blood dripping into the sand and disappearing as it vibrated deeper. His smile turned maniacal and he raised the knife high so I could see it coming at my chest. "Let the games begin," he drawled with sadistic glee.

I didn't even try to fight him or run. I knew I was no match for this demon. I regretted not allowing Priest to stay with me. His power might have been strong enough to save me. As an afterthought, I remembered Priest had not left me defenseless.

Jimmy drove the knife down, eliciting a gasp from the audience members who had caught on to my predicament. At the same time, I raised my own hand, seemingly to slap Jimmy's face, but instead of a quick assaulting impact, I pressed my hand to his cheek.

His body jolted as Priest's blessed cross came into contact with his skin. I felt the impact of a soul movement, but this time it didn't feel energizing. The shockwave left me feeling dirty from the inside out.

Jimmy's body fell to the ground in a heap, but unlike when Priest dispelled Adrian, he didn't get back up again. I looked down at the young shuddering body. Blood dripped from Jimmy's nose and mouth. I could only assume there was no coming back from a full demon possession.

I looked around, trying to find the bookmark in my life's story. Since I hadn't died, I frantically put my "to do" list back together. I found my friends. Devin was already stumbling to me over the unstable sand. He grabbed my arm and ducked under it to help carry my weight. Between the increasingly turbulent ground and the blood gushing from my back, I was more than happy to have a crutch.

The audience murmured at the impromptu earthquake in the stadium, but they didn't start screaming until the eardrum-popping thunder started. The rolling crackle was only slightly muffled by the building walls, but the sonic boom that followed shook the structure. The metal creaked all around us and dust filled the air, falling from no discernible location.

"What the hell is that?" Devin asked as he ushered me forward.

"Maybe the skies are finally falling," I suggested humorlessly as another boom threatened to collapse the building.

"No, *that*!" He nodded behind me and I looked behind us as he pushed me along, ignorant of the pain I was in.

My former puddle of blood had already fallen through the sand, but now the sand was sifting into a small hole in the floor. I couldn't see what was inside the hole, but I could see it was still growing. The vacancy enveloped Jimmy's body, peeling it away from the surrounding ground.

"What's happening?" Haden screamed in my face when I reached her. Another boom from outside paused my response.

"I think the battle is beginning!" I panted.

"What do we do?" Garrett asked.

The ground in the center of the arena split, breaking up our pleasant conversation. Unbalanced by the shift, I fell into Haden. Sand spilled into the crevice between us and the men. The audience erupted into nonstop screams and started jumping over each other to get to the exits. Though they weren't technically locked in, it didn't stop them from using their fellow man as battering rams to get them open.

"Quick, jump back across!" Devin reached across the rift and his hand shot downward, dragged into the darkness within. Haden screamed his name and reached after him but I stopped her. Garrett pulled on Devin, forcing him back and away from the rift. He wasn't wounded, but he looked terrified.

"What is it?" Haden asked, looking over the narrow trench that now divided the arena floor in two.

"We can't cross that." I shook my head at Garrett. He was still gripping Devin as he reached mournfully for the dark fissure. "We'll find another way out."

I pulled Haden back even as her curiosity pulled her forward. Garrett looked at Devin and then back at me. He didn't want to leave us behind.

"Whatever this is, it's not safe and its growing," I explained.

"No!" Devin wailed. "There's no hope."

"He's right," Haden whispered next to me. "We might as well just give up."

"Garrett!" I yelled even as his eyes started to fall to the trench. "Get him out of here! Get away from this thing before it sucks you in!"

Another thunderous boom from outside helped shake him from his piteous thoughts. He nodded and started yanking Devin away. He had to fight him at first, but the farther away they got the easier it was to convince him to move.

"Move, Haden." I winced and pulled her along by the arm.

We were on the lesser expanse of the arena and the exits on our side were mobbed with people. Everyone was trying to get out the fastest, and no one was getting anywhere. The ground shuddered and the rupture spread. The fluid darkness consuming the floor took even more of our tenantable space.

"Climb, Haden." I pushed Haden to the arena wall and gave her a foothold to start her climb. I shoved her butt, easing her ascent into seating. She reached back for me and I did my best to help her lift my weight. I huffed after the exertion and tried in vain to clutch the gash on my back.

I looked out into the fleeing crowds and caught a glimpse of Devin's and Garrett's worried and infuriated faces as they pushed their way through the river of people exiting on the other side. That was the last thing I saw before the lights went out.

Somewhere After Midnight

T HE INTERPRETATION OF DARKNESS is different no matter who you talk to. A sunny day has shadows. The night has the glowing moon. Caves are as dark as the world ever really gets.

The light, what little of it persisted to leak through the damaged panels in the canopy, bent to the growing crevice in the floor. It was like a black hole, pulling in anything that got close enough. The sound diminished as echoes of people's screams were swallowed.

It wasn't gravity, though. Because even gravity couldn't pull at your mind, demanding you to give up all hope.

I watched desperate men and women try to maneuver around the crack, seeking a clog-free exit. They slowed as they passed until they were at a dead stop. If they were screaming and grappling with the attacking force it would have been better, but they weren't. Their forlorn faces turned back to the fissure, and without deliberation or opposition, they threw themselves in.

One by one the remaining audience members who hadn't escaped in the melee walked to their deaths. The live sacrifices fed the silent beast beneath and the hole widened. The cold, tangible silence wasn't the fire and brimstone of folklore, but it was the scary, blank, black nothingness that people feared from death.

"There's no point." Haden gravitated to the edge and I pushed her back up the steps. "It's over. This is it."

"What do you mean? Just because the Earth is about to be ripped apart by the mouth of hell—that I inadvertently helped open—doesn't mean we should be pessimistic!" I yelled, trying to distract her from the blanket of depression. "Follow me!" I pulled on her, drawing her up the rising stands, away from the vacancy.

I could feel her trying to pull away from me. I drew on what strength I had to keep a grip on her arm, but my injury was making it difficult to see past my human half.

"What's the point?" Haden asked and pushed me away. I fell, landing on my wound. I groaned and rolled up as fast as I could, but she was already down a half dozen steps.

"Haden, stop!" I half ran, half tumbled down the stairs, and grabbed her before she could swan dive like the others.

I could feel the pressure of the emptiness demanding the same from me, but I couldn't give in. There had to be some advantage to having an angel for a friend, and if it wasn't to keep you from going to hell, what else could it be?

"Haden, look at me!" I clamped my hands on her face and forced her to look at me. I could see the pain in her eyes. She was crying. It was probably the first and last time I would ever see it. "Listen to me! She *chose* you!" I shook her face. "Do you know what that means? It means you are stronger than everyone else. You will fight this and you will win!"

Her eyes glazed and for a moment I thought I had lost her, but a certain determination in the form of a pissy glower took hold on her face and she nodded at me. We stood and, despite a few very difficult first steps, we were well on our way up and away from the clutches of hell.

To Fight the Rising Odds

Haden and I finally made our way outside of the building that was disappearing in a veil of darkness behind us. The gates of hell had opened, and so long as it had willing sacrifices, it wasn't likely to close. Haden pulled me clear of the immediate luring threat and we looked back on what we had just escaped.

The convention center disappeared within the tangible darkness, leaving no evidence of rubble or debris. The flat expansion that maintained the new address was the blackest hole I could fathom. It had no topography or substance; it was just... nothing.

We moved past the line of semitrailers to get a better view of the melee that was inducing torrents of gut-wrenching screams from the previously elated party-happy people. On the other side, I froze and stared at the carnage unfolding in the parking lot and streets surrounding us. I hadn't had much hope of a happy ending with the depths of hell only a hundred yards away, but the secondary gaping hole in the middle of the sky pretty much assured me that shit had officially hit the fan.

The turbulent vacuous tornado in the atmosphere above us burrowed unfathomably into a separate dimension. The twisting gray tunnel and lightning weren't the typical picture of heaven's gate, but fluffy clouds and flying cherubs didn't really scream *kill the infidels!*

The ground was showered with sparks as huge men and women with wispy auras pummeled smaller humans with blackened auras. The battle between angels and demons had begun.

The successive sonic booms signaled the arrival of new angels. They landed like meteors, shattering concrete and crushing any unfortunate person who might have wandered onto their landing pad.

The people were terrified and trying to get away, but the swarms of grim, trickling from their former captivity, were herding them like cattle, forcing them to remain for entertainment and to bear witness to the massacre.

Humans were being eviscerated for sport. Raped for amusement. And in the midst of it all the *noble* angels were batting them aside to clear a path for their combat.

I gripped Haden's hand tight as I looked over the bedlam before me. She either didn't notice or she didn't object. I thought Adrian had been exaggerating about burning down the trees to make room for his war, but it was true. This battle was the beginning of the war. This was what we had been waiting for. And the only part humans were playing in it was to feed the demons a steady supply of fear and offer soft footing for the angels when they walked across our broken bodies.

I heard a fizzle and an explosion in the north. I looked over and saw one of the many buildings, containing the hordes of collected grim, collapse into a dust cloud of debris. Another fizzle from a rocket launcher downed another building, squashing untold numbers of grim. I followed the sound to its source and saw Ian on top of a nearby factory building. He had indeed made some friends. Six men were on the roof with him, sharpshooting troublesome grim below. Three others guarded the perimeter below, using machine guns to subdue any invading swarms.

I could see Devin and Garrett ahead of us, slicing their way through the onslaught of grim, defending who they could. Devin had traded in his bloodied fists for a machete. Priest was nowhere to be seen, but a path of grim fell in his wake as he made his way through the crowd toward us.

I scoffed and smiled. I was losing hope by the minute, but my team was in fine form. Haden pulled her hand from mine—suddenly aware of it, I assumed—and pushed me toward Priest.

"She's been stabbed!" Haden yelled over the bevy.

"I've got her." Priest turned me and pressed his hand to my back. His warmth spread over me and I was instantly out of pain. I watched the roiling angel/demon battle as he finished. It looked like death-matches between David and Goliath. Only, David packed as much punch as Goliath.

"Who did this?" Priest finally asked.

"Jimmy the Card," I admitted sheepishly. Priest must not have believed me, because he didn't answer until Haden nodded.

"Jimmy was a demon."

"Not a demon. *The* demon," I clarified. "He's been pulling the strings. He was the head puppet master." I grimaced. "All this time I thought it was the mayor. I never suspected a thing."

"I imagine that was the point," Priest assured me.

Haden raised her gun and shot two grim that were sneaking up on us while we were chatting. "We need to get out there and help them," she grumbled. "You two are the only thing that is going to save us now." She glanced back at me, putting a majority of the compliment on me.

"Okay, let me just get my not-so-zen on."

Priest stepped back and I concentrated on my purpose. I accessed that special little kick-ass place inside of me and I felt a wave of power tingle over my extremities. When I looked up, the battle was clearer than before. Monsters of every variety infested the streets; wings or horns... they were all enemies of the Earth.

I Need a Hero

ANNOUNCING MY POSITION AND identity probably wasn't the smartest choice, but somewhere deep in my throat the guttural, screeching roar bloomed. Perhaps it was just instinct, a necessary part of the uniform that was my dual angel costume. Of course, it might have also been the fact that I was super pissed-off.

I had watched the pain and suffering long enough. If they expected us to just stand by and watch, while they destroyed our home, then they should have chosen another planet, or at the very least another state. We may have been ten years late on fashion, and hell if you could get anyone here to comprehend the purpose of energy conservation, but what the Midwest *could* comprehend was the value of our land.

Two lifetimes of anger boiled to the surface and I shattered the already raucous battle din with my announcement. The crowds of people and monsters alike paused, giving confusion and acknowledgment a moment to cross everyone's face before the battle shifted and continued.

For the most part, the angels had no interest in me, but I got the sense that they would not be coming to rescue me from the sudden onslaught of grim that I had invited to challenge me.

I didn't waste time questioning my abilities or planning an escape route. I just ran into the mob.

Two steps were ten. I was on the first of the line in seconds.

My weapons were no longer necessary. I was the weapon. My ghostly outlined hands ripped through the papier-mâché grim. Their skulls burst under the lightest pressure of my strength.

Two jumped on my back, attempting to bring me down to an approachable level, but I threw them as easily as dolls. I tore through the line, only leaving a few for Haden and Priest to finish off.

At this rate, I might have finished off the grim with a steady pace and a few hours, but after the first forty fell with ease, the rest retreated to pursue easier prey. The scattered attackers made the battle slow down and I was forced to seek out my enemies one by one.

I heard more sonic thunder and I could see an arriving angel's intended landing site. I raced inhumanly fast and barreled over a young couple that was hiding behind a car. The angel touched down as gracefully as a bombshell, crushing the car and impelling glass shrapnel at me and the couple. I managed to block most of the glass, after which the couple thanked me by screaming in my face and scrambling away.

"You're welcome," I mumbled and turned back to glare at the newly arrived angel.

He unfurled his body, and rose to an astounding eight feet. He eyed me carefully as he stepped down from the mangled car and approached me. I could see the cocky manner in his walk and his blue-eyed gaze lured me to him just as his was hooked on me.

I stood and faced him, flaunting my angelic aura. In my attuned state, I could see his human form and his angelic one overlapped, much like mine. His human hair was fair, and his skin was unblemished. His wings were tucked discreetly behind him, but they shifted slightly, as if he were flexing for me.

I tipped my chin up, daring him to test me. To my surprise he responded by bowing to me. I wasn't sure if this was supposed to be a mutual bow, but I waited to see what would follow. When he rose, he was smirking. I still didn't remember my previous existence, so for all I knew this angel might have known me. Maybe they all did.

He glanced behind me and frowned. I looked back and saw an unfamiliar face, drenched in black from her thick evil aura.

"Careful, *achot*," the angel whispered behind me, close to my ear. "It's a prince." I felt a waft of air on my back and I knew the angel had gone.

The woman approached me sporting a number of offensive accessories, including fishnet stockings, a nose ring, and a swastika tattooed around her belly button. "You know you can't win, don't you?" she said with a deep voice that didn't seem to match her frame.

"Jimmy?" I asked to clarify. "Nice choice."

"Finding a new body is as easy as shopping for a car to drive."

"Frustrating and slightly demeaning?" I said flatly.

"Even now you can't take this seriously?" She shook her head.

"What do you mean? I got dressed up, didn't I?" I opened my arms to show off my angelic highlights.

He opened his arms, mimicking my movement, but instead of the darkened looming shadow of a piggy-backing demon, highlights of red and orange bloomed into an aura. From that a new outline was born, growing to match the height of the street lights. The shades of red deepened to the unfathomable black I saw in the arena pit. Fully formed he was barely more than a blob, but he was a substantial blob.

He chuckled. "Are you finally losing your humor?"

I tried to focus on the human face before me, but my eyes drifted back up to his expanse. "What are you?" I asked.

"What would you like to hear? Shall I say that I am what nightmares are made of? Or perhaps I should claim to be what goes bump in the night."

"Are you...?"

He chuckled again. "I am the beginning and the end. That is all you can comprehend." The hand of his female host swept gracefully through the air, and I felt the air leave my lungs. I tried to inhale, but my body was no longer under my control.

My eyes watered as I stared at the all-powerful being before me. She twisted her hand, and I felt my heart cease momentarily. I was allowed a shallow breath to prolong my consciousness as my heart raced faster and faster, pounding against my chest. Her long fingers pressed delicately together, but the pain it offered my legs was enough to collapse me.

I tried to reach for my strength, but the pain in my chest demanded my attention. The euphoria of lack of oxygen was a blessing, and I hoped the pain would end soon. No matter what the outcome was.

A gunshot sounded distantly in my mind and I felt the pain release. I heard the round twice more and I inhaled sharply, securing my consciousness, but not my steadiness. Priest's familiar arms wrapped around me as my dizziness subsided. When I opened my eyes, I could see Haden standing over Jimmy's host with her gun still aimed at her just in case her pesky houseguest came back.

"Haden, what the hell?" I scolded and she looked at me, baffled. "That demon was a freaking general. He was ten times more powerful than Adrian."

She turned back to me, irritated by my reprimand. "So what?" She shrugged. "Dumb fuck wants to keep coming back in human bodies, then I'll keep shooting him."

I stared at her, dumbfounded by her ignorant arrogance. I glanced at Priest for backup. He looked to me and translated my frustration.

"She's right, Haden. You shouldn't risk giving him permission to harm you."

"He was killing you," she complained and clotheslined an attacking grim before slamming her boot heel into his face.

Priest looked back at me. "She's right, Lenore, you did look a little... overwhelmed." He frowned.

I wanted to object more, but I decided Haden wasn't as ignorant as I was giving her credit for. Even if she had known the danger the demon posed to her, she still would have shot him.

I stood up with Priest's help and looked around the continuing battle. I could still see Garrett and Devin making a dent in the populace. A good number of men and women had taken up arms near them, but every one of them looked exhausted and bloody. Ian's newly acquired team was still doing well, but once the ammunition ran out, they would be down to punching and kicking with the rest of us.

I lassoed a passing grim by the neck and shoved it to the concrete, shattering it. Haden lined up one in her sights and pulled her trigger, but the gun clicked ineffectively. She cussed and reached for her back pocket. When she didn't find another clip she cussed a little quieter.

"We need to clear out more of these grim before the others get too tired to fight," Priest mumbled beside me, seeing the same future play out. He turned his attention to me. Once again, I had unintentionally volunteered for the position of savior.

"Okay," I exhaled. "Just so you know though... I might be useless after this."

"We'll deal with the aftermath," Haden said, flanking me with a newly acquired hammer. "Just do what you can," she murmured and glanced back at me.

I nodded at her and looked to Priest. He kissed my cheek and whispered. "I'm right here."

I wanted to kiss him, but I didn't want to make the moment feel like a goodbye. I shut my eyes and visualized my targets. One, twenty, one hundred, two...

Somewhere Just Beyond My Reach

I REACHED OUT AND grabbed onto everyone my mind could touch. I waded through human and grim, tagging each one to hold or release.

I avoided the power emanating from the angels. It was similar to my own, but as repellant to me as magnets with the same polarity. The true demons were as problematic as the grim, but I knew better than to take them on. I wanted to extinguish as many threats as I could, but their connection to hell was too strong for me to defeat all of them. I could try to subdue them in a second round—assuming I didn't pass out from the strain.

I harnessed the tattered souls occupying the plague of grim around me. I felt the concussive effect of the lingering human memories still inside them. I blocked the emotions that threatened to still my executioner's hand. I started to squeeze the life out of my collected prey, when I remembered what August had said before I left my dream pep talk. I hadn't killed the grim that had attacked me the day I met her.

What did she mean? What else would I do with a grim?

They had to die. That was my purpose. I couldn't just shove so many into heaven. The majority of the fragile souls wouldn't survive and even if they did, they didn't belong there as they were.

I felt the souls squirming in my mind—angry, weeping, and desperate for more. More of their cocaine addiction to hell. I shifted gears, hoping it was the right answer.

I relaxed my grip on the souls and instead offered a sweeping cleanse to the destructive links that fed them. I snapped the innumerable connections to hell like cobwebs. I severed their life's blood and released them; not from existence, but from torment.

The grim threads yielded easily under my power, but they were sticky. And the call to hell was strong. As strong as the darkness that tempted Haden to throw her life away. The lingering webs tangled in my thoughts, demanding and threatening that I surrender my endeavor.

Despite the risk, I pushed through and snapped the connections. The puppet strings had been cut. The marionettes were free to be real boys and girls. I, on the other hand, had snarled myself in a tapestry of evil intent. The barbed wire influence seared my mind... and enveloped my soul.

Like a Fire in My Blood

B EING HALF LIGHT AND half dark meant I was still vulnerable to influence. The love I had inside of me made a demon's manipulation as irritating as a gnat, but harmless. However, I wasn't being oppressed by the mind of a demon. I was trapped in hell's snare.

It was the same infinite, insatiable *hunger* that was eating a hole in the street not far from me. It was an ageless, boundless power that fed the demons, so they could in turn feed *it*. An awakened consciousness that was the backdrop of the universe, until a presumptuous God dared to paint on his perfect blank canvas. The infinite pain that pooled within its core was harvested from the very first tear and the very last drop of shed blood. It fed on it all.

The intrinsic evil wrapped spiny tentacles around my mind, luring my sanity with promises of power and pleasure. To submit to madness on Earth as a demon was a significant torture to endure, but as with the dual citizenship of a Principality, my domain transcended the boundaries of my physical body.

I was being pulled into hell.

All of me.

Perhaps a phase shift through a dimensional schism was a more appropriate phrase. Whatever it was, I was killing myself trying to stay on the Earth. I could taste the blood dripping from my nose, and, I suspected, my eyes.

I could hear the others were trying to help me, but their frantic questions couldn't be answered, and their wrenching grips would never be enough to hold me to my physical form. No amount of angelic power would either.

I had saved them all. There wouldn't be a standing grim for ten miles. That would have to be enough.

I was, at long last, the hero. And like my predecessor, I would have to leave them.

I gave in to the blackness that was absorbing me body, mind, and soul.

There's Someone Reaching Back for Me

I FELT A NEW hand grab hold of me and I snapped taut between the two worlds. Here and there, but not quite anywhere, I overlapped the two realms. I knew it was Priest. His warmth was familiar and comforting. The power he exuded was magnificent. It was enough to hold me still. I was on the precipice, but at least I might have sixteen seconds to offer him.

I managed to open my eyes to look at him. His hands had moved to my face and his eyes were pinched as he murmured prayers, or maybe they were pleas. He no doubt wanted God to save me, but what about His edict? Was it against the rules for him to help me? I wasn't human, and the hungry vortex trying to suck me in certainly wasn't human. I wasn't even sure if it was classified as a being.

Priest opened his eyes and looked at me. His expression surprised me. He looked almost smug. He wiped the blood from my upper lip and kissed me. I wasn't opposed to one last kiss, but it did seem ill timed.

A heat rose inside of me. The protective warmth of Priest's soft fuzzy blanket was on electric blanket setting. He continued to kiss me, his tongue roaming into my mouth. Now this was really getting inappropriate.

He pulled me in tight, pressing my body to his before he released my lips.

Before I could fathom what was happening, wave after wave of unforgiving, relentless, authoritative power bypassed Priest entirely and came straight through my own tether. I screamed at the force turning my body into a private battleground. I didn't know what to do but lay my head back and let it happen.

The power clashed with the death grip hell had on me. The insatiable hunger slackened with every bombarding surge.

Priest gripped me tighter, protecting me with the strength of his love. I wasn't sure what would happen to me if he let go, but I was willing to hypothesize that standing in the path of God's offensive attack would not be good for my health.

The darkness released and I was back—fully on Earth—fully attuned to my human body.

The overpowering presence stopped almost instantly, leaving me confused, angry, relieved, and so very sad. That was about the right balance, I supposed.

Fresh from the Fight

I DIDN'T REMEMBER COLLAPSING, but I was down on the concrete and Priest was kissing me not so chastely. "Matthew," I mumbled through his kisses. "I can't breathe."

"Sorry," he said, reluctantly breaking from our *thank-God-you're-alive* make-out session. I couldn't wait to get home for the *thank-God-you're-alive* sex.

"What happened? Did I kill the grim, or just kick them out?"

"You stopped them," Haden said.

I peeked over and saw Garrett and Devin next to her. "Where's Ian? Is he okay?" I asked, fearing the worst.

"Ian is just fine," he called over as he limped into view with more than a few friends behind him.

"What's wrong with your leg?" Priest's face lit with concern and he jumped up to meet them. With my bolster suddenly gone, I flopped limply to the ground. Priest looked back, mortified that he had abandoned me to drop six inches.

I laughed and waved him off to help Ian.

"I don't know if you'll want to heal me when you find out what it's from." Ian smirked and chucked him on the shoulder.

"What did you do?" Priest asked, waving Garrett over for some healing attention instead. He seemed to have retained the worst injuries, but Devin was starting to look a little wobbly. I hoped that Priest could heal internal bleeding.

Ian plopped down beside me and positioned his arm under me so I could sit up. I was virtually dead weight after my encounter with the two divergent powers, but other than that, I felt good. I felt alive. And that was very good.

"I tried to duplicate that famous celebratory sailor kiss with a hot chick outside the factory. I was expecting a slap, but she kicked me in the crotch instead."

I chuckled. "Modern women." I rolled my eyes. "Where are the grim?" I asked, looking around at the panicked milling people. The angels and demons were all but cleared out. I wasn't sure if they were scared off by my display, or if they just decided to relocate the battle to a spot with less riff-raff.

I got the sense that the two invading holes in our world were going to be there for a while. The wall was breached, and short of an intervention from God, or a massive influx in the human population, it wasn't going to mend itself. However, I was confident that the humans could eventually raise their numbers and balance the two dimensions again.

Ian looked at Devin and Haden. They exchanged a glance before nodding, giving him permission to answer me. "You cleared out most of them with whatever you did. They just... poof." He made the one-handed explosive gesture. "Fairy dust."

"Good. What about the ones that didn't go poof?"

Ian twisted his mouth. "They didn't go poof, because..." He narrowed his eyes. "...they turned back into humans."

The silence ensued for several seconds on both ends. I glanced at several faces, trying to get a straight answer that made sense.

"The day we met you," Devin ended the silence, "you were being attacked by a grim. August hopped out of the truck to help you, but before she got to you, the bugger was thrown off and she was pushed back. She went over and checked on you, but you had passed out."

"What happened between my passing out and waking up in the truck?"

"The grim got back up," Haden continued and Devin put an arm around her, to steady himself. "August picked up her sword to kill it, but the damn thing cowered away from her and begged her to stop. That's when we realized it wasn't a grim anymore."

"I brought the people back that God took?"

"No," Priest answered for them. "You saved hundreds of souls from hell. The lost souls that possessed the grim have been placed inside the bodies they were puppeteering."

I looked around. "Living demons?"

"No; broken, confused, humans." Priest pulled his hands from Garrett's mostly healed face. He put his hand out for Devin to come to him and he shuffled over. He poked and prodded at his ribs until he nodded, and he focused his power there.

"It's like a mental ward out here," Ian chimed back in. "These people have no freaking clue who they are or what they are doing here. I don't even think they know they aren't in the right bodies."

"Can that be right?" I asked. "How will they function in a different body?"

"So, the number of transvestites goes up." Ian shrugged off my concerns.

"It's a clean slate," Priest interjected. "Male, female, young, old, it doesn't matter. They're not in hell, and they aren't dead. They have a second chance. A chance to be forgiven and more importantly, to make peace with themselves."

"What do you make of that, Chief?" Ian asked, flexing his bicep to bob my head.

I surveyed the apprehensive dazed faces around us. "They look so lost."

Priest opened his mouth to respond and Haden raised her gun at him. "If you quote *Amazing Grace*, I will shoot you."

He sighed and tried to glare at her, but he couldn't hide his amusement. "I was just going to say that what you've done is a good thing. They are no worse off than they were. In time, they will find their way."

"Speaking of finding our way," Devin said, exhausted, "let's find our way home."

"I second that," Garrett added.

Someone Somewhere Watching Me

I WAS HAPPY TO discover that my *thank-God-you're-alive* sex lasted for hours. Priest was beyond overjoyed that I was alive, and in his bed instead of another dimension. I had no objections to the extra attention, though I imagined the couple sharing our wall didn't agree.

I had told everyone about my dream with August on the way home, and how her words had fueled my hope for the future. I warned everyone that the coming years would be difficult, and I even offered them another opportunity to leave. They all laughed. I was stuck with them, which was fine with me.

I stumbled downstairs in the middle of the night to get a drink of water. I was sore and dehydrated from my superhero feat, as well as my extended tryst. I found Ian sitting at the table staring off into the wall angrily.

"Oh crap, we aren't keeping you awake, are we?" I asked him as I chugged down a glass of water from the tap. "Ian?" I asked and moved around to get a better view of his face. He was sweating and his fists were balled so tight I could see drops of blood on the table from his fingernails digging in. "Ian!" I gasped and moved toward him.

"Go away," he growled.

"What's wrong?"

"I can't stop him. Please just…" He groaned and looked up at me. "Kill me, Lenore!"

"What? No!" I shook my head and reached for his mind. My supernatural sight revealed a thick shadow looming over him, pressing to inhabit his body. I could sense Ian weakening against the familiar demon parasite. "Adrian!" I snarled.

Voicing his name was probably a bad idea.

Ian leapt at me, grabbing my throat and slamming me back into the drywall. "You are going to die!" Adrian's original voice overlapped Ian's.

I struggled to breathe and grabbed onto the demon threatening my friend. He was strong, but not *drag-me-into-hell* strong. However, I was weak from taking on a city of grim and he was latching onto Ian so tight that I wasn't going to be able to hurt one and not the other.

I shoved Ian off, and he landed against the fridge, rattling the glass bottles within. He looked up at me, himself again, but only momentarily. "I can't stop him. You have to kill me, or I'll kill you."

"No, I won't do that." I crawled toward him.

He frowned, his lips slowly turned to a sneer. "Your friends will be the death of you someday." Before I could plead with Ian to fight harder, he sprang to the counter and grabbed a knife from the wood block. He slashed at me and ripped my pajama top before I could draw back.

"You should have listened to him," Adrian's voice said.

I scrambled to my feet as he corralled me to the living room. I heard several feet arrive on the stairs and a gun cock.

"No, Haden!" I waved my hands, not taking my eyes from Ian as he licked his lower lip. "It's still Ian."

Ian clicked his tongue. "Sorry, Ian isn't home anymore." A gravelly voice took the place of Ian's and Adrian's. He glanced to Haden and winked.

"Haden, put your gun down," Priest admonished her. I could feel his presence rise in the room, preparing to force Adrian out of Ian.

"Matthew, don't," I objected.

"I can get him out," he argued, but I could already feel his power recede.

"No. He has to fight him off himself. These bastards mark you for life."

"He won't fight," Adrian answered for him. "He is weak. His past is all I need to control him. He is mine now. I'm going to make him rip your fucking head off."

"He isn't weak!" I yelled back. "Ian, listen to me. I can sense evil from a mile away. The day I met you, I invited you into my home. Do you think I would have done that if you were evil? Don't let your past dictate who you are."

"He's a killer!" Adrian hissed.

"He *was* a killer, but now he's a warrior and a good man and my friend. Do you hear me, Ian? I know you want to hang onto those bad memories and hate yourself for them, but that is not the point of memories. We remember it all so we can learn from our mistakes."

"I can't, Lenore," Ian panted. His body drooped. "He's too strong."

"You have to. If this sick prick gets inside you fully, demons will always be able to get inside you. Force him out, and then I'll rip him to shreds."

"I can't," he rasped as if he were in pain.

"It's *your* body, Ian. It's as much a struggle for him to invade you as it is for you to fight him off. That's a fair match, and you can win. Don't think about your past. Think about your future." I gave up my surrender and returned to him. He growled and grabbed my throat again, but the pressure on my windpipe was minimal. "You are one of us now, Ian, and I'm not letting you go." I caressed his cheek and I could see tears forming in his eyes. "I love you, you idiot."

Ian looked into my eyes, and I let my angelic form rise within me. His eyes skirted my outline. I could see his lips move, but his response was inaudible. I felt the demon release after the sentiment.

I reached after the retreating shadow and snatched the lingering trail of his sickly anger. I didn't offer ceremony to the death, nor did I allow him any last words. I just slowly ripped at his essence, letting him howl in agony for sixteen seconds before I tamped out his existence for good.

Ian dropped to the floor and panted. I returned to my human form and bent down to hold him. He looked me over. He was still crying. I patted his head and pressed his back gently, encouraging him to embrace me. His forehead bent down to rest on my shoulder. He wept hard, releasing some of his life's pent-up pain.

I glanced back at the stairs, but I could see Haden's and Devin's feet trudging beyond my view. Priest had turned to go up, but was waiting for my instructions. My face must have been a mixture of pain and relief, because he looked concerned. I swallowed my pride and put my resentment in the back seat. "Will you bless him?"

He looked notably surprised by the request, but it passed and he walked to us and knelt down behind Ian. He held my gaze a moment, before touching Ian's back. He closed his eyes and I felt his warm fuzziness rise as his litany began.

So, this is the end... Or is it the beginning?

MINOR AND MAJOR BATTLES broke out all over the world, after I ignited the war between demons and angels. Not everyone fared as well as us, but there were rumors spreading of select people with astounding abilities. At first I thought it was just a recap of my and Priest's performance, but the superpowers were unlike anything Priest or I could do.

I wasn't sure if their power was stemming from God or angelic origins like ours, but it was nice to know that we weren't the only ones putting the grim in their place. As for those outside the circle of *special*, they were being inspired to fight for what was rightfully theirs. And so far, they were winning.

I knew the result would inevitably be a massive annihilation of grim, reducing the number of souls I could purge from hell. But, I couldn't and shouldn't save them all. There was still a balance to be maintained. The darkness may have been a disease to the human race, but it was never going to go away.

Ian traded in his contract with the mayor for a contract with me. He would hunt and capture grim to deliver to me for a proper soul transplant. Anyone still alive when I was through was blessed by Priest and taken back to the O. They were developing a hospice for lost souls there, and in this case, it wasn't meant metaphorically. The pressure of so many new people on the food supply was pushing us to hunt and garden, but it wasn't anywhere the human race hadn't been before.

We still had to fight a few uber-demons who were none too happy about us leading the fight to essentially reverse the apocalypse. I kept expecting an attack from Jimmy's demon, but with a war to coordinate, he probably didn't have time for petty revenge.

With hope returning to the world, reports of babies were popping up left and right, including in our own home. Haden made a very bitchy pregnant person, but I knew deep down inside she was happy. To help with the labor we invited a midwife to stay with us. Ian was very accommodating to her, which made me think we might have another pregnancy on our hands soon.

Garrett chose not to stay with us, which didn't surprise me, but he visited often enough that I didn't have to worry about him. Ex or not, he was still August's brother, and he would always have a place in my home and my heart.

As part of my weekly routine, I laid new flowers down on August's grave. I was now glad I had destroyed her body. As beautiful as she was, I couldn't bear the thought of a strange soul living in her body.

I pulled my jacket as tight as I could to keep out the cool breeze and took in a deep breath before speaking to the presence behind me. "I'm really not in the mood to kick demon ass right now." I turned and found a slightly familiar face and body leaning against a tree. He was handsome and tall. He had dark hair and wispy bangs that should have been combed back. A fine set of taut muscles stretched the long-sleeved shirt he was wearing. He might have been tempting to a girl if she didn't sense the danger from him.

"Hello Lenore." His voice was softer than I expected, soothing and deceptive.

"Do I know you?"

"Not officially. We met in passing the day of the first battle," he said.

I vaguely remembered bumping into him, and the coy smile he had given me. I did, however, remember the power coming off him that day… as strong as today. "What brings you to my neck of the cemetery after all this time?"

He smiled at his own private thought. "I've come to congratulate you. You seem to have incited a fire in humanity."

"Congratulations aren't necessary. Certainly not in person. Why don't you go back to where you came from? And by that, I mean *go to hell*."

He smiled again and pushed off the tree to take a few lingering steps around me. "You are strong. I'll admit that. Stronger than most, in fact. But not me." His intense stare after that statement gave me pause.

"So, why haven't you killed me yet? It's been almost a year. Have you been lurking in the shadows just to pop out and flaunt your laziness?" I shouldn't have been trying to piss off the uber-demon, but my logic was getting ahead of my common sense. I hadn't faced him yet, but I assumed if he was powerful enough to kill me he would have done it a year ago at the battle.

Since I couldn't sense his mind, I had to assume he was telling the truth about his strength. Maybe he wasn't even an uber-demon. Maybe he was one of the princes as the angel had mentioned. Was he Lucifer? Satan? Beelzebub? Or were they kings? Nevertheless, the lesser demons were knights and pawns by comparison. The only question was: knight or king? I could save pawns, and kill knights, but what could I do to kings?

"Save me the trouble of figuring out your endgame, because honestly, I really suck at that. I'm not sure I'm innately naïve; I think I just like surprises."

"Then you'll like this surprise," he said with a smile.

I was slow to react to his attack. His hand gripped my neck, and his power resonated against mine, jarring my senses. He was strong, as he said, but the energy reverberating against mine was not the sticky tendrils of darkness that I was so familiar with sloughing off. It was luminous.

Magnanimous authority pressed against me, demanding my respect even while it bristled against the darkest part of me, the part of me that refused to keel to man or myth no matter how hot they looked in Earthen form.

"Get off me, you angelic prick!" I yelled. Now that he was touching me I could see the wispy outline of his wings. He was not unlike me. He could take a physical form to interact with humans as he saw fit, but unlike me, he was not a Principality. He was an archangel.

"To answer your question, the reason I have waited to kill you is because you have been doing a tremendous job cleaning up the Earth for us. My fellow brethren are more than happy to let you do the dirty work, but now it's time for us to take over."

"Why? I still don't understand why angels want the Earth. What is the point, when you have heaven?" I choked through his grip.

"In heaven I am a servant of God. Here... I could be a god."

"So, that's it? You're just as sick and twisted as the demons."

"I certainly am not." He lowered me back to the ground and pulled me closer to him. "I do not wish to make your people hate me. I want them to *love* me. To worship me." He said the words in earnest, but the sadistic tone made him sound like a cult leader. He would love and value his servants, so long as they obeyed him. It was heaven on Earth, so long as he was treated as a god.

"Not gonna happen, birdbrain. I won't let it. I don't care if you're an angel or a demon—the human race belongs to the Earth, and the Earth belongs to the human race. I'll revise my earlier statement. Go back to heaven."

He lifted me again, squeezing my neck and capping my deep-rooted power at the same time. I hated that there was always someone stronger. There was always someone ready to one-up the hero.

"The beautiful part of all of this, Lenore, is that you aren't strong enough to stop me."

He was right. I wasn't strong enough. Fortunately for me, my baby was.

I felt a tiny kick in my belly just before the angel was flung back, hitting the tree he was previously leaning against. His head chipped the bark before he landed flat on his back. I landed safely on the ground and stood up, tall and unafraid of him.

He looked at me, aghast by this new painful revelation. I rubbed my barely noticeable baby bump.

"I may not be strong enough to fight you, but he is." I took a step toward him and he had the good sense to tense. "Get this straight, feather-head: humans have dominion over the Earth and that's the way God intended it. You want a war? Then by all means, bring it on. But I would advise starting elsewhere. Unless, of course, you want my baby to sever your connection to God." His eyes widened at this prospect. "How does that sound? Eternity on Earth, as a human, forever locked out of heaven? I've heard there are more than a few fallen angels in our midst already. Maybe you could form a club or something."

I started walking back to my car. I wasn't about to hang around and watch him babble about taking over the world or getting revenge on me. In the end, it was all the same stuff I had heard from a thousand grim. He might have been driven by a power free of hatred and pain, but damn if pride and piety didn't look just as ugly close up.

Sister Witches

FELICIA JEDLICKA

Sister Witches

Felicia Jedlicka

FOLLOWING THE DEATH OF her father, Hennie goes off the rails. Her mind is weakened by thoughts of suicide, making her vulnerable to an evil influence. Under the illusion of revenge, Hennie is forced to direct her harmful actions outward. Following an attempted murder, she is led into a life of poverty, chastity, and obedience. At least, that's what she appears to be doing.

Hennie may be wearing a black veil, but her loyalties to God start with the women of her coven. She and her fellow sisters aren't just teaching bible school. They are ridding the world of evil, one exorcism at a time.

If prayers are ineffective, the members of this convent will cast spells instead. Hennie's natural inclination to magic makes her an asset to the coven, but when the devil takes notice, the witches will need more than hexes to ward him off.

About the Author

A s a Nebraska native, and a small-town girl at that, I have very little to occupy my time beyond imagining a world outside of my own reality. By the grace of God and the seat of my pants, I have kept my waning attention span on the task of becoming an author.

So here I am, an indie author, peddling my words in cyberspace and enduring my comeuppances with an unwavering determination. I may not be a professional, and I certainly am not perfect, but if you've made it this far, you have to admit, this smart-ass yoke does spin quite a yarn.

From the self-inflicted sweatshop conditions of my unairconditioned childhood home to the arthritis-reaping positions of a sedentary lifestyle, I bring to you: my sarcasm, my oddity, and my heart. Take it with a grain of salt or a teaspoon of sugar, but take it for what it is: a story born of the mind, translated to paper, and gifted to you.

I thank you for your readership and even more for your support.